YO-BLS-881

BCPL-WA

| DATE DUE | | |
|---|---|---|
| OCT 08 2004 | | |
| OCT 22 2004 | | |
| DEC 14 2004 | | |
| JAN 05 2005 | | |
| APR 12 2005 | | |
| June/05 | | |
| AUG 10 2005 | | |
| | | |
| | | |
| | | |

FIC Ashe
Ashe, Elisabeth,
The jade pendant /

SEP 6, 2004                30.95
   BRUCE COUNTY PUBLIC LIBRARY         hq

Bruce County Public Library
1243 MacKenzie Rd.
Port Elgin, Ontario  N0H 2C6

© 2004 by Elisabeth Ashe.
All rights reserved. No part of this book may be reproduced, stored in a retrieval system, or transmitted in any form or by any means without the prior written permission of the publishers, except by a reviewer who may quote brief passages in a review to be printed in a newspaper, magazine, or journal.

First printing

ISBN: 1-4137-2098-6
PUBLISHED BY PUBLISHAMERICA, LLLP
www.publishamerica.com
Baltimore

Printed in the United States of America

*This book is dedicated...*

...to my son, Kevin Deon Folstrom,
and my granddaughter, Taylor Leigh Marchment.

# Acknowledgements

I wish to thank my family and friends whose encouragement and support has kept me going while writing this book. Special thanks goes to my friend Sharon Leblanc for her wonderful editing skills, but mostly for her expertise in being the best friend anyone could ever hope for. I love you all.

# Chapter One

Lydia glanced out the window as the cab pulled up to the terminal. *Thank God*, she thought relieved to be out of the cramped quarters. The driver had talked to her incessantly during the thirty-minute ride, gesticulating wildly with his lit cigar, until she finally asked him firmly but politely to put it out. As she waited for the driver to retrieve her luggage from the trunk of the vehicle Lydia thankfully followed the porter to the top of the stairs and into the rotating doors of the International Departures Building. Exhausted, she mindlessly wound her way through the chaos before her, mentally reeling off the enormous list of hurdles she had to overcome just to get to this point today. Lydia considered the last few hectic weeks carefully. Somehow she had managed to keep her wits and humor intact – no easy feat considering the circumstances.

There was the advertising business she co-owned with her partner Dee. Their company, the Prince George Directory had just launched for its first season and had faced some stiff competition from the giant in the industry, The Yellow Pages. Overcoming the distrust and fear of the unknown her clients faced them with on a daily basis. It had taken every last bit of strength and determination the pair could muster to reassure their clients.

Coupled with that was the packing and moving the two had to do, first from Kamloops to Prince George and then back again when the sales campaign had finished six months later. On top of that, the Franchisor had decided that Lydia's success with her own franchise was reason enough for him to bring her to Vancouver to assist in training other less successful branch offices. Although he had compensated her richly for her expertise, she was now exhausted and looking forward to a long month of R & R. *You're on holiday*, she reminded herself sternly. It was time to forget about business for a while. She brushed a long strand of honey colored hair from her face as she dogged the porter's steps, wishing she were already lying on a beach in Mexico with a tall cold drink of something fruity in her hand.

The Vancouver terminal was a frenzy of people from all over the world, either rushing to depart or anxious to reach their final destination. Mysterious, East Indian beauties, sloe-eyed Native Americans and bespectacled Japanese businessman to name a few, made up the mix. Harassed looking young and not so young mothers wearily chased after rambunctious children intent on getting themselves lost while bored teenagers congregated along the walls, legs sprawled before them amid a scattering of knapsacks. Indeterminable minutes later, Lydia found herself in the line-up to check her bags and validate her ticket. As she waited with as much patience as she could muster she smiled at the thought of John Mathews, the man responsible for her being here today.

Lydia had started dating him shortly after her arrival in the northern city of British Columbia and she was amazed at how much he had come to mean to her in such a short time. All her free time had been spent with him in quiet dinners and conversation or walks along the beautiful paths by the park near his home. Unfortunately, due to her short relocation to the Vancouver office, she had not seen him for over a month, since before her birthday. Although they had called each other regularly, she missed the intimacy of being with him more than she would have thought possible. She wondered what he was doing this moment. *Probably working like a maniac cutting still more deals and drinking more than he should.* The idea popped into her head unexpectedly, startling her. After all, wasn't that what had attracted her to him in the first place? It was true that John worked hard. Most people would say he was a workaholic. As well, in his circles his ability to drink was nearly legendary. They would be right on both accounts. Most times she overlooked those aspects of his personality. Wondering why she thought about these things now she shook her head gently and concentrated instead on remembering the first time she had laid eyes on him.

Behind schedule and over-booked with appointments as usual, she had rushed into his office almost seven months ago. It was an especially hot day for June and one of the few Prince George experienced all that summer. She had put the top down on her Mazda Miata convertible, so that her shoulder length hair had an attractive wind-blown look to it and her "power suit", a hot, red number showed off her tanned, slim legs to perfection. Weeks later as they sipped icy glasses of champagne while sitting in his Jacuzzi tub, John had laughingly told her she'd reminded him of a wood sprite blown by a hurricane.

The sales call itself was of particular importance to her because he had been so difficult to pin down for an appointment. That fact alone had made her even more determined to sell him, thereby confirming her reputation in the business as one very tenacious sales representative. In fact at a magazine she once worked for in Calgary, her sales manager had laughingly likened to her a dog with a bone. After weeks of repeated calls she had finally confirmed a meeting with John, not at all daunted by the fact he had given her no more than fifteen minutes to state her case. Used to dealing with difficult clients she had readily agreed to his terms. From past experience, she knew that if he became interested she could easily stretch the fifteen minutes into thirty or forty, which was really all the time she needed. Confident in her ability she rushed into his office and headed to the counter behind which a tall and decidedly handsome, rugged looking man stood. Pleasantly surprised by his looks, she grew even more confident with each step she took. At first the man did not even glance up from the order form he was writing on, allowing Lydia the time she needed to appraise him closer.

Judging from his face she guessed him to be about forty-five or so, trim and compact looking. Definitely looks like a man who takes care of himself, she had thought, as she gazed at the arms bared from sleeves rolled back. His tousled dark brown hair, a little on the long side, curled around his forehead, giving him an appealing boyish look, touched as it was by gray on both sides of his face. When he looked up, as if just realizing she was there, his cool green eyes slowly raked her petite figure. For a minute she saw a flicker of surprise register and she grinned inwardly at the obvious interest he was careful to hide from her as he bent again to the form he was working on. Patiently she waited until he was ready to acknowledge her, taking the time to quietly and shrewdly assess the office and acquaint herself with her surroundings.

Eyes roaming the room she saw for the first time that they were not alone. With a small smile she greeted an older gentleman seated in one of the armchairs in what appeared to be a lounge area. He looked amused as he returned her silent greeting. Deer heads and antlers were mounted on the office walls; their glassy eyes staring vacantly at her from their lofty perches. With a slight shudder she moved her attention to the right of her. Through the open doorway leading to what was possibly a shop she spied a collection of RVs, snowmobiles and a large Ali-Craft speedboat. *This guy takes his toys seriously.* She knew from previous accounts that Ali-Craft boats were custom built to owner specifications and very expensive. Her innate business sense told her that the place reeked of money. She was determined that the man in front of her would be parted with some of it. She made the first move.

"Hi." She stuck out her hand to the man across the counter. He looked up, surprised as if he had forgotten she was still there.

"You must be John Mathews." She introduced herself, "I'm Lydia Jordan, your two o'clock appointment." She smiled brightly, her eyes crinkling at little at the corners, momentarily disarming him. Without thinking, he stuck out his hand firmly and met hers across the gap between them.

"Yes I am John Mathews," he rumbled with a small smile, "Nice to meet you."

By now the other gentleman had joined him behind the counter so that they both stood facing her. Both men towered over her but Lydia noted that John was taller by a few more inches and broader across the shoulders. John introduced his friend as Bill Johnson and Lydia obligingly shook his hand as well. Bill smiled back openly, his warm friendly eyes nearly magnified by thick coke-bottom glasses.

"Hope you don't mind me sitting in do ya? John told me you were popping by and the fact is I have a small business myself. Maybe you've heard of it? Johnson's RV and Marine?"

*Good! Lydia gloated silently. Two birds with one stone.*

"I don't mind at all" she spoke agreeably her head tilted back to eye her potential customers, barely peeking over the countertop. "In fact you've saved me a trip because you are definitely on our list as someone to call on."

John's next words cut into the air like a knife.

"The only thing is, little one, if you're here to sell me advertising I can save you some time and trouble. I never advertise."

Undaunted Lydia replied brightly, "That's okay."

The two men exchanged glances and eyed her warily.

"You wouldn't happen to have Yellow Pages handy though would you?"

Eyes questioning, John reached below the counter and silently handed one to her, its thick pages so heavy she had to use two hands to grab it.

"Thanks" she smiled as she took it and promptly dropped it at her feet with a loud bang, causing them to start a little. Stepping nimbly on top she managed to raise herself several inches above the counter, enough so that she was able to put her elbows on top and afford herself a better view.

"That's better," she declared satisfied. "Now that we all know what this directory is good for maybe you owe it to yourself to see how much better mine is and what it can do for you."

Amused the two men burst into laughter. Then amiably they settled down to hear her pitch.

At the end of the business day, sipping martinis and sitting by the pool with Dee, Lydia related the story of her hilarious sales call.

"The look on their faces when I pulled that stunt was worth it Dee. I wish you could have been there. Best of all, not only did I get a firm commitment from Bill today for several ads; I was able to set another appointment with John, too. So I guess the gamble paid off in spades."

"There is no doubt you have a horseshoe," Dee kidded her affectionately. "Too bad you didn't get a commitment from John today. Now you have to go back."

Lydia laughed. "Yes, I know, but I have to tell you that John Mathews is one of the most interesting men I have met in a long time. He is also incredibly handsome, if you like the strong rugged type. I would bet my last dollar that the real reason I didn't sell John today was because he wants to see me again."

Dee groaned. At just a few years older, tall, willowy Dee had appointed herself Lydia's guardian. Inclined to be more careful than her impetuous partner and best friend, she regarded her worriedly.

"What are you up to this time Lydia?" she asked half-jokingly. "You know in a town this size you can only go out with one man while we're here, so you'd better make it a good one. After all that, I sure do hope you sell him."

Lydia had flashed a wicked grin before replying to the underlying caution in her friends' voice.

"Don't you worry Dee. John Mathews is a good one all right. As for selling him - well it's just a matter of time, isn't it?" Dee groaned again as Lydia clinked glasses with her friend and burst out laughing.

"May I help you?"

Startled Lydia looked up into the brilliant blue eyes of the male representative behind the reservations counter.

"Ticket and passport please," he requested politely holding out his hand.

"Oh…of course." For a moment Lydia fumbled in her handbag for the required documents.

"Sorry," she apologized. "I guess I was daydreaming."

The clerk smiled as he glanced at her ticket.

"Well no wonder," he remarked still pleasantly. "I see you're off to Ixtapa Zihuatanejo for over a month. I have been there many times myself. Lucky you!" He handed back her folder and she replaced it in her handbag.

"Is it nice?" she questioned eagerly.

"You'll love it," he assured her warmly. "Have a wonderful time *Senorita*. Next please!" he called over her shoulder as she smiled and moved away to the customs line up in front of her.

Later on the plane, with a celebratory Margarita in her hand and travel book guide on the tray before her, she casually surveyed the plane and fellow passengers around her. *Always good to know who's going to die with me when the plane goes down,* she joked.

At one time she had taken pilot training in order to get over her fear of heights and flying. Despite the lessons she was still a white-knuckle traveler in large planes. The confined feeling of so many people around her made her claustrophobic as well.

A feminist to the core, Lydia always found it difficult to give up any of her hard won independence. At thirty-four she was still unmarried with one disastrous marriage behind her. At the thought of her age Lydia frowned. She was more than a little miffed that John had not made it down to her birthday party in Kamloops, nor had he thought to send her a gift or card. All day she had half expected some acknowledgement from him. In retrospect she was surprised at how disappointed she had been by his thoughtlessness.

At her party thrown by several of her closest friends she had tried to make excuses for John's absence. Although they had never met him, Lydia had told them about the times they had shared. Lina, a vivacious brunette had looked thoughtful but merely smiled her serene smile as Lydia stumbled her way through a shaky explanation of why John was not in attendance. *That's why I love her like a sister. She never says I told you so even when she told me so!* Her live-in lover and soul mate Len was not so reticent.

"What the hells the matter with the guy Lyd? And how come he hasn't come down to meet us yet? I don't know. I don't like him already and I haven't even met the guy...." He broke off as Lina gave him a not so gentle nudge.

"Lydia says he's busy right now and can't get away, Len." She turned back to her friend. "Give him another chance Lydia. After all, he did say he was going to join you in Zihuatanejo didn't he?"

"Yes he is." Lydia brightened momentarily and then frowned. "Problem is I just can't seem to pin him down to an exact date. All he says is that he will try to be there around the middle of January - maybe sooner. The worst part is I don't even know if I am going to be able to get a room at the Citlali Hotel yet. When I asked him how was he going to find me if I couldn't, he just laughed." She deepened her voice and managed a fairly accurate imitation of his.

"Why honey, I'll just look for the biggest crowd in Mexico and you'll be in the middle of it."

Lina laughed appreciatively. "It sounds like he has you pegged fairly well for someone who hasn't known you for too long. That's good news. Don't worry. I'm sure you'll find each other. You've already done it once."

Lydia smiled at the support in her friends' voice. "You know me – I'll manage anywhere. I told the lady on the phone in absolutely atrocious Spanish that I would take a hammock if that was all they had until a room became available."

Lina sighed wistfully. "I wish I were going too. I've been so tired lately."

Lydia looked closely at her friend for the first time that evening. She did look a little wan and her eyes seemed puffier than usual and....

"I don't know Lydia" Len interrupted. "I don't like the idea of you going to a strange country by yourself with no confirmed reservation."

Before Lydia could reply, Lina turned to him and began to ease him away, patting his arm in the calming manner with which she did everything.

As he followed her she threw a grin at Lydia who shook her head at the woman of steel beneath that fragile appearance.

"Don't worry honey, Lydia will be just fine. If anyone can take care of herself it is Lydia. Now let's get some food."

Lydia sipped her drink, suddenly weary as the Boeing 747 jetted across the skies. *It would be nice to have someone take care of me for a change.*

When she had first encountered John's powerful personality she had hoped he might be the one. Not financially of course, although he was certainly wealthy enough to do so. Lydia was many things but she was not a gold digger. She took pride in the fact that she was self made, a woman who had succeeded in life with a great deal of hard work and a healthy dose of luck thrown in. And, as young as their company was, she and Dee had managed a decent profit in the first year, enough so that she was able to take this time out for herself and recharge her much depleted batteries without worry or stress. Meanwhile, Dee had chosen to stay at home and do absolutely nothing but tend her sadly neglected gardens and lawn for a solid month.

When Lydia had first approached Dee about buying the business and going into partnership, she was understandably reluctant. Married to her husband of over twenty-five years and mother of three very active teenage daughters, she was leery of starting an unknown venture at this point in her life. After some thought however, the same reasons that made her hesitate were the very ones that made her decide to risk all and take the plunge. Having lived in Kamloops all of her married life, Dee shocked everyone by deciding it was time to move out of her comfort zone and look at this as an opportunity for change. Lydia knew that leaving her family behind for six months with only weekend visits to sustain her had proved more difficult than she had imagined. On the other hand Dee had seen the new level of maturity the girls had attained as they pitched in to keep the home fires burning. Her husband Jim had taken to being a little more romantic than he had over the last few years and she often glowed for days after a weekend home with her family. All in all the experience had proved to be a good one in many ways. Still, there was no question that Dee was happy to be back surrounded by her own treasures in the home she and Jim had furnished and loved all those years. In no time at all she had reestablished control of the house; much to the relief of both her husband and daughters. Soon they announced they were ready to forgive her for the summer of "Mom's Great Adventure", as they secretly called it among themselves.

*Of course what they don't realize is that come next May, we will be doing it all over again,* Lydia grinned to herself.

The plan when they first bought the Franchise was to get the business up and running and then resell it to someone else a few years down the road. They already had their eye on another Franchise in Kamloops owned and operated by a sweet young couple just out of college. Dee and Lydia had already discussed the possibility that they would be interested in taking it off their hands at a future date.

Lydia considered her friendship with Dee gratefully. If it hadn't been for her, she would never have had the opportunity to have a business of her own. It was only through Dee's considerable clout with bank managers in town and a willingness to use her land as collateral that had allowed them the capital they needed to start their business.

*Thank God we succeeded,* she thought; relieved they had been able to pay off the loan in full by the end of the campaign.

This accomplishment made them both very proud of themselves even while it completely surprised the naysayers when they had first broached the idea. In fact, even the banker they had borrowed from had been surprised by how soon he received his money and assured them that next year all they would need was a line of credit to cover their start up expenses.

No, money was not the problem for her, Lydia realized as she pulled her mind back from the past. At this stage in her life all she really needed and wanted was someone special to share her life with. Someone she could depend on for emotional support and someone who would want to lean on her too, when times got rough. She got the feeling that John, as attentive as he could be when he put his mind to it, not only didn't really need her, but he also seemed to withdraw whenever it looked as though she might need *him.*

*You're being silly,* she chided herself.

John had been a strong supporter of hers since the beginning. He constantly told her how much he admired her business savvy and strength. He wasn't the most romantic man in the world she realized, perhaps clearly for the first time, but he had so many other good qualities.

*Yeah? Like what? What about love, romance, candles and champagne?*

*Stop it!*

She buried the sound of her inner voice deeper until it quieted. Another part of her knew full well she should be content with the obvious admiration of such a successful man. Then why did she feel such disenchantment? Pushing the negative thoughts away from her overstressed and taxed brain, she took a long sip of her pre-mixed, canned drink and pretended that she was already basking in the sun on a quiet beach in Mexico.

"Another drink, Ma'am?" the flight attendant asked brightly, poised over her cart to fill an order. Lydia handed her glass with a shrug and smile. *Why not,* she thought. *I'm on vacation!*

# Chapter Two

Lydia stretched languorously as she lay on the small bed of her hotel room the next morning, peering around her with a self-satisfied smile on her face. It hadn't been easy to get a room at the Citlali at the late hour she had arrived but thankfully, this last one was available for her. It was just before New Year's Eve and the town was packed with tourists from all over the world for the festive season. Driving into the village of Zihuatanejo from the airport she had hung out the window of the cab in an effort to take in all the frenetic commotion, lights and colorful ambience. Delighted by everything she saw as the cab whizzed her to her final destination for the night, she couldn't wait to stretch her legs and experience all that was before her.

John had recommended both the town and hotel to her early on in their relationship when she told him she wanted a nice quiet place to get away to once the campaign they had launched was finished for the year. That night he had taken her to the infamous Log House Restaurant for dinner – their first date – and she had mentioned her wishes for a holiday at the end of the year.

When she said, "Mexico somewhere sounds good to me," he'd laughed and told her about this place.

"If you really want a great place for a vacation that has the best of all of Mexico and is a little off the beaten track, I suggest you try Zihuatanejo. You will love it, I think."

"How do you pronounce that?" she asked.

"Zee-wah-ten-eh-ho" he pronounced the difficult word phonetically. "It is only 8 kilometers away from the better-known resort of Ixtapa. I have spent every year there for the last eight, usually a week or two in each place and, usually in January. First I stay at a charming little hotel in the village. It's small and although not really luxurious it is a very clean family owned operation. Best of all its very cheap," he added, mindful of her budget.

"Then for the latter part of my trip I go stay at one of the mega hotels like the Radisson. That way I get to experience true Mexican life and spoil myself a little too, by just hanging out around the pool and sipping Pina Coladas."

"It sounds wonderful," she agreed. "I think I will check that out. Where did you say I should go to find out more?"

The next day Lydia, true to form, combined a sales call with an excursion to the travel agent who answered her questions about a personal vacation to Mexico. Her agent was only slightly less enthused about Lydia's product initially but there was no mistaking her enthusiasm when it came to talking about Zihuatanejo. By the end of the hour appointment Lydia had all the info she needed as well as a contract signed for a modest ad campaign.

As she came to know and like John more, she began to harbor fantasies that maybe he would want to join her for his annual trek to Zihuatanejo next year. Perhaps even fly down with her?

With the wishful thoughts gathering momentum, she began to make initial inquiries as to departures with her new client, delaying as long as possible as she tried to gauge his timetable. Finally, when the travel agent warned her that time was running out, she laid down her deposit to hold the reservation to leave right after Christmas.

To her dismay, she discovered that she had miscalculated the timing when John would be able to get away and all hope of flying together to Mexico was dashed.

"Sorry kid," he threw out nonchalantly, seemingly unaware of her disappointment. "I'm afraid I won't be able to leave when you do. I have too much work to do getting in the bids to the government agencies before the end of the year. There's no reason you can't go ahead though. I could catch up to you later."

"Yes I guess so," she had agreed reluctantly. "Any idea when that might be? I plan on staying at least a month."

Pondering for a moment he finally came up with the possibility of sometime soon after New Year but refused to be pinned down to an exact date.

"Don't worry though. I'll be there, I just don't know when. I'll call the hotel and give you plenty of notice. At least enough time to move the Mexican boys out before I get there," he teased her lightly patting her head affectionately. She hated when he patronized her in that way but she swallowed her disappointment with a forced grin and then changed the subject.

Continuing the inventory of her room, Lydia spied a small dresser in the corner, with an even smaller mirror above. Several hangers in the closet reminded her that she should unpack and that she should squeeze a few more from the owner of the hotel. She had, as usual, brought more clothes than one person could reasonably expect to wear. Her motto was that it was better to be prepared than caught short. So, over the protests of Dee, she threw anything that looked vaguely tropical or festive into her overstuffed bags.

Further inspection revealed pretty white lace curtains doubly lined and adorning her window overlooking the courtyard. The tiny bathroom contained a shower, sink and toilet but not a countertop and she wondered where she was going to put all the toiletries she had with her. Thankfully however the room did have a full-length mirror behind the bathroom door.

The room resembled a broom closet but it was immaculately clean as John promised it would be, and she was not about to complain. She was lucky the hotel had believed her good intentions to come and had set aside this room for her arrival. Her travel agent told her she was extremely lucky to get a room this close to New Year and in such a prime area of town close to all the amenities. As it turned out, because she had stalled with her booking as she tried to wait on John's timetable, she almost didn't even get a flight until well into the second week of November. This, of course left her wondering how John was going to manage but then she shrugged it away.

*He's a big boy! He'll get here when he gets here. Stop fussing.*

It had been nearly 10:00 last night when the taxi deposited her and her bags on the sidewalk in front of the hotel. Looking doubtful when she assured her driver that this was the place, she wondered at his reluctance. From the outside and in dim light at least, she was charmed by the place. Brightly colored window boxes were filled to overflowing with flowers, spilling over the balconies of the three-story building. What she didn't realize was that her driver had taken an almost fatherly shine to her, recognizing a vulnerability about her that surprised him, given the fact he was happily married with ten brown-eyed children of his own. It was easy to see that this was her first time to Mexico, if the way she gawked shamelessly out the window was any indication.

"What's wrong with Canadian men?" he had questioned her on the drive, his English broken but surprisingly good.

"What do you mean?" she had laughed, somewhat surprised by the question.

"Why are you here alone in Mexico? A pretty woman like you should not be alone." And then he added before she could formulate a reply, "Don't worry. You'll find a man in Mexico for sure. *Mexico es muy romantico.*"

Lydia only smiled from the back seat, not bothering to tell him that her boyfriend would be meeting her here later. *Let him think what he likes. John will be here soon and all will be great.*

*Yes and so will New Year's Eve and you will be alone again this year.*

The thought depressed her almost immediately and she sighed. The taxi driver hearing her shook his head sadly once more secretly thankful for his faithful wife in his own home and vowing he would give her an extra kiss and a squeeze tonight.

As she rose from her bed, Lydia glanced out the window on the far side of the room. From there she could see out over the rooftops of some of the smaller buildings nearby. Mostly whitewashed, the buildings were covered with flowers that seemed to grow out of the cracks in the walls. Breathing deeply, she inhaled the fragrant air around her. In the distance she could hear the sound of roosters crowing, dogs barking and venders crying their wares. Peering out the corner of the window she could see children playing exuberantly in a nearby playground, attached to what looked like it could be a school. Later, over a leisurely breakfast on the pretty little rooftop café of the hotel, she asked Xotchel, the owner of the establishment, about the neighborhood.

"Yes, there is a schoolyard around the corner from here" Xotchel answered in perfect, heavily accented English. "My son goes there. I hope the sound didn't disturb you too much? The holidays are here now. It will be much quieter in a few days time when the children are let out for vacation."

"It's no problem at all Xotchel, *gracias*." Lydia graciously smiled at her host. She decided to purchase a pair of earplugs at the first drug store she came across.

After breakfast Lydia packed a few things in a small rucksack and set out to explore the surroundings. The travel guidebook she had inherited from John before she left "to make sure you hit the high spots" said that Zihuatanejo meant A Place of Women.

*How very apt since I am here without a man,* her inner voice whined pathetically. She shook it off and continued walking.

Following the small map she headed toward the ocean, stopping to window shop as she strolled. At this hour the streets were already busy with both tourists' and locals alike. Children and dogs, equally unattended roamed the streets freely, darting in and out of slow moving traffic. At only 10:30 in the morning the sun was already starting to heat up, beating mercilessly down on Lydia's unprotected head.

*First thing you need to do is buy yourself a hat,* she reminded herself.

She continued on following her map as closely as she could until she found the Native Market, located conveniently across from a rather large Catholic Church. At the very first stall she came across she noticed wide brimmed and colorful sun hats on the wall. She approached the friendly looking vendor standing in the entranceway. After much good-natured haggling and bargaining (the guide-book pointed out quite clearly that it was acceptable to do so there), Lydia walked away from the shop the proud owner of a rather ridiculous looking straw hat. Although she felt that the price was fair, she wasn't so naïve as to think that she had the better end of the deal. Still she was satisfied with her purchase and decided it was time to head for the beach.

Raising a white arm she caught the first of many taxis that were cruising the streets and was soon riding in cool comfort to Playa La Ropa, Zihuatanejo's most popular beach. She was intent on a relaxing day of sun, sand and refreshing seawater.

Deep in thought as the town sped past her window, she started when the driver spoke to her.

"*Habla Español?*"

Looking up she smiled and shook her head no. He persisted.

"Who are you here with?"

"I am here by myself," was her quick, unthinking reply.

He leered suggestively in the rear view mirror.

"*Si?* I could be your guide, no?"

"No" she said firmly, amused. "My boyfriend will be coming here in a few days. Thank you anyway though."

The young driver shrugged good-naturedly not particularly bothered by her answer. There would be other *gringas.*

"Too bad for me," he smiled philosophically.

Turning halfway around in his seat to face her, he winked. She couldn't help it and burst out laughing at his audacity.

At last the taxi arrived at the little restaurant that Xotchel had recommended. It was next to the Mexicana Fiesta Hotel. Xotchel had told her that *Patty's Seafood Bar and Grill* was a favorite of both locals and tourists. She waved goodbye to her would-be guide and entered the *palapa* to the right of her. Seeing a small bathroom off to one side, she slipped in and proceeded to change into one of the five new bathing suits she had splurged on before leaving Vancouver. This one, a bright melon colored bikini, flattered her rather voluptuous figure. She was a little self-conscious as she stepped from the tiny stall, unaware that all eyes of the waiters were upon her. She made her way to a chaise lounge under a beach umbrella and quickly placing her towel flat on the cushion she made a nest for herself. A waiter magically appeared a moment later. She ordered a fresh squeezed orange juice. Closing her eyes, she felt the tension of the last few months slowly ebb away.

It was short lived.

"*Buenos dias.*". A musical voice broke into her dreams. With a soft groan she reluctantly opened her eyes. Deep brown eyes regarded her thoughtfully, a smile on full lips.

"You want to go fishing? Maybe snorkeling? You here with your husband? Maybe you come with me?" The questions came rapidly.

"No gracias." She smiled back at him. "Not today."

"*Mañana?*"

She complied quickly in the hope of dissuading him. "*Si*, maybe mañana."

Lydia closed her eyes again in the hope that he would take the hint and go away

"What time *mañana?*"

*This guy does not give up. I sure could have used him in our advertising campaign this year. God knows the salespeople we did hire were pretty hopeless.*

"*Senorita?*"

"What? Oh sorry. Listen, maybe tomorrow ok? Maybe not. I'll let you know." she told him as gently but firmly as she could, wishing wholeheartedly he would just go away and leave her alone.

"Right now I need to rest ok?"

He smiled good-naturedly.

"No problema *Senorita*. My name is Felipe. I see you on the beach *mañana.*" With that he swaggered away, his tiny bathing suit hugging narrow hips that swayed to a rhythm only he seemed able to hear.

Still smiling she closed her eyes again, enjoying the sound of the surf a few meters away. Just as she was drifting off, a woman's voice sounded in her ear.

"Necklaces? Bracelets? Good buy. Very nice."

"No *gracias*," she mumbled without opening her eyes.

"Look, I'll show you." The voice was more persistent now

"No gracias!" she repeated more firmly, refusing still to open her eyes until she felt the shadow move from the lounge chair.

*Gee, it's going to be harder than I thought to get a siesta today.*

Slowly she sat up and reached for her drink as she surveyed her surroundings.

Ahead of her was a long stretch of white beach, dotted with brightly colored cabañas. It was a little crowded today with mostly Mexicans as Xotchel had warned her it would be until at least after the ninth of January when most people would head back to the larger cities.

"Zihuatanejo is the preferred holiday destination of Mexicans during the Christmas and New Year season, while most *gringos* seem to prefer the resort area of Ixtapa just a short 10 minute bus ride away."

When John had mentioned that perhaps she would feel more comfortable there than in the village, Lydia determined that she would prefer being closer to the locals. He seemed to approve her choice.

"Best way to know the country and the people I always say."

Surprisingly though, he then suggested that maybe she would join him for a week in Ixtapa sometime after he arrived. Just so she would have a taste of both Zihuatanejo and Ixtapa and of course it went without saying that the tab would be on him. Pleased by the suggestion and slightly mollified in her disappointment that he was not going to be with her on New Years Eve, she heartily accepted the invitation.

Even while her mind was on the events that led up to her vacation here, she couldn't help but be fascinated by the activity around her. Young fathers played tirelessly with their children in the sand while mothers indulgently looked on or took pictures of their offspring as they dug castles on the beach. Large teams of teenage boys kicked soccer balls up and down the length of the beach, scoring goals between makeshift goal posts of discarded coconut husks. They laughed wildly and slapped each other on the back when someone made an exceptional play. Pretty Mexican girls in modest and not so modest bathing suits strutted nearby, giggling and pretending not to notice the would be soccer stars while the boys themselves often stopped dead in their tracks as they passed by, wolf whistles following the girls.

Laying in the lounge chair observing was soon making Lydia sleepy and sliding lower in her seat she decided to risk trying once again to finish her nap.

Many hours later she emerged from a deep sleep, hot, tired and thirsty. Blinking stupidly she sat up in her chaise lounger and gazed blearily around her. She could see that the sun was much farther to the west than it had been when she first arrived and dismayed, she looked down at her body. Gingerly she poked her thigh with a finger, gasping as she saw the imprint become white for a long time.

*Pretty in pink,* she giggled to herself, hurriedly standing up to cover herself in the matching sarong she had brought with her.

Taking a deep pull on her now warm beverage, she signaled to the waiter for her check then walked slowly behind the restaurant to hail a cab. A long, tepid shower an hour or so later did much more to revive her than she would have thought possible. Already her skin was deepening to a becoming shade of gold in the shadow of the fading sun. The combination of a warm breeze and a healthy hunger for sustenance beckoned her outside her hotel once again. Instinctively she turned in the direction of the ocean in search of an early evening meal.

For her first real night out on the town, she'd chosen to wear a clingy blue and white dress that hugged her curves becomingly and showed off her figure. The simple scooped neckline dipped tantalizingly low, while her bold silver earrings gave the garment a certain pizzazz.

Admiring glances from appreciative Latin men followed her progress but she was oblivious to the attention as she rambled through the cobbled streets. Passing a mix of tourists of both American and Mexican heritage, she smiled at the vendors, her eyes taking in the usual mob of children and street dogs as they darted in and out of traffic and people. Eagerly her senses drank in the sounds and sights before her. She felt as if she had landed not only in a different country, but on a different planet. The festive atmosphere combined with a blend of pop rock/Mexican music, filled her with an excited feeling of abandon. She nearly felt like dancing down the street to the seductive beat. Restraining herself, she thought that she could live here the rest of her life.

If only that were possible. I wonder how John would feel about six months a year in Mexico.

Lydia dismissed the idea almost as soon as she thought it. Impossible to imagine the powerful John Mathews leaving his business in someone else's hands while he lay around in the sun doing nothing. Sure he had his trusted assistant, Curtis, who could be left in charge. This was highly unlikely, given John's controlling nature. Still, for her though, it would not be an unreasonable or farfetched idea, given the fact their campaigns lasted only six months of the year, leaving the rest of the year fairly open to do whatever they wanted to do.

This year she had committed herself to working the next few months in the corporate head office assisting the other franchises with winning national accounts. Any ideas of moving here permanently would have to wait for at least another year, but for now it was definitely something to think about. She shook her head to chase away her fantasy for the moment and crossed the wide expanse of courtyard before her. It held a basketball court along with the occasional vendor along the sidelines.

Tonight the court was not being used to play the sport but rather looked as if there was to be some sort of entertainment about to happen. Anticipation crackled in the air and she decided to take a seat in the crowd on the concrete steps that led to the court.

She didn't have long to wait. Soon *Mariachis* began to line up along the edge of the makeshift stage, striking up what sounded to Lydia's untrained ears like a traditional folk song. As people around her swayed and clapped in time with the music, a troupe of handsome young people sashayed onto the stage, bowing and dipping in perfect harmony to the dances of the region, their colorful costumes a blur.

Her hand was grasped by a handsome, Mexican youth in his early 20's and before she could anticipate his intent she was laughingly dragged to her feet to dance on the court floor. White teeth flashing at her wickedly, he swung her around and around until she was breathless and giddy. Other couples joined them and soon they were dipping their way in a wild, madcap polka while the real folk dancers swirled expertly on the stage above them.

The music stopped and Lydia was able to gasp for her breath as the lad led her to her chair, whirling away with a smile of thanks on his open, handsome face. For the next two hours Lydia remained enthralled as the variety show played on, sometimes dancing with any of the Mexican boys who asked her, other times simply content to become a spectator in the crowd.

As the show neared its finale, Lydia realized that by now she was ravenously hungry. Waving goodbye to her new friends, she once more set off in search of a good meal.

Taking the promenade to her right she passed several boutiques and shops before reaching a promising looking restaurant, filled to near capacity with both Mexicans and Americans. Sensing that *Elvira's* would be a good choice she stopped in front of the menu board at the open-air eatery to peruse its contents. The maitre d' noticed her immediately and introducing himself as Enrique in perfect English, began to explain some of the specialties that Elvira's was most famous for. As he seated her and took her drink order, which he himself served, she took a moment to decide on which of the many delicacies Enrique had recommended. She settled on the *Camarones en Salsa Coco,* which was shrimp in coconut sauce and served on a bed of rice with baby carrots and buttered green beans. While waiting for her food she laughed and flirted with the staff of virile waiters who were determined, it seemed, that she would never be alone or lonely.

When her food arrived a little over 30 minutes later, they left her to enjoy her meal in peace. With real appetite she set upon her dinner, doing full justice to the chef's efforts. Her hosts responded with pleased smiles.

It was nearly 11:30 before Lydia, replete and content from the delicious dinner, paid her bill, leaving a generous tip to the waiters and bid goodbye to the friendly staff, promising to return many times during her stay. *Time to hit the hay. Just a quick stroll around the block and I'll turn in for the night.*

Realizing that tomorrow was already New Year's Eve, Lydia wanted to make sure she would be up and ready for a night of revelry, despite the fact she knew no one and had no plans of any kind to celebrate the event. She felt sure that anything and everything was possible in this magical place. Stepping down an interesting side street off the boulevard, Lydia followed the sounds of laughter and guitars to yet another restaurant whose neon sign proclaimed it to be "Coconuts Restaurant." On impulse she decided to stop in for a quick nightcap before going back to the hotel.

As she stepped over its portal, Lydia stopped in what appeared to be the lounge area and looked around slowly. Both sides of the massive bar to her right were ringed with tourists who seemed to come from everywhere in the world. She heard snatches of English, German and a smattering of what sounded like French and perhaps even Japanese. The only Spanish she heard spoken seemed to be from the staff as they rushed from table to table clearing plates and delivering food and drinks to the somewhat affluent looking clientele. Lydia searched for a place at the bar to squeeze in while watching the crowd. She felt an unaccustomed stab of loneliness and thought that it would have been nice to have been with John this evening and in particular in this place.

Just then the hostess, a tall, stunningly regal looking woman noticed her. She introduced herself as Tonita and offered to seat her. She was relieved when Lydia opted instead to sit at a space that had just become vacant at the bar knowing it would have been a long wait for her lone guest. She left with the promise that someone would take her order soon then hurried off to seat a table of four who had appeared out of nowhere in the doorway.

Lydia climbed atop the tall barstool beside a florid, gregarious looking man who sat with his back to her. Sensing a new body beside him, he turned to give her a wide welcoming grin.

"Well howdy there, little lady," he boomed in a classic Texan accent.
"How ya all doin?" Just get in, did ya?"

He stuck out his right hand leaving Lydia no choice but to take it, a faint smile on her face.

"Name's Earl. And this little darlin' here is my wife Bunny." He leaned back so Lydia could see the tiny blonde peeking around him, a warm smile on her freckled face.

"Bunny's mah wife," he said proudly, throwing a meaty arm around the object of his affection in such a way that he nearly upset her onto the floor. He soon righted her though and placed a smack on her cheek at which she giggled and snuggled closer.

Of course she is, Lydia thought wincing a little as the meaty hand shook hers but she managed a smile anyway. *Bunny! What else would you name someone who looked like that?* And this time her grin became genuine as Bunny's nose twitched in her direction.

Aloud she responded. "It's nice to meet you Earl and Bunny. I am Lydia. Is this seat taken?"

"Just by you," Earl guffawed. "Just set yourself down there and make yourself at home."

At that moment another group of people arrived to stand by his chair. Texans by the sound of it! Much to her relief, Earl turned his back once again as the boisterous group grabbed his attention. As inebriated as they were, they soon lost interest in her and became engrossed in the usual back slapping kind of hilarity that effectively excluded her. Thankful for the reprieve, Lydia turned her attention to the lounge part of the room, scanning hopefully for a single table at which to have a drink before retiring for the night.

It was then she noticed a small, attractive woman sipping a glass of wine from a long stemmed glass and staring straight at her, a small smile on her lips. Wearing a simple deep blue dress with a long flowing scarf wrapped dramatically over her shoulders, Lydia thought she looked elegant, almost regal—a sharp contrast to the people beside her at the bar. Behind the woman was the dining area. Intimate tables with snowy white tablecloths dotted the Terra Cotta floor, candles glowing softly on each of them. High walls enclosed the section but the roof was open to reveal the velvety night sky. White fairy lights strewn over the many plants and full-grown trees in the courtyard twinkled behind the woman, giving her an almost magical appearance. As Lydia watched, several people stopped by her table on their way into the dining area for several minutes before moving on. *Almost like she's holding court,* Lydia thought alternately amused and charmed by the scene.

Lydia turned back to the bar and placed an order for a Kaluha and Cream with "Pauley" the bartender. Paying for the drink immediately, she sipped from it as she rotated once again to continue her vigilance of the scene around her.

At that moment the woman in the corner looked up and regarded Lydia from across the room. Glancing quickly and somewhat disdainfully at the rowdy group at the bar, she imperiously raised her hand in greeting and beckoned to Lydia to join her.

Why the hell not, Lydia thought as she gracefully slid unnoticed by the Texans from her perch and crossed the room. *I haven't spoken to an interesting woman in two days except for Xotchel of course. This woman certainly looks like she's that.*

She stopped and smiled down at her hostess, extending her hand in greeting.

"Hello," she began gratefully. "It is nice of you to…"

Impatiently the woman waved her hand, ignoring Lydia's outstretched one and motioned to her to sit down on the chair beside her.

"Never mind that," she interrupted as Lydia complied with a smile. "I saw you at the Citlali last night when you checked in and since I'm staying there too, I certainly couldn't leave you with that crass bunch of people over there now could I?"

She smiled mischievously, her beautiful face seeming to glow in the soft candlelight as she continued.

"We single women have to stick together. My name's Ana. I've been coming to Zihuatanejo every year for 17 years now. I see a lot of people come and go, like those people over there," she indicated the spot where Lydia had just vacated.

"I presume you are *solita?*" she asked pointedly. Smiling Lydia nodded and introduced herself to the interested woman. This time the hand she proffered was accepted. Curious, she looked more closely at Ana as she talked on.

At first glance it was hard to determine her age but Lydia thought that Ana was probably in her mid-fifties, albeit a well preserved one at that. Her small face was virtually unlined, but it was her sweet smiles that even when speaking with such obvious dislike as she was now, captivated the expressions on her face and gave her the youthful glow she wore.

"Thanks for the rescue Ana," Lydia smiled gratefully. "Those people are not really my type either although where I'm from in northern Canada we have many people just like them. Friendly and nice enough, but I'm not much of a drinker so I prefer to distance myself whenever I can."

*Is that so? Funny you picked John, as a boyfriend then isn't it?*

Quickly she changed the subject, not wanting to investigate the inner voice that was intruding on her. Especially not now!

"You've been coming here a long time Ana. How long do you usually stay? What brought you to Zihuatanejo in the first place? Do you like it? Can you speak Spanish?" Lydia fired off the questions and Ana held up a hand laughingly.

"I came here quite by accident many years ago. A friend of a friend introduced me to this place and so here I am. As to how long I stay, it really varies over the years. Now I am able to stay here at least five months out of the year. How long will you be staying Lydia?"

"Not as long as you unfortunately, but I am here for a month."

"Wonderful," Ana enthused. "I meet so many people who come only for a week or two and frankly I find it a complete waste of time. A month at least will really enable you to get to know the area, the people and the surprisingly good shopping we have here."

"I agree," Lydia concurred, thinking back to her last short vacation to the Caribbean last winter. It seemed she had just arrived when it was time to turn around and head home again. This time she had been determined to treat herself to a real vacation – with or without John.

Ana was asking her a question and Lydia forced her mind away from further thoughts of her errant boyfriend.

"What do you do?"

Lydia launched into a brief discussion of her business and product, skipping over the details of her partnership with Dee and their franchise agreement.

Ana nodded politely as Lydia added quickly, "And sometime in the next couple of weeks my boyfriend John will be joining me. Maybe you know him? He has been coming here for the last eight years himself and always staying at least a week at the Citlali. His name is John. John Mathews."

Ana gave the question some thought. "The name doesn't ring any bells with me. Maybe if I saw him. Is he a writer?"

Lydia almost laughed aloud at the idea of the hard-core businessman as a writer, bent diligently over a typewriter. John much preferred to be outside in the lot pouring over his trucks with his head mechanic. It was either that or with local government officials or some cronies over a glass of Canadian rye whiskey in the back room of Bill's store.

"No, Ana. I would say that John is more the tycoon type." Lydia laughed and for the next few minutes described his attributes to her new friend who listened intently, a small half-smile on her face.

"You're not very happy with him that he's not here now are you Lydia?"

Ana pointed out shrewdly when she finished extolling his virtues. She waved an elaborate Spanish fan carelessly.

"Never mind! Tomorrow is New Year's Eve and Zihuatanejo is a magical place. Anything and everything can happen here." She laughed deep in her throat.

"Who knows? Maybe you will meet someone else?"

Lydia joined her laughter. "You sound like all the taxi drivers and waiters I have been meeting. They all seem to think I must be a crazy woman for being single and Canadian men are crazy for allowing me to leave the country alone."

For the next hour the pair talked about everything imaginable. Finding an amazing number of similarities in each other, Lydia marveled at how easily they fell into a comfortable friendship. She discovered that Ana was a writer of some renown in New York City while Ana realized that Lydia had once owned a large talent agency in Calgary supplying actors to various film companies that came through the area. Ana was now in the midst of writing her first screenplay and when she learned of Lydia's background she suggested that it would not be improbable that one day they might even work together. They laughed at the idea while at the same time realizing that stranger things could happen and often did.

At last Ana glanced at her watch.

"Well, my darling girl, I must be off to bed to get some beauty sleep if I want to look perfectly wonderful tomorrow. What are your plans for New Year's Eve?"

Lydia replied slowly. "I haven't given it much thought. Since I'm alone this year I thought I would let whatever happens, happen."

She paused. "You know I have this theory about New Year's Eve."

"Oh? What's that?"

I believe that how you spend your New Year's Eve is how the rest of your year will be. Now how silly is that?"

"Not silly at all," Ana affirmed. "In fact I believe something similar, too. So my dear, what we need to do is change your fortune for the coming year. If you feel like it why not join me tomorrow night? Everyone generally meets at Coconuts about 11:30 for drinks, at least those of us who are having dinner elsewhere as I am, and then we all go dancing later, after midnight. The management here hands out the usual party favors and sparklers, though not, thank god those silly hats. It is really quite beautiful."

"That sounds lovely Ana and I accept. I will meet you here at 11:30 tomorrow night. Thank you."

"Perfect, Lydia – be sure to wear something wonderful. Everyone will be very dressed up. Now I must be off. See you tomorrow."

Without waiting for a reply Ana whirled away into the night, her long scarf floating behind her."

Lydia sat quietly for a few minutes before leaving. It would be fun tomorrow she was sure and much better than being alone in a strange country. *But what will I wear?* She thought practically, doing a mental inventory of her wardrobe as she slipped from the restaurant to return to her room.

# Chapter Three

Sunlight streamed into the windows of Rodolfo's bedroom in the projects, effectively turning all that it touched to spun gold. By Mexican standards you could call the neighborhood he lived in as a suburb. Most would have laughed at the lofty title, preferring to call it simply just another *bario* in a city filled with them. Having lived among Americans in the past, Rodolfo knew that most tourists would be appalled by the crowded living conditions in which many people lived. City planners had wisely placed such districts, called *Infonivits* off the beaten path, so as not to offend visitors who came here searching for the natural paradise. Tourist dollars meant jobs and money to Mexicans who depended on it for their livelihood. Many such workers only made an average of less than four dollars a day. The real money came for those who catered to foreign tourists in tips, not wages and was something Rodolfo was adept at making sure he got his fair share of. Rodolfo and his family were definitely among the lucky ones.

Rolling over in bed Rodolfo gazed out one of the small windows of his room, seeing only the dirty walls of an opposite apartment building in desperate need of paint and upkeep. He knew that the dirt street outside would be littered with debris and strewn garbage left by any one of a dozen stray dogs that hung around waiting for people to place their trash outside.

The one bright spot in the neighborhood was the small oasis he and some of his neighbors had planted last spring between the buildings, taking turns weekly with the upkeep, which meant watering and hoeing. It was a small improvement but one that made a difference to Rodolfo and his meticulous family. Some days his people's lack of concern for sanitary habits was the one thing that made Rodolfo almost ashamed to be Mexican. *Almost, but not quite,* he grinned to himself.

He lay reveling in the glow of a new day, listening to the daily resonance of vendors and hawkers as they called out their wares of *pescado, boleos, pollo* and *agua* (*fish, buns or bread, chicken and water*) below his window. He grinned wider even as he pulled the pillows over his head in a vain attempt to drown out the noise. Not to be outdone by the human contingency, stray dogs and roosters started and kept up an almost steady chorus, while the shrill whistle of the local knife sharpener clashed with the sounds of housewives jabbering like seagulls in the courtyard outside his open window.

Babies began to cry in protest, although not for long. There was always someone around who could quiet a fretful child. Latin music began to blare from several other open windows, blending surprisingly well in a chaotic sort of way.

Giving up on getting anymore sleep that morning, Rodolfo threw off his covers with a sigh and sat up, swinging his feet to the floor and cradling his head in his hands for a brief moment. *There is no question that Mexico is a noisy country,* he thought for about the umpteenth time.

Swaying a little on his feet, he viewed his small sanctuary with satisfaction, noting favorably its cleanliness and order not only here but in the rest of the house as well. Last year they had painted every wall a different color, giving it a unique look that was the envy of everyone in the community. Warm bright Mexican colors that reflected the family itself.

Going to his closet, that unlike most peoples in the vicinity boasted real wood doors on it, he opened one, trying to decide what to wear. He noted with satisfaction the crisp white shirt and pressed black pants he would wear to work tonight, ironed as usual to perfection by his sister-in-law, Roberto's wife, Yola. Together with their only child, a young girl of ten, Andrea, the four of them made up the family group.

Tonight was New Years' Eve and as a waiter at the famed Coconuts Restaurant, he stood to make a great deal of money in tips. His position was envied by many of the other, lesser waiters in town simply because Coconuts was the best place in town to work—and the most expensive. It was not unheard of for Rodolfo to make two thousand pesos in gratuities in this night alone. He made good money he knew compared to most, and saved more now that he was once more living under his elder brother's roof. It hadn't always been like that though he remembered with a sigh, thinking back to the days when he had his own household and family to care for. Sitting down on the bed as he buttoned up a favored shirt, his mind raced back to the day his life changed forever.

Next to Coconuts, The Bay Club in Zihuatanejo was noted as a top restaurant and bar for miles around. As its general manager, Rodolfo hired his wife Beatrice to work as cook there. Together the two of them made the astonishing sum of twelve thousand pesos a month. It was more than enough to afford a small apartment, nice furniture and a little Volkswagen bug to drive back and forth from work and sometimes to the beach on Sundays.

Still, Rodolfo had been noticing a certain discontent and restlessness in Beatrice these days, her usual cheerful self edgier and sharper than warranted when they did manage to find the time to be alone.

His questioning of her only seemed to make matters worse and she would only shrug and roll over in bed, her back cold and unyielding to him when he tried to approach her. She began to take time off work, asking a distant cousin to fill in for her, paying her out of her own wages. Rodolfo became annoyed then downright angry as he demanded answers to her behavior and they began to have an increasing number of arguments, escalating until one or both left the other standing alone and confused.

To make matters worse, Victor, one of his newest employees seemed to be taking more time off work, too sometimes on the same days as Beatrice. This left him doubly short-handed and even more resentful. Rumors began to circulate around town that the happy marriage of Beatrice and Rodolfo was not all that it appeared to be, and suspicious notions were whispered into his ear concerning Beatrice and the new waiter. He did his best to ignore them, doubling his efforts to appease his wife and get back into her good graces.

The day everything exploded came on the heels of a phone call from Victor saying once again he would not be in to work that evening. Knowing it was also Bea's day off, Rodolfo suddenly grew cold as months of rumors finally dug their way into his heart. Removing his apron he excused himself to the owner and made his way to the door of his apartment.

As he began to turn the key into the lock, he heard the peal of Bea's laughter coming from within, followed by the low rumblings of a male voice. Slowly he turned the handle and with cold dread, stepped inside.

That incident had been over four years ago. Rodolfo had responded to his wife's infidelity in the only way he knew how. As his family watched helplessly, he got drunker than he ever had been in his whole life, and made sure he stayed that way for three solid months. During that time he sold everything he owned, including his car and small fishing boat. Leaving the apartment and furnishings to his now contrite wife, he decided he needed to leave the country in order to forget his troubles and disastrous marriage. He headed for the United States.

Hearing the news of his imminent departure, his mother cried and pleaded with him not to cross the border illegally at Tijuana, the horror stories of thousands who had tried and failed still rampant and fresh in her mind. Sure he would come to a similar fate she held onto him as he came to say his goodbyes, hoping against hope she would be able to change his mind.

His father stood by quietly and calmly in the face of his wife's hysteria and finally stepped in to remove her arms from their son's stiff and unyielding neck. Holding her tightly against him, he bowed acceptance.

"Come back safely my son," he whispered. "Mexico needs more men like you here."

With a final blessing to protect a favored son, he then turned away, his sobbing wife in his arms. Leading her gently inside, he closed the door on the modest home he had built for her so many years ago.

Crossing the border had been every bit as dangerous as Rodolfo's mother feared, and then some. Initially he had turned over nearly all the money he had to his contact, a man named Chico. He knew that Chico would first buy drugs with his money, and then sell it to eager customers before he would have enough to pay the people he needed to pay. This would turn his paltry two hundred pesos into ten thousand, the right amount needed to smuggle a live body into a new life.

For the first three days he had waited for the "Flesh Peddler" to give the word that they could leave, meanwhile trying to conserve as much of his funds as he could by eating sparingly and drinking little.

Even with careful conservation, Rodolfo was soon scrounging restaurant bins for enough food in order to survive while he waited word that the time had come to go. Determined to see this through to the end no matter what, he did whatever was necessary, no longer concerned about the outcome.

At last word was given and he and almost twenty other men from south of the border were herded into cattle cars to be driven as close to the border as they could be before they were to be led by foot across the dangerous terrain.

As long as he lived, Rodolfo would never forget the terrifying sounds of the helicopters whirring close to the ground, or the equally frightening bedlam of barking dogs and men's authoritative voices through loud speakers urging them to give up and turn themselves in. Terrified of being caught, his heart raced madly as he ran hell bent for leather, darting behind bushes when sweeping lights threatened to expose him. All around him he could almost hear the sound of men's heartbeats hammering in time to the din. Men just like him – looking for a better life, or running away from something as he was. For a brief moment he wished himself back in the warmth and safe haven of his mother's arms as he had when a child, but the snarl of a guard dog seemingly close on his heels soon brought him back to reality. He started to run.

On and on he ran through the stillness, keeping as much distance between himself and other men as he could, not wanting to be herded with the rest of them, only trusting himself in this venture to stay free. And then suddenly he was.

As he collapsed on American soil, free but still not entirely safe, he kissed the ground and offered thanks to the Creator. Watching the early morning sun as it began to rise above the earth, he saw for the first time a new day begun in a new land and suddenly he felt a new hope; as if a new life were possible for him, too.

Hitching a ride in the back of a pick up truck, he made his way to LA, a city he had only seen on TV. Once safely there he called Daniel Forbes collect from a pay phone far away in Butte Montana. As he waited for the operator to place his call, he reflected on his friendship with the man he was reaching out to.

Spanning several years, his friendship with Daniel was something he felt he could depend on. An authentic Indian Chief of immense power, Daniel had been a favored customer at the Bay Club. Every year he came to Zihuatanejo, bringing up to 23 family members with him. They took up three deluxe condominiums at the luxurious Villa del Sol on Playa La Ropa at a whopping price tag of $500 a night for each of them.

Despite their economic differences, Rodolfo and he had struck up a friendship and he had become like one of Daniel's sons. More than once Rodolfo and Beatrice had invited Daniel and his entourage to their home for fiestas and special occasions and soon the two families grew close and intertwined.

Daniel had often suggested to Rodolfo that he come to Montana to work for him at one of his many businesses. In addition to a trading post, he also owned apple orchards, an art gallery and a service station to name just a few. There was even a position for Beatrice if she wanted one. At the time they had politely declined, preferring to stay in the country of their birth. Now that was all changed and Rodolfo was soon to find out just how sincere Daniel's offers and friendship were.

He needn't have worried. Daniel answered his private line on the first ring and immediately accepted the call. Surprised to hear from his longtime friend, he listened intently to Rodolfo as he briefly explained the circumstances of his call. On hearing where Rodolfo was, he started the wheels in motion that would bring Rodolfo from the city of angels to what he always referred to as God's country.

A few days later Rodolfo arrived, hot, tired and hungry but eager to begin a new life with an old friend.

For the next five months Rodolfo worked for $5.00 an hour under the table, doing whatever was required of him. Living rent-free in Daniel's luxurious ranch-style house, he soon felt at home in his new surroundings. His social life became once more active with any one of the local town's nubile young girls, for whom he cared little but who sometimes quelled the pain of Beatrice's betrayal on hot summer nights. He was always kind to them and grateful for the warmth their bodies afforded but they knew that they would never be able to reach below the wall he had built around him. Still, they never felt used and accepted what he could give them with the grace of the young and wisdom beyond their years.

Life was good in Montana and although he missed the tranquiller life of Mexico, he quickly adapted to the new pace of his adopted country. He discovered a latent talent for beadwork and soon his designs were being sold in the trading post where Daniel had decided he best fit in. His outgoing personality and wide-open smile made him a favorite with customers and tourists alike while Daniel's daughters flirted with him all day long in the back room where he worked on his creations. Life was good and he became happy again. With some surprise he woke up one morning realizing a whole day had gone by when he hadn't thought once of his errant wife. He was beginning to feel that there was another world out there that he had yet to explore and that just maybe it would be worth living again, although not perhaps in the way he had first envisioned.

A call from his mother in late September changed his life once more and his newly found optimism was sorely tested as he listened to her pleas to come home. His father, always a robust and healthy man in the past was diagnosed with terminal cancer. It had spread rapidly and without warning was already inoperable. His time left was not long and his last wishes included seeing Rodolfo one last time before he died. Without hesitation, Rodolfo packed his few belongings and bid goodbye to Daniel and his family. Although it was doubtful he would be able to return, he did promise Daniel that he would keep in touch and made sure he knew he looked forward to the annual visit the family made to Zihuatanejo each winter.

Visiting his father on his deathbed in the room he had shared with his mother for over 40 years had been difficult and painful for him but he knew the trek was necessary.

"I knew you would come," his father had whispered triumphantly, a mere shadow of his former self, although his coal black eyes still burned brightly in his dying face.

Rodolfo, thoroughly shocked by the destruction the cancer had wrought, bent to kiss his cheek, gingerly lest he hurt him in his clumsiness and grief. But his father caught him in a fierce bear hug, clasping him firmly to his bosom.

After several undeterminable minutes he released him, studying his son's face and seeing the sorrow etched in his newly formed lines. Rodolfo was becoming a man, he thought, proud of this person he had helped to create standing before him.

"Tell me son," he demanded. "I have never been to America. What was it like?"

For the next two hours, Rodolfo regaled his father with stories of his adventures, skipping over the more brutal ones such as the escape over the border. His father was not a stupid man however, and he was quick to feel the terror and difficulty his son must have endured. He gave silent thanks for his son's safe return to him. As he listened to Rodolfo's tales of the people he had met and loved, the job he was assigned, and the new skill of beadwork making that he had learned, the old Shaman slowly drifted off to a peaceful sleep.

From that day Rodolfo sat beside his father every afternoon. Sometimes they talked quietly, sometimes not a single word was spoken as Rodolfo worked on his beads and his father watched in companionable silence. The rest of the family left the two alone during this time, allowing his mother a much needed break from the constant nursing she provided and his other siblings a chance to grieve away from their father's eyes. It was an arrangement that suited everybody. Sometimes Rodolfo could almost believe that his father's health was even improving, but of course it was a false hope.

His father's last day on earth began as so many before with Rodolfo entering his room as he had each day since his arrival. This time however his father lay gasping for breath, his eyes wild and glazed in a tortured face.

Rodolfo immediately filled the syringe with morphine as he had been taught by the doctor and injected it slowly and carefully into his father's veins.

"Not too much, not just yet," his father instructed as Rodolfo eased the needle out of his bruised arm.

"There are things I must say to you first my son…before I die. Come closer."

Rodolfo leaned over his father and watched as his face gradually cleared slightly as the drug began to take its effect. He spoke again.

"My son, will you be returning to your wife again now that you are here?"

Rodolfo bent his head, ashamed but decided to be truthful. He owed his father this much at least.

"No Poppa. I don't love her anymore."

His father's next words surprised him and he raised his eyes stunned.

"*Bueno*," he stated firmly. "That is good. I had a dream…last night and I dreamt of you. There is a blond woman coming for you…a white woman…she will make you happy again…don't worry."

Rodolfo smiled wondering if perhaps he had given his father too much of the potent drug.

His father continued, "There's more that I have to ask of you. You know you have always been my favorite," he held up his hand as if to stop any protest Rodolfo might have.

"Let me finish… I do not have much time."

"*Si* Papa," Rodolfo replied meekly, humbled by his father's words.

"Remember when you would take me fishing in your boat…so…far…out?"

Rodolfo nodded surprised.

"I never told you…how scared I was…"

Rodolfo laughed quietly, a smile playing lightly around his father's face as he continued.

"I have always been so proud of you…to have such a fine brave son."

By now tears streamed down Rodolfo's face and he let them go unchecked as he strained to hear the words.

"I need you to be brave now my son. Braver than you have ever been." His eyes went to the syringe on the nightstand and immediately Rodolfo knew what was required of him.

Anything but that Papa, his eyes pleaded but his father's need was stronger.

Finally, he nodded. As he prepared to honor his father's wishes his father gave him a look of such complete and pure love that Rodolfo knew he would never forget it.

Once more he picked up the needle and began to fill it, his own eyes never leaving the grateful ones of his father.

As the end neared, a ferocious expression glinted in his father's eyes. With a warrior's cry, Chief Joseph Miguel Perez-Perez lunged upright, his hands reaching out claw like before him at a vision only he was privy to. A moment later he collapsed in his son's arms.

As his father breathed his last, Rodolfo gently laid him down and closed his eyes for the final time. He stayed with him for several hours, reflecting on his life with the greatest man he had ever known, Then, rising he pulled the snowy white sheet over his face and went to tell the rest of the family that his father, the last Shaman of the Tarhamaraha Indians, was no more of this earth.

Rodolfo got up off his bed and stepped into a pair of cut off shorts he had left on a chair beside his bed. Pulling his thick black hair into a ponytail he walked into the kitchen where his sister-in-law was fixing the family's midday meal. She smiled a warm greeting and indicated a pan of *huevos a la Mexicana* heating on the stove. Grabbing a plate he heaped it high. He added a few handmade tortillas and sat down at his empty chair opposite his brother, to enjoy his food.

## Chapter Four

The same sun that shone brightly on one side of Zihuatanejo's town glowed as golden at the Posado Citlali. Already Lydia was enjoying an early morning breakfast on the hotel's rooftop, sipping her third cup of coffee after having just devoured fresh fruit, two eggs and a basket filled with toast. *I have to stop eating like this or I'll be as big as a house,* she thought guiltily, adding a spoonful of jam to still another buttered piece of bread.

As she chewed she thought about all the opportunities before her today and finally decided to take Enrique's advice as to how to spend her day. She would take a horseback ride along the beach at Playa Linda, about a half hour or so away by bus. Riding was one of her favorite pastimes in Canada although not one she had been able to indulge in much recently. After that, she would play the rest of the day by ear, assured that as always some interesting prospect would present itself in due time.

The rickety bus that transported her to Playa Linda careened to a stop on the nearly deserted beach and briefly Lydia drank in the wonderful feeling of being totally alone in the world. Following the crude sign to her right a short distance to the stables, she noted with approval that the horses appeared to be well fed and cared for. Almost immediately a groom appeared at her side and she spent the next few minutes agreeing on a price for the hour and a half ride. As luck would have it she was the only one out for a ride so early in the day, which meant that it would be just she and the groom.

Quickly assessing her riding ability, Miguel as he introduced himself, matched her with an appropriate horse. She was delighted with his choice—a quick-footed roan mare named Cometa. Miguel explained that Cometa meant Comet in English. True to her name, Cometa was lively and eager to move out while Miguel readied his own mount.

The silent caballero led her down the beach. Lydia remained slightly behind and closest to the waves that crashed to shore. She had often dreamed of riding along the surf with the sound of the waves like music to her ears. As she breathed in the salt air Lydia closed her eyes and reveled in the sensations of the moment.

A discreet cough from Miguel interrupted her reverie and she opened her eyes to find him regarding her with amusement. *Gringas,* he thought with a small smile. He turned his horse gently to the right and away from the beach.

Somewhat embarrassed to be caught daydreaming but feeling light-hearted nevertheless, Lydia flashed her famous grin and followed meekly behind.

A few hundred feet from the shoreline they found themselves in the midst of a coconut plantation. Enthralled by the great height of the majestic trees and enjoying the cool shade, Lydia wondered if a coconut had ever struck someone riding below.

Wouldn't that make great headlines back home? 'Native Kamloopsian Killed By Errant Coconut In Mexico.'

She giggled aloud, earning another puzzled glance and smile from the Mexican cowboy. Taking the camera slung around her neck she snapped his picture and smiled back.

"*Muchas gracias,*" she called gaily with a wave.

"*De nada,*" was his soft reply as he turned forward once again in his saddle. The gentle swaying of her horse lulled her and her mind drifted back to another time, many years ago.

She was that questionable age between fifteen and sixteen. Not quite a real woman but no longer a child anymore. While most girls her age were boy crazy, Lydia was horse crazy. Unfortunately her family was dirt poor and there was no way they would be able to afford anything as outrageously expensive as a horse. Her father, a loud, beer-bellied blue-collar workingman had enough trouble putting food on the table for the family of eight, let alone provide extras. It seemed that there was never enough of anything to go around.

Her mother, a mousy, downtrodden woman constantly chided her for the holes tomboy Lydia put in her clothes, convinced she would never grow out of her manly ways.

"Lydia," she would admonish her, "it's time you grew up and acted more like a lady."

That year Lydia drifted aimlessly, hovering belatedly on the edge of childhood and womanhood. Her late blooming body finally filled out, leaving her with high pert breasts, a twenty-four inch waist and softly rounded hips. Long golden hair hung shimmering down her straight back from a precise part in the center of her perfectly formed head. Her lips were full and she had unusual green eyes, which had a piercing quality that upset most people with their intensity. Until she smiled.

"When my Lydia smiles," her father would boast, usually while in his cups, "the whole world smiles with her."

At nearly seventeen, Lydia was a wonder—having what some referred to as a "Marilyn" body. High school boys vied for the chance to be alone with her but Lydia never gave them a second look.

Many a life changing situation can occur when you are least expecting them. On one particularly bright summer's day, Lydia was at her job at the Mcleod 9 Diner, where she worked for her Uncle Max slinging hash and flipping eggs for truck drivers and locals alike. She had started the job at an age when she was barely big enough to see over the counters, which she had to wipe with greasy dishcloths. Back then she had nurtured a dream of someday being able to buy herself a horse. Over time however, that dream had changed to the "how am I ever going to get out of this town?" kind of dream. She saved every dime she made.

Like the high school boys, the male regulars at the Diner had long ago given up hope of ever dating Lydia and often watched gleefully while she shot down first one, then another stranger, looking to score some action. They all thought she refused them because she was still an innocent but they couldn't have been more wrong. Lydia had lost her virginity a couple of years back to a callow-faced boy at the stables where she sometimes rode at, five miles from town. Thinking he might have gotten her pregnant, he slipped away sometime during the night, never to be heard from or seen since.

Lydia's reasons for holding back were much more calculating than that. She was looking for someone who could get her away from here and on the road to a better life. Her chance came in the form of Dennis Jones, a traveling salesman all the way from Calgary Alberta.

Lydia watched the white Cadillac as it pulled up to the parking space directly in front of the restaurant. With vague approval she noted the soft bucket seats were leather—at least that's what it looked like from her vantage point anyhow. They were in fact cheap imitation vinyl but by the time she found that tidbit out her panties were around her ankles and she was lying on its backseat, too excited to care.

As it was mid-afternoon the restaurant was fairly deserted and Lydia was bored beyond belief. Happy for any diversion, she perked up considerably as a tall, elegantly dressed man unfolded himself from behind the wheel and walked purposefully into the store.

As the door chimes rang merrily, he approached the counter and sat on one of the low stools in front of her. Reaching for the plastic menu from the metal folder, he read the contents while Lydia patiently waited, order pad and pen poised.

Without looking up at the girl in front of him he gave his order rapidly, with the arrogant authority of someone who is used to getting his own way.

"I'll have the eggs and ham, brown toast, no butter and coffee black," he read aloud as he ordered. "Eggs over please."

He looked up and Lydia found herself starting at one of the handsomest man she had ever met. He had two of the bluest eyes she had ever seen.

She breathed.

"Will that be green eggs and ham?" she quipped before turning on the full magnetism of her smile.

It didn't take long for sparks to ignite between the two of them. They saw each other as often as they could over the next few days. As district Sales Manager for a major publishing company in the east, part of his duties included recruiting new salespeople to sell subscriptions to various publications door to door across the country. From the beginning Dennis saw her raw talent and potential. She quit her job at the diner almost immediately to go to work for him. Between bouts of passionate lovemaking either in his motel room or the back seat of his Cadillac, Dennis tried to convince her to go with him.

"It's a good opportunity for you Lydia," he coaxed with one eye on the naked curves of her body. "You're a natural, I can tell and what better way to see the country than this? Next week the crew is heading for Vancouver Island. Come with us." He added slyly, "You'll make a lot of money. We'll make a great team, you'll see."

Lydia was tempted to say yes immediately but instinct told her to hold out so she refused him time and time again.

"I can't go with you Dennis."

"Why not?"

As if to a child, Lydia explained. "We're not married, that's why not. My parents would never allow me to go with you." Lydia held her breath during the endless pause that followed her remark.

Finally, slowly he answered her.

"Then I guess we'll just have to get married then, won't we," he grinned as she threw her arms around him in relief and gratitude.

A justice of the peace married them the next day. Her parents managed to throw a small going away party for her the following week, secretly relieved that not only would there be one less mouth to feed but that they were spared the expense of a big wedding.

The next two years were good and Lydia not only proved Dennis right as a natural in the business, she was soon exceeding even his own sales records before he became the manager. Lydia learned how to cajole, flatter and close sales to people who couldn't afford, didn't want or would never need, what she was selling. Head office noted the progress, sending letters of congratulations to the couple on the road aimed mostly for Lydia's benefit and often excluding Dennis's contributions to the company. Over time, resentment began to build and fester in the couple's idyllic relationship.

Moving frequently from town to town, city to city, the places they visited soon became a blur to Lydia. Most of the time she had no idea where they were. As money flowed, so did the endless stream of parties. After a sales day any number of the people they worked with would join them. It seemed as if they never had any time alone together anymore. When Lydia mentioned it to Dennis he shrugged her concerns away.

Lydia found herself drinking more, sleeping less, and working harder than ever. Her new slender, sleeker figure had matured and ripened. Though still curvy, time had erased any sign of the baby fat she carried as a teenager. Curiously enough, as her body changed, so did Dennis's attitude towards her. It seemed to her that he was avoiding any contact with her unless it related to business. He slept in the other double bed of the motel rooms. As he withdrew from her, she felt the coldness coming from him. Eventually the situation became unbearable for her.

One night, pleading a headache, Lydia decided to stay in the motel room she shared with her husband instead of joining him at yet another party down the hall.

"Are you sure babe?" Dennis asked with rare concern, stroking her forehead with a tenderness he hadn't exhibited in awhile.

She shook her throbbing head and waved him away with an effort, the blackness threatening the beginnings of a full-blown migraine.

The sound of thunder woke her many hours later. Muffled sounds, through paper-thin walls further irritated her still throbbing head. Reaching out to feel the other side of the bed and finding it empty, she glanced at the clock on the dresser beside her. Three AM.

Instantly alert, a foreboding feeling starting in the pit of her stomach. She switched on the night light above her bed, wincing as the glare pierced the remnants of her migraine, temporarily blinding her. Moving carefully she eased herself off the bed.

The sounds from the next room were getting louder, punctuated by a woman's giggles and sharp shrieks of laughter. Lydia knew that the room belonged to Dennis's newest recruit, a buxom redhead with long legs that practically started at her neck. Glenda something or other, she thought annoyed.

Sounds like someone is getting lucky. And, where the hell is Dennis?

She decided what she needed most of all was a breath of fresh air. The small room was stuffy in the storm and threatened to engulf her. Wrapping her housecoat around her, she stepped onto the balcony of the motel room, which overlooked the parking lot. She breathed deeply as the air assaulted her senses. Dennis's car was still in the lot. She wondered where he could still be at this hour of the morning.

Just then the door to the room next to them opened. Lydia watched in shock as Dennis stepped out into the hallway with a naked, clinging redhead wrapped tightly against his body. With a familiarity that sickened Lydia, he patted the woman-child's rear and shoved her, still giggling, inside the room, shutting the door behind her. As if sensing a presence, he turned and peered drunkenly in to the semi darkness.

Lydia stepped back into the open doorway, praying that he hadn't seen her. She was unsure as to what she was supposed to do next. She ran to the bathroom with her hand over her mouth and got quietly sick. Dennis reeled in. Half lying on the cold tile floor in the bathroom, she waited until she heard him stumble toward the bed. The squeak of the bedsprings indicated that he had fallen across the mattress.

Giving him a little time to make sure he passed out, she let herself out of the bathroom quietly and crawled between the sheets of the opposite bed while Dennis, still fully clothed snored loudly in the other.

The next morning, Lydia feigned illness and took the day off work. A haggard, sheepish Dennis left to round up the troops for breakfast before their usual morning hurrah session. Once sure he was safely out of the way, Lydia packed her belongings, slipped the weeks sales proceeds into her purse and caught a cab to the bus station. At the end of her journey she filed divorce papers. She never spoke to Dennis again.

The best revenge is living well. Her favorite saying came back to her as she swayed on the back of her horse in time to the breezes on the wind. Feeling gloriously alive and well, she kicked her heels into the sides of her now complacent mare and started her at a nice easy lope toward the beach. Her guide had no choice but to follow. Soon they were racing down its silky length, heads bent over the necks of their mounts, gaining speed as they flew. Finally, Lydia pulled up on her reins and slowed the panting Cometa to a quiet walk. Smiling at her guide she followed him as he turned his horse toward the stable, indicating her ride was at an end.

Saddle sore, but unaccountably happy, Lydia slid to the ground from the beautifully wrought leather saddle. Tipping Miguel generously, she limped her way toward one of the restaurants that dotted the beach. She wanted a cool *cerveza* and a chance to rest her stiff bones.

Although her joints and backside already ached from the unexpected exercise, she knew from experience she would be even sorer tomorrow. Settling gingerly in a plastic chair, she ordered a beer from the waiter and leaned back to view her surroundings.

Her quiet enjoyment was interrupted when a rusted out VW Van roared into the near empty parking lot. Six tourists wearing loud cotton shirts, cameras slung around their necks got out. The driver's side opened and an energetic Mexican man, possibly the tour guide, in his late 50's or early 60's, leaped from the vehicle. Expertly he rounded up the group and herded them toward the pier. As he passed her table he tipped his hat to her. He had caught her amused expression so he stopped and looked down at her, a wide smile on his face.

"You want to go snorkeling? We're going to Ixtapa Island. Why don't you come along?"

He stuck out his hand. She took it, allowing him to pull her from her chair to stand beside him.

"My name's Jose." He introduced himself.

Lydia smiled, charmed by his easy manner.

"Thank you Jose but no. I don't know how to snorkel and I am terrified to learn."

"*No hay problemo,*" he said. "I'll teach you. Twenty pesos and that includes the rental of your equipment. I've been snorkeling all of my life and I promise you in one hour you will be an expert."

Lydia thought for a moment, glancing at the other tourists standing nearby who smiled their encouragement.

"Come on," they chorused. "What do you have to lose?"

Good point, she considered. *What did she have to lose, except quite possibly her life?*

Aloud she said, "Ok Jose, you've got a deal."

Gathering her small knapsack, she paid for her beer and followed the boisterous group to the end of the pier where water taxis awaited to transport them to the island. Jose informed them that the island was a mere short five-minute ride away.

Lydia waited patiently while Jose organized the group. She grew more comfortable as she watched him instruct them on the use of the equipment before sending them into the shallow end.

He turned to her confidently and took her by the hand, leading her to a path winding over the hill and down to the stony beach on the other side.

"Now your turn. I'm going to take you myself," he promised her.

Waves crashed ominously on the rocks near shore, striking terror in to her. Sensing her fear, he quietly explained the equipment and how it would work. Adjusting the straps of her mask, he taught her to seal it around her face with one quick inhale through her nose. Placing the snorkel in her mouth, he showed her how to breathe with the unfamiliar apparatus until she felt comfortable.

When he was satisfied that she was at ease with the basics he showed her how he would guide her when they were in to the water.

Still apprehensive, but feeling slightly more confidant, Lydia followed him into the surf, clutching his hand in a death grip as they waded thigh deep in to the water.

Now Jose crouched down and donned his gear, indicating to Lydia she was to follow suit. She followed his example and bit gently into the snorkel as he taught her to do.

Stretching out on the water he pulled her down on top of him until she was riding his back into the waves, one hand around his incredibly taut middle, the other gripping tightly on his right shoulder. In this strangely sensuous way they swam away from shore until Lydia began to feel more and more relaxed, her grip lessening with each gentle lull of the waves.

God, I'm almost turned on, she realized giddily, almost laughing aloud in her snorkel at the thought.

Suddenly, a world she had never known existed opened before her and enfolded her in its magical embrace. Fish of many colors—electric blues, yellows and deep red swam idly before her, fins twitching effortlessly in the tide. Occasionally the teeming marine life darted around and through them in search of food, nibbling gently at her toes and fingers before flitting away. Brilliant coral shone in the water as if lighting the way to other treasures.

From a pocket of his trunks Jose procured a packet of crackers and he banged it on a piece of coral while easing the contents from the wrapper.

The effect was instantaneous. Enormous schools of fish of every species imaginable engulfed them, and Lydia found herself surrounded by nothing but moving color and light. Enthralled for the second time that day, she reached out her hand in an attempt to touch as many of them as she could but they eluded her. Time stood still as they drifted languorously in the warm waters of the Pacific. She never wanted to leave.

Eventually Jose indicated that the lesson was over and they surfaced easily from the waist high water a few feet from shore.

"Very good Lydia. Now it's time for you to try it on your own. I know you can do it. Don't worry I will be on shore watching you. You'll be alright," he assured her watching as a flicker of fear crossed her face.

A wonderful sense of accomplishment followed her as she rode in Jose's van back to the hotel. Exhausted, but immensely proud of herself, she quickly showered then lay down for a much needed siesta before the festivities of the evening.

## Chapter Five

John shut down his shop exactly one hour before his usual closing time, his only concession to New Years' Eve. A self-made man, his first priority had always been his business; his family came second. His two grown children, Erica and John Junior, often complained to their mother that he hadn't spent enough time with them as youngsters, a fact she knew all to well.

Hard to teach an old dog new tricks, he soothed his conscience, turning off the lights of the shop and closing the door behind him as he stepped back into the office.

His pickup truck idled in the parking lot outside as he went through the normal routine of shutting down for the next couple of days. Glancing at his watch he realized he had time for a leisurely supper at the neighborhood pub before he had to shower and change for the party he was invited to.

The whole month had been a whirlwind of parties celebrating the Christmas season. It was an important time of year for him business wise. Opportunities for schmoozing old clients—primarily in the forest industry he catered to, and for attracting new ones. In the north, that often meant a bottle or sometimes even a case of the fine scotch he bought in Vancouver. If they insisted that he join them for a glass or two to help solidify a deal, that was all part of doing business, as far as he was concerned.

Sighing, he gave the front lock a final twist. He shivered in the bitter cold outside his shop and jumped quickly into the now warmed up Ford. The cold reminded him that soon he would be basking in the heat of a Mexico sun. Mexico reminded him about the woman he had been seeing the last six months or so.

He was surprised at how often his thoughts turned to Lydia. This was an unheard of phenomenon with most of the women of his past. He admired her, he knew that much, and appreciated her sassy manner and go-getter attitude.

As he shifted the truck into reverse he turned his thoughts to Theresa. She had fooled him badly, he thought with a wry grin, still amazed at his gullibility. He had found out after the fact that he had been just one of a whole string of men she had cast aside or burnt in one way or another.

He'd met Theresa at the popular country bar known as Viva's in the Yellowhead Inn. It was a great place for people who loved live country music. You could have a few laughs and beers and it was also known as an excellent pick-up joint. Filled with hungry divorcees, usually between the ages of 35 and 50, all looking for Mr. Right, any man looking for a way to score usually got lucky on any given night. In fact it was rare when a person didn't.

In Prince George odds were in favor of the women with a male to female ratio of three to one. The trick, John's friends joked, was to find a woman late at night still standing and still definitely alone.

When John and a couple of his buddies from the local Ford dealership arrived, it was nearly 11:00, a couple of hours away from closing time. The three of them were already three sheets to the wind, and looking for action. Casing the joint, they quickly found a place at the bar and ordered a round of drinks.

Spinning slowly on his bar stool, John saw her, staring at him from across the room. A small smile played around her mouth as she looked away. She whispered something to a female companion and then looked back over at him. It was all the encouragement he needed.

While his buddies watched with amused interest, John lurched slightly unsteadily to his feet, and walked over to the object of his desire, and introduced himself.

Knowing he was fairly drunk, and fully aware of who he was, Theresa didn't pretend to be hard to get. A half hour later found her driving him home and hopping into his bed – a place she occupied for the next year.

At first Theresa had seemed almost too good to be true. John thought he had died and gone to heaven. He had never remarried after the bitter divorce from the mother of his offspring. He sometimes missed what it seemed most of the world but he had – a real home and someone to come home to. There had been many women over the years, but they never lasted, especially once they realized how much time and energy he spent on his business. He had been ripe for the picking when Theresa came along and charmed her way into his home and heart with ease.

Their first night in the sack convinced him that she was the woman for him. Bells rang that hadn't been rung for a long, long time. The other thing that appealed to him was that she never complained of his late nights and the amount of time he spent carousing with his friends, often getting up when he stumbled in late and helping him into bed. Long hours he put in at the shop never seemed to concern her either. He always arrived home to a hot cooked meal after work – when he bothered to that is. She never complained no matter what he did and John began to see a future – one that included her in it.

Six months after living together she dropped her bombshell on him. Informing him that she didn't like sex and in fact never had, she moved her things out of the master bedroom and into the equally spacious spare one. Rocked to his core he managed to finally get an explanation out of her.

"I have an inverted uterus," she informed him flatly. "Sex hurts."

Emotionally, it was like pouring hot oil over him. Occasionally she allowed him access to her body but on the rare times it did happen John finished the act as quickly as possible, with her lying absolutely still below him. Theresa's former pretense of enjoyment gone, he often felt more like her rapist than her lover. It certainly had the effect of dousing his desire for her. The question now was what was he going to do about it?

John was reluctant to admit to his family and friends that the relationship had soured. At first he tried to make it up to Theresa in other ways, showering her with gifts of clothes, jewelry, and furniture – anything she wanted. For Valentine's the following year he bought her a new car and a mink coat and on her birthday presented her with the keys to a new house.

For her part she kept herself beautifully and immaculately coiffured as was befitting a woman of her new financial status. While his private life left much to be desired, in public John was the envy every of man he knew. Unfailingly polite to his clients, family and friends, she always looked wonderful on his arm at any public function they attended. Alternately miserable and content, John knew he was trapped into a deal of his own making—one he didn't know how to get out of.

His hopes rose just after Christmas. His longtime friend and confidant Bill had whispered that the rumors that were spreading all over town about the carryings on of Theresa while he was away on business trips to Vancouver were true. Suspicious of her from the beginning, Bill told him her love interest was a small town celebrity and TV host, Tom Savage. Young, handsome and heir apparent to the top position at the station his father-in-law owned, Tom was definitely a rising star in the industry. The only fly in the ointment was Tom's marriage to the boss's daughter. A scandal could cost him everything he had worked for and John was fairly sure he wouldn't risk that for a bit of fluff like Theresa, no matter how attractive she might be.

John was also fairly sure that Theresa was not about to leave him unless she was sure her next target was firmly and completely hooked. It was definitely going to take some planning but one thing John had on his side was time. All he had to do was catch them in the act, but how was he going to do that and get rid of her without it costing him a ton of money?

In Canada property laws were strict; common-law partners were entitled to a 50/50 split after a certain period of time – undisputed. While gathering evidence and baiting the trap, John quietly bided his time. After all, he was a northern boy born and bred and up here in this relatively isolated part of the world. Patience came like second nature to men like him.

Several months went by with Theresa's behavior becoming bolder and riskier in light of what she viewed as John's indifference to her and her extracurricular activities. It was this lax attitude of hers that he had been waiting for.

It all came to an end when he had pretended to accept her excuse of a Women's Auxiliary meeting at a hotel downtown. Telling her he was going to be late himself that evening, he borrowed one of his company's newest vehicles from the shop—one she wouldn't recognize – and followed her, hoping to catch her red handed.

Not noticing his presence, she parked the car he'd bought her in front of a somewhat run-down apartment building on 15th Avenue that he was sure didn't belong to any of their mutual friends. He watched from a safe distance as she hurried up the stairs to the entrance, produced a set of keys and let herself in. He waited a little while and then followed her as far as the glass doors.

It was a security door and for a minute he debated whether he should just give up and go home or wait to see what happened next. Perseverance won out and he was rewarded by the departure of another tenant from the building, which allowed him admittance.

Scanning the row of names on the board, he searched anxiously for a name he would recognize. He needn't have worried. There in bold letters proclaiming his guilt was the name of T. Savage.

This guy is really, really stupid or he wants to get caught. John grinned to himself. Not waiting for the elevator he took the stairs two at a time to the penthouse suite.

When the door of the apartment opened to his knock, John stuck out his hand to the startled man in front of him, smiling even wider at the pale, angry face of his former lover.

"Thanks buddy," he quipped brightly. "You've just done me a real big favor."

There had been the usual tears and recriminations, but John managed to steel himself against Theresa's games and threats. After three stressful weeks she signed the papers against any future claims and took the $50,000 he offered her. Hauling away the many gifts he had bestowed upon her she packed up everything, including all the furniture, into a U-haul trailer and, like a gypsy in the night, folded her tent and left town for good.

He tried not to begrudge her the money, knowing that it could have been a lot worse. Thankfully Tom had turned out to be a real sap and had forced her into taking his offer in order to save his own skin. As Theresa found out all too soon, Tom never had any intention of leaving his wife for her, a fact that bruised her pride and made John feel almost sorry for her. Almost.

*She walked away with a hell of a lot more than she came with,* he grimaced as he pulled into the driveway of his house and stepped inside.

He met Lydia on the same day that Theresa was leaving town, a fact that was not wasted on John even now. Grinning, he recalled the way she had handled both her and Bill with the grand standing stunt she had pulled with the Yellow Pages. Even now as he opened the door to his house he remembered the way she had dealt with the situation with aplomb and a self-deprecating smile. Stepping into the now bare living room, *I really have to furnish this place,* he saw her lively face, admiring the courage and business sense that he had easily discerned at their first meeting. She had even managed to charm his old friend Bill, not an easy feat at the best of times.

His friends and family were shocked when he took up with Lydia so quickly after Theresa's departure, pointing out to him the uncanny resemblance the two women had to each other. It was true—they did look alike—both blonde and on the petite side, but there the resemblance stopped as far as John was concerned. While he saw now that every move that Theresa made in any situation was always coldly calculated to put her in the best light, Lydia on the other hand was completely without guile or subterfuge.

At first he had kept Lydia at arms length, not anxious to get involved with someone who resembled his last girlfriend and for once heeding to some extent his friends advice to be more careful. For her part Lydia seemed to ignore his reluctance, not really understanding what came before her, and kept up the friendship they had tentatively begun since the first day they met. Popping in on him sometimes just to say hello or to have a quick cup of coffee with him before running to another appointment, he began to relax and see her for who she was.

Time after time again it seemed he tested her in small subtle ways and each time his admiration for her character became stronger as she handled things with grace and style. He decided to follow his instincts and soon even the most adamant naysayers began to see what he had from the first day he met her – a substantial woman he could depend on.

Entering the kitchen to make a sandwich to go with the beer he had just opened, John eyed the telephone on the wall.

I should call Lydia and wish her a Happy New Year.

He realized he had been cool towards her since she had moved to Vancouver to work in their head office and he felt a pang of regret. It wasn't her fault that he was being more cautious towards women, and judging from what he could see so far, Lydia certainly wasn't anything like Theresa in temperament or character. Sighing he picked up the phone and dialed the number he had noted in the address book on the counter.

# Chapter Six

When Rodolfo arrived to begin his shift at Coconuts, the restaurant staff was already brimming with anticipation. Tonita was carefully going over the seating arrangements with Debra, the owner, while trying to accommodate them all. It was proving to be a Herculean task. The pair couldn't afford to make any mistakes tonight as they painstakingly checked and rechecked every detail.

In the dining room, Marcos, the busboy assigned to Rodolfo at the beginning of the season, was already laying down the snowy tablecloths and setting the cutlery in perfect, precise rows. Elsewhere, other waiters and busboys busied themselves with the minute details of their own sections, racing back and forth in an effort to be ready by the time the first reservations arrived at 6:00 P.M.

Generally these early arrivals were seniors who had seen more New Year's Eves than they cared to count, and didn't mind turning in early after an excellent meal. The "in" crowd however would show up to dine starting from eight 0'clock onward, while the partygoers tended to flock through the doors of the lounge at 11:30, just in time to ring in the new year.

As Rodolfo returned from punching in his time card, he surveyed his section with satisfaction and busied himself with setting up the banana flambé and special drinks tray he would undoubtedly need throughout the evening. He worked until it was perfect.

As if on cue the first customers arrived. Since it was still early, these customers were casually dressed. Some of the men were still wearing the same shorts and flowered shirts they had put on early in the day. The women, although slightly more formally attired, hardly looked more appropriately dressed than their male counterparts. Rodolfo sighed and thought how little style most Americans had despite the excess dollars they earned. Then in typical Mexican fashion he shrugged philosophically. As long as they had money in their pockets and were good tippers, who cared what he thought about the clothes they wore. Smiling broadly at his own folly, he hurried forward to greet his first customers.

    Lydia clipped on her rhinestone earrings and eyed herself critically in the mirror. Shoulder length hair swung invitingly in a bell to her shoulders, lightly streaked from her last two days in the sun. Her tan had given her a natural, healthy glow so that her make-up was minimal.
Less is more
The old adage from fashion magazines resounded in her brain.
    She pulled a deep midnight blue dress, simply and elegantly cut from her closet and slipped it over her head. Smoothing the clean lines over her body, she had kept adornments to a minimum, knowing bows and flounces would look ridiculous on her small voluptuous figure. Her only concession to frivolity had been the matching rhinestone beads on her sandals that she now bent to strap on. They matched perfectly the jewels in her ears. Completing the outfit was a finely wrought silver bracelet. She left her finger bare and carefully applied a bronzer to her arms and legs, which gave her a shimmering, festive look. Satisfied with her appearance she once more sprayed her favorite perfume, Coco by Chaannel and headed out into the night.
    Behind her the phone rang shrilly in her room several times before it finally stopped.
    As she walked down the stairs she thought about Ana and wondered if her invitation had been sincere. Thinking back over the conversation last night and the rapport that had built so rapidly between them she concluded it was and decided to drop by Coconuts at the appointed time. She wondered what John was doing tonight, a little disappointed that he hadn't called. Guiltily she wondered if she should have called him instead and almost headed back to her room before dismissing the idea.
    Let him make the first move for once, she thought.
    For a moment she stood still on the sidewalk, wondering where she should go for her dinner.
    All dressed up and nowhere to go. She giggled aloud earning her a puzzled glance from a Mexican woman about to close her shop for the night.
    Lydia smiled warmly at her and was rewarded by a friendly smile in return. Feeling better and more confident now, she straightened her shoulders and headed toward the Marina in search of another great dinner.

*THE JADE PENDANT*

Resplendent in a black tux and white hand-made linen shirt John buzzed the doorbell of his brother's house. As he waited on the sweeping porch a sense of Déjà vu overcame him and he wondered how many more inane parties he would have to attend before people would simply stop inviting him. He had done everything he could to get out of coming here but his brothers Jeff and Kevin had refused to let him off the hook. They had informed him their wives insisted it be black tie. John would much rather have preferred a quiet get together with his buddies at his fishing lodge drinking scotch and smoking Cuban cigars in a pair of old jeans and worn plaid shirt.

The front door opened and he automatically plastered a smile on his face. His sister-in law Maude urged him to come in out of the bitter cold. With a welcoming hug and kiss, *as if I didn't just see her yesterday,* he groused inwardly, she took his overcoat and ushered him into the living room.

Someone stuck a scotch in his hand amid greetings without asking him what he wanted to drink and he wondered not for the first time if he was that predictable. Shaking off the feeling he shrugged philosophically and took the first of many sips of the night, silently toasting the room filled with everyone he knew and saw on a regular basis.

In one corner he noticed Bill and his wife Molly chatting to a young couple from down the street. Catching his best friend's eye he raised his glass to him. Bill grinned and returned the salute before continuing on with his conversation. Near the kitchen his lawyer, and sometimes poker buddy, Brock Jefferson had cornered a prospective client, while his brother Kevin circled the room looking for an ashtray.

Since both his brothers worked in one form or another in the auto industry, John easily recognized many people. Debating whom he would talk to first, he sighed, bored with the prospect and took another deep gulp of his smooth scotch, nearly draining the glass.

I wonder what Lydia's doing tonight, he thought for the second time that day, sorry he hadn't been able to reach her when he called earlier.

The hotel clerk had informed him that the *Senorita* had stepped out for the evening, giving no indication as to when she would be returning.

Looking around the room he knew that Lydia's cheery presence and sunny disposition would have made this party more bearable. This time as he took another huge swallow of his drink he did drain the glass. Heading toward the kitchen for a refill before he joined the fray, he wondered what in the hell he was doing here when he could have been in Mexico with Lydia.

A winding back alley near Coconuts led Lydia to Hauchinago Restaurant, where she had an excellent meal of red snapper, the house specialty that had fairly melted in her mouth. Sitting at a stool at the bar she topped it all off with an extremely potent liquor recommended to her by the owners.

Throughout her meal her kind and gracious hosts, Jorge and his wife Olga had kept up a steady stream of conversation with tales of Zihuatanejo and the antics of their many children. Several of them worked at the restaurant and occasionally stopped their duties from time to time to offer her shy, welcoming smiles.

Invited by other tourists who had stopped in to join them at the bar, she consumed glass after glass of wine, appreciating the company and conversation. Her initial feelings of loneliness were completely dispelled by the group she was with. They came from all over the world, the hot tropical weather somehow making it easier for them to start conversations with a perfect stranger. Or perhaps it was simply because they were on holiday and so normal constraints no longer applied. At first Lydia wondered why that was, but as she became more engrossed with the group, she decided it didn't matter and settled in to enjoy the excellent wine and company.

At nearly 11:30 she realized she had to go if she was to meet Ana on time. Kissing her hosts and new friends goodbye she wished them a happy new year and promised that she would return soon. Lydia made her way down the alleyway to Coconuts.

As she picked her way in the dim light she once more wrestled with the idea of walking into the popular place alone and unescorted.

I'll just walk by and peek in the back door, she assured herself. *If Ana isn't there I'll head on back to the hotel.*

The thought depressed her.

Moments later she found herself looking in at large groups of fashionably dressed people standing around the bar, drinks in their hands, chatting casually to each other. Red and white streamers and balloons hung or floated from heavy wooden beams while huge potted plants placed strategically around the room glowed with fairy lights, which cast an iridescent glow. The effect was festive and inviting and Lydia hesitated a moment more, taking in the colorful sight before her. At first glance Ana was nowhere in sight. Disappointed but unwilling to appear gauche, Lydia decided to move on.

Halfway down the block she stopped abruptly and turned to look back to where the party was going strong. To this day she never knew what made her go back – she only knew she had no intention of spending this New Year's Eve alone.

Nervous but determined, Lydia walked boldly into the restaurant where

Ana appeared magically by her side. Looking a vision in an understated but elegant black dress, the ever present scarf which Lydia later learned was her trademark, wrapped loosely around her neck. Ana threw her arms wide, engulfing her in a warm embrace.

"Darling," she enthused dramatically. "What took you so long? I was afraid you would never get here. Come, there are some people I want you to meet." With that she pulled Lydia deeper into the room.

The last of the fashionable moneyed crowd were enjoying their brandies and coffee after dinner. Champagne to toast the New Year chilled in silver ice buckets next to their tables. Rodolfo took the opportunity in the lull to stroll back to the bar area, grab a beer and take a much needed break from his duties. He had been going non-stop since he arrived, but the tips he raked in tonight were worth it and the night was not over yet. Thankfully he patted the pockets of his pants that bulged from his efforts.

Across the room he noticed Ana signaling to him, a pretty blonde woman next to her, eyes sparkling as she looked around her. The pair weren't in his section, but his curiosity about Ana's friend caused him to answer her imperious summons.

Rodolfo had known Ana from almost the day she first arrived in Zihuatanejo and he was a mere busboy at Coconuts. Unlike anyone he had ever met before or since, she was a favorite of his from the beginning, always interested in his life and how he was doing. She fascinated him with her "New York ness" and eccentric mannerisms, amusing him with the dramatic storytelling of her life in the Big Apple.

"Rodolfo!" Ana exclaimed playfully tapping his arm with a finely wrought fan from Spain, "Where is that necklace you promised to make for me?"

"I'm making it Ana. I'll have it for you *Mañana*."

Ana laughed a deep throaty chuckle that caused nearby heads to turn to see who the source of such undisguised amusement was.

"*Mañana, mañana*. In Mexico everything is *mañana*." she chuckled again as she turned to Lydia in mock resignation.

Rodolfo smiled at her and moved slightly to eye her companion.

"I'll make one for you too *Senorita*," he promised, turning on the charm of his deeply dimpled smile in Lydia's direction.

Lydia, startled, stepped back from the intentness of his gaze and his sheer animal magnetism. Then she too relaxed and smiled back at him.

This time it was Rodolfo who was taken aback. Without thinking he reached for her hand as he stepped closer. His chocolate colored eyes never left her iridescent green ones. Lydia blushed as she tipped her head back to look at him towering over her.

Ana watched the by-play with great interest—a secret smile playing on her face as she looked at first one and then the other.

Well will you look at that?

She smiled as the two before her stood grinning foolishly at each other, eyes locked as if unable to look away. She decided to step in.

"Lydia, I want to introduce this gorgeous hunk of Mexican man to you. Rodolfo meet my friend Lydia. She's from Canada and she's here for a few weeks. She's staying at the Citlali, too."

Rodolfo smiled into her eyes, mesmerized by the unusual color. "*Mucho gusto,* Lydia," he said.

Tearing his eyes away he addressed Ana. "Where are you two going after, Ana?"

"Dancing of course," was the prompt reply. "Do you want to come with us? We're going to Mr. Mike's."

He faced Lydia again, "And you *Chiquita?* You will be there too?"

Lydia looked at Ana who nodded regally.

"Yes I will," she grinned back inanely. *Did he just call me a banana?* She decided to ask Ana about it later.

"Okay," Rodolfo promised. "I will be waiting for you later. *Hasta lluego.*"

Kissing the hand he still held unnoticed throughout conversation, he reluctantly departed to wait on his customers who by now would be clamoring for his attention.

Lydia laughed self consciously, curiously affected by the old fashioned charm. She couldn't remember the last time if ever someone had kissed her hand, grinning wider at the thought of John attempting it and realizing how foolish he would look if he were to try. Or for that matter any of the "good ole boys" from Prince George.

Her friends had told her how romantic Latin men were and she was pleased to see they were right. She decided she could get used to that kind of chivalry in a hurry.

"Who was that masked man," she quipped to Ana as she watched his retreating back and pretended to fan her face with her fingers to cool down.

Ana laughed at the joke, stating firmly, "That is the most evolved man in Zihuatanejo. Make that the most evolved man I have ever known."

Lydia could only stare after him, her heart beating a little faster than before.

"Well, whoever he is, he sure is cute," she giggled aloud. "Did you ever see such dimples in your life? They should be illegal. Too bad I have a boyfriend on the way."

"I know what you mean," Ana agreed. "If only I were a bit younger I would take a run at him myself. Rodolfo is without a doubt one of my favorite people in the world and has been a good friend to me these last fifteen years or so." She smiled while Lydia continued to watch the man they were discussing across the crowded room. She nudged her friend.

"Lydia, for heaven's sake you're positively drooling. Come on, there are some people I want you to meet."

Lydia laughed as she broke her eyes away and followed Ana into the lounge where a large group of party goers greeted them warmly.

At a few minutes to midnight, as Ana predicted, the staff handed out sparklers and horns to patrons who began the countdown to midnight in earnest. When the clock struck twelve, hundreds of balloons were released from the nets hung high over the crowd, floating gently to the earth to the strains of *Auld Lang Syne* and joyous cries of "Happy New Year."

Lydia hugged first Ana and a few of the people she had just met, then stepped back out of the way as was often her wont, to view the scene as it unfolded before her.

Beautiful women in sequined gowns and elegant chiffon, which flowed to the floor, spread like a sea of color while their rich, tanned escorts stood guard nearby. The younger set sported a more casual look in shorter, sexier dresses, cut low and daring in the front or back, their dates looking no less handsome beside them.

Waiters flitted in and out of the crowd, stopping frequently to fill champagne flutes and light cigarettes. Lydia held out her glass and a smiling waiter obediently filled it, winking audaciously as he moved away. She was still smiling when a soft, low, male voice whispered close to her ear, sending a shiver down her spine.

"*Feliz Año Nuevo,* Lydia. Remember to save a dance for me later *Senorita.*" The presence moved away.

Whirling to catch sight of the owner of the phantom voice, knowing deep inside whom it must be, she saw Rodolfo's retreating back and smiled widely at the sheer silliness of it all.

"Penny for your thoughts?" Ana broke into her musings.

Lydia laughed throatily.

"I'm afraid they're a little X-rated," she admitted candidly, pointing in Rodolfo's direction.

"God but that man is sexy."

Ana nodded her head in agreement. "He sure is. Too bad John is on his way, however if you were to have a romantic interlude with a Mexican man that would certainly be my choice."

Mine too, she silently concurred with her friend feeling slightly guilty for the disloyal track her mind was taking. She shrugged.

Good thing looking is not the same as doing though or I would be in real trouble.

Lydia laughed aloud lewdly, realizing that too much champagne was beginning to cloud her judgment. She set her glass down on the vacant table next to her. Ana took her by the elbow and steered her away to a quiet table in the opposite corner.

"Let's sit there," she suggested, "and I'll tell you about some of the people here."

When they were both comfortably seated she pointed to a young attractive couple standing alone in the center of the room, eyes intently on each other, oblivious to everyone around them.

"See that couple there? That's Carla and Michael. I'll introduce you later. They met here four years ago and if there ever was a couple meant for each other, it would have to be them.

Lydia looked harder.

They look alike, she thought with some surprise. *How interesting!*

It was true. Dressed simply, she in a short black dress and he in white jacket and black trousers, they maintained a certain air of understated elegance. Tall and thin, nearly matched in height, their classic features gave way to the same slightly turned up noses. They could easily have passed as brother and sister. Lydia turned back to her friend, the gleam in her eye already anticipating the story. Ana began her tale.

## Chapter Seven

Walking down the beach at La Ropa, Carla barely saw anything, so lost was she in her own thoughts. She had arrived yesterday afternoon, leaving a bewildered husband behind in the hopes she could find something to salvage when she got back—some sense out of her muddled life.

She and Joe had been experiencing serious problems with their relationship. Lately it seemed as if everything was about to come crashing down around her ears. She needed to distance herself from the situation that was becoming increasingly unbearable with each passing day. Carla tried unsuccessfully to explain to Joe her reasons for going, and her need to re-evaluate their relationship alone without his presence distracting her. He in true Joe-like fashion had not understood her reasons for leaving at all. With a sigh, Carla recalled the last ugly confrontation they had the previous night.

"I don't know why you have to go Carla," he whined. He stopped, his manner becoming suddenly sly.

"Unless of course you're meeting someone there. Is that it?" he demanded.

She protested adamantly but when she saw he was not about to accept her word she began to pack in a quiet fury. Pacing unceasingly around the bedroom they shared until she wanted to scream at him to get out, he alternated between demands, threats and professions of love. Closing the lid of the suitcase she refused to budge.

It was a familiar story with them she realized, like a bad dream from which she would never awake. Of course it was the drugs that that made him so paranoid. That's what had brought them to this point in their seven-year marriage and would continue to do so unless he finally decided he needed to get help. It was obvious to her that he would never kick his habit without therapy of some kind. His reluctance to do so was one of the many reasons she was leaving now. She tried again to explain this to him, but as high as he was, it had been as useless as spitting into the wind.

"Look Joe, you know what we agreed to with Dr. Daniels. If our relationship is to work we both have to clean up and stay clean. I've done my part now it's up to you to do yours. Maybe while I'm gone you'll check into the rehab center on your own. It's up to you Joe. I'm going."

Despite her harsh words though and his incessant complaining that she was deserting him just when he needed her the most, at the last minute she had almost changed her mind at the airport. Her flight was called over the loudspeaker and kissing her husband quickly on the lips, she fled into the waiting room before she relented and returned home to her doomed marriage.

Well here I am and I have nothing but time to think, she thought, already missing the Joe she used to know before their problems began.

From the balcony of La Perla restaurant, Michael sat staring moodily out at the ocean crashing to shore. A buxom blonde giggled next to him as she flirted with one of the waiters, while her other hand played with the fly on his jeans under the tablecloth. He thought her name was Debbie something or other, he couldn't really remember. Not that it mattered much anyway. A bit of a playboy, every year he showed up at the resort town with a new "flavor of the month". The relationships usually lasted no longer than the vacation itself. He would send them packing soon after. Most people thought he was a real son of a bitch and most people would have been right. On the other hand, he congratulated himself, he didn't get where he was today by being Mr. Nice Guy and if he ran over a few people here and there, well what did it matter to him?

Right now despite the expert attentions of the hand at his crotch, he was incredibly bored and his head ached from yet another party last night.

Shifting slightly in his chair his attention swung to a lone woman walking aimlessly on the beach. World-weary but deciding to get a closer look anyway, he lifted the binoculars from the string around his neck and peered out over the wide expanse of sand. His heart lurched as he trained the glasses on her incredible body. Michael slowly wound his way to her face that had, at that instant, turned to look his way. He almost dropped them as he removed the cord from around his neck and sat them down.

"That," he proclaimed loudly to the group of hangers-on around him. "Is the woman I'm going to marry."

With that he removed the hand of the protesting blonde from his lap and stripping to his trunks, jumped the rail to the beach below to meet the woman of his dreams.

"You're putting me on," Lydia exclaimed, fascinated but skeptical.

"I am not," Ana, chided her seriously. "Do you want to hear the rest of the story or not?"

"I do. I do." Lydia clamored for more the way a child would and Ana mollified, continued.

"Hi there." Michael stepped in her path. *How original!*

. He tried again as startled, she stopped and looked him steadily in the eye, waiting. At her hard, unfixing stare he was surprised to suddenly find himself feeling so awkwardly inept. It was not a feeling he was used to.

"Come here often?" *Brilliant Einstein.*

"Hi," she responded, eyes downcast once more and stepping to her right to bypass. He stepped to his left, successfully intercepting her move, forcing her to stop again. This time when her own brilliant blue ones met his again, they flashed in anger and something deeper than that. Hurt, sorrow, he couldn't be sure but for some reason that look pierced his soul. They stared at each other a moment as the surf swirled around their ankles.

"Is there something you want?" she asked bluntly, angrily.

He relaxed, once more confident and grinning broadly asked her out to dinner. She refused.

"Oh," Lydia said disappointed. "So, it wasn't love at first sight?"

Ah, Ana thought with a smile of satisfaction – *there beats the heart of a true romantic after all.*

Aloud she hedged, "It was and it wasn't. For Michael, he thought it was, which is ironic given his past, but for Carla it most definitely was not. She took some convincing. There were many obstacles in the way. This relationship certainly didn't happen overnight."

It didn't take Michael long to find out whom Carla was and where she was staying. Convinced this was just another one of Michael's passing romantic interludes, everyone was curious to see what would happen next and so provided him with all the information he wanted.

Carla did everything she could to avoid him whenever she saw him. This happened far too often for her liking. Michael of course planned it that way. He showed up wherever she was going to be and tried to catch her attention any way he could. She ignored him completely.

Finally, when even he was about to give up, without meaning to, he hit upon the perfect way to capture her interest.

He had followed her one-day to Las Gatas, a white-sanded beach around the bay of Zihuatanejo. She was hiding, as usual, behind a big hat reading a novel in front of one of the many restaurants.

Despondent that she would not even glance his way as he strolled past her chair, he stopped at a spot a short way down the beach to where young Mexican children were making castles in the sand. Joining in, he soon became totally absorbed by what he was doing.

Carla laid aside her book with a sigh, realizing she had been trying to make sense of the same page for the last five minutes. As she stretched her cramped muscles and debated whether she should take a dip or not, she noticed the happy group a few feet in front of her.

There's that guy again, she thought wearily. *He just won't give up. I wonder if he's seen me.*

Slightly annoyed, she watched him as he dug in the sand, seeming to direct the process at the same time.

Figures he's the kind of guy to just take over. Still, it does look like fun.

She sat up and edged herself to the end of the lounger, careful not to tip it and watched some more. Curiosity got the better of her and she stood up and walked to the happy group.

Her shadow cast long and dark across the sand castle and Michael looked up momentarily distracted.

"Mind if I join in?" she asked.

Lydia breathed happily, "Then what happened, Ana?"

"Why, it was the beginning of a beautiful friendship is what happened. As I said, Carla was married and she told Michael that at the very beginning. If he wanted to be friends that would be fine, but that was all. They could go for walks, talk, have dinner once in a while but there would be no funny stuff as she called it. She wouldn't let him kiss her or hold hands or anything. *Nada.* She stuck to her guns, too."

"So how did they end up together?"

Ana answered her. "That was kind of sad at the time anyway. When it was time for Carla to leave, I mean. She had decided after being here for a few weeks that she should give it a try with her husband one more time. The problem was, of course, that she was starting to have feelings for Michael too, even though up to now their relationship was strictly platonic. I will never forget how heartbroken Michael was the day her plane left. He sat right where you're sitting now and cried."

"How sad."

"I told him what I tell everyone who comes here," Ana smiled with some secret wisdom.

"I told him that Zihuatanejo is a magical place and anything and everything can happen here." She nodded sagely pointing her fan to the couple in front of them, as Lydia looked on, still doubtful.

"Fate intervened," Ana pronounced solemnly as Lydia sat back to hear the rest of the story.

Five long months passed and Michael had returned to Canada for the summer. It was ironic that they were both Canadians and only lived a few hours apart, but Carla had decided that it would be better if they didn't stay in touch as long as she was married and Michael had no choice but to accede to her decision. She was determined to make a go of her marriage and did not want or need the distractions of another man, no matter how much she was drawn to him.

Her reunion with Joe was bittersweet. For the first few months it looked as if Joe had finally kicked his habit and turned over a new leaf. His eyes became clearer, his paranoia lessened and he began to be the man who she had married so many years ago—the one she had first fallen in love with. Still, no matter what she did, she couldn't get Michael off of her mind. With each passing day instead of forgetting him, she found herself remembering their brief time together. She tried harder to push thoughts of him away and concentrated even harder on her marriage.

It wasn't long before Joe noticed the change in her. He stood by and watched as she became more despondent, her old carefree personality a shadow of her former self. Afraid to ask but knowing that something or someone had happened during her trip to Zihuatanejo, he was unsure as to what to do about it. In an attempt to forget, he turned back to drugs.

Carla soon found out and used it as the excuse she needed to get out of the loveless marriage she was in. She still had no idea what she wanted. With thoughts of Michael still haunting her, she moved to Vancouver. The uncontested divorce would be final in just three months.

Michael, too, was having his own problems dealing with the absence of the one woman he felt he could be happy with for the rest of his life. Throwing himself into his work with a renewed vigor in an attempt to forget only succeeded in making him more money but it did not bring him the peace he was striving for. Despite his promise he decided to call her from his office one day.

Joe answered the phone. At first Michael was at a loss for words. On some flimsy pretense he passed himself off as a bill collector who needed to speak to a Mrs. Carla Adams immediately. It was then that he learned the truth about their marriage. A disgruntled Joe was only too happy to give Michael his soon-to-be ex-wife's address, certain that he was causing her some grief in doing so. Michael, elated, leaned back in his chair to plan his next move.

Carla gave her last customer a final brush on her neck to sweep away any trace of stray hairs left behind. Her back and feet ached from her long hours at the salon. She looked forward to a hot bath, a comfy terrycloth robe, and perhaps a cozy fire before she turned in for the night.

She enjoyed her job as hair stylist in one of Vancouver's trendiest salons and most of the time made excellent money in tips. It was a hard way to make a living as her aching body attested to. Often she tried to imagine herself back on the beaches of Zihuatanejo. As always, thoughts of Michael intruded and she experienced a pang of regret when she thought of him.

Peering out at the night from the windows of the street level store, she noted there was a blizzard blowing outside. She dreaded the drive home this Friday evening in rush hour traffic. Sighing, she headed for the back room to clean her brushes and soak her scissors in an antiseptic solution before leaving.

As she was finishing up, Amie, one of the apprentices, stopped her.

"Carla you have a visitor," she cooed with admiration, rolling her eyes and making her laugh despite herself.

"Who is it Amie?" She asked sighing. "You know I'm finished for the day and I don't have any more appointments booked till 10:00 tomorrow. Can you ask them to come back tomorrow or, better yet, just make an appointment for me?"

Amie laughed mysteriously.

"I think this is one customer you might want to talk to yourself Carla," she said as she whirled back into the main salon before Carla had a chance to say anything more.

Exasperated with the air-headed assistant and more than a little put out by a client who would ask to speak to her so late in the day, Carla put on her best face and went to greet her nameless visitor.

"It was Michael wasn't it?" Lydia interrupted excitedly. "Was it Michael?"

Ana laughed delighted with her friend's enthusiasm.

"It certainly was Michael. All six feet of him carrying at least five-dozen long stemmed roses and what seemed like a million heart shaped balloons. The place went crazy. All the employees and even the clients started to cheer. Carla told me it was the most romantic thing that had ever happened to her in her entire life."

"That's a wonderful story Ana," Lydia smiled even as she stared at the couple across the room, arms loosely around each other in a comfortable embrace.

"Yes it is. They call me their fairy godmother. As a matter of fact they know Rodolfo. He is a very good friend of theirs, too," she mentioned casually.

"You should get to know them while you are here if you can."

"Good idea, Ana," Lydia agreed. "I think I will. And thank you again for such a wonderful story."

Ana waved her hand airily, smiling impishly. "There's much more where that comes from. I am a writer after all. Besides where do you think I get my best material if not from the people who come to Zihuatanejo? And who knows? Maybe you'll end up as one of the characters in my next book." She laughed again.

If only, Lydia smiled warmly at her new friend.

Ana stood abruptly and caught Lydia's arm in one smooth motion. She hauled her out of the chair.

"I think it's time for you and I to do some dancing. Why don't we see if we can stir up some excitement in this town?"

Laughing, arms linked, the two of them sailed out the door leading to the alleyway as a lone waiter followed their departure with interest.

As Lydia matched Ana's steps, she glanced casually over her shoulder to see who might be watching before averting her head.

Probably looking for me, Rodolfo thought conceitedly, unaccountably pleased with the idea.

After all she is just another *gringa* and he had seen many of those in the years he had served in the hospitality industry. It was a well-known fact that most Americans and Canadians came to Mexico to find themselves a little diversion before going home to reality and to their husbands and boyfriends back there.

He was constantly amazed that these women who were probably extremely conservative and respectable in their home country could act so wanton and irresponsible when on vacation. They threw away their inhibitions it seemed the minute their planes landed on foreign soil. His few months living in the United States had educated him quickly as to the ways of the women there, and he was very selective if, and when, he dated a tourist on vacation here. For one thing he was extremely careful not to let infectious diseases touch him and always wore protection whether they protested or not.

There was something about this one that intrigued him. Although she had flirted with him lightly it was in a quietly amused way. She seemed to have a firm hold on her emotions and behavior. He made up his mind he would definitely meet them later at Mr. Mike's when his shift ended.

Wild rock music blared from Roca Rocks Nightclub where Ana and Lydia danced to exhaustion with beautiful Mexican boys in tight jeans, their smiles pearly white in the black lights.

Taking a breather at their low table closest to the dance floor, Lydia shouted a question to Ana, pounding with the gyrating music.

"Do you think Rodolfo will be upset when he goes to Mr. Mike's and doesn't find us there?"

They had arrived at Mr. Mike's only to find it nearly empty of customers; the waiters looking bored and ready to close for the night. They opted instead for this popular club downtown, and judging by the crowd it had been a good choice indeed.

"Don't worry," Ana yelled her reply. "He'll find us."

Lydia started to protest then gave up as a handsome blonde tourist leaned over their table and spoke close to her ear in an effort to be heard.

"Have you been kissed yet this year?" he smiled wickedly as he pulled a stunned Lydia to her feet.

Without waiting for a reply his arms encircled her and in one swift motion he planted a heart-stopping kiss on her lips.

For a minute she was too surprised to react. Then instinct kicked in and she found herself. She kissed him back, hard.

When they finally came up for air they stood staring at each other, breathing hard.

"You should be honored to know that you are the first real kiss of the year for me," she teased him flirtatiously, her breathing still fast.

Another Mexican boy approached and asked her to dance. She left the blond standing there with a befuddled, amused look on his face.

Shrugging good naturedly, the stranger winked at Ana and swaggered back to collect his winnings from his buddies who were holding up the bar in the corner of the darkened room.

"Pay up boys," he demanded arrogantly as they made lewd comments and slapped his back, congratulating him for a job well done.

Several hours later, Ana and Lydia emerged, arms linked, from the smoky bar. They were breathless with laughter as they compared notes on the best lines used that evening.

"Wasn't that guy with the impossibly tight jeans hilarious?" Lydia gasped.

"No more so than the girl who asked me to dance? At least I thought it was a young girl until I looked closer. There were more transvestites there than I have ever seen in one place in New York at the same time."

"No!" Lydia laughed. "Really? I would never have guessed," she said still laughing.

"Let's take a last stroll past Coconuts and see if there is anyone still around. That way you can apologize to Rodolfo for standing him up," Ana teased her lightly. Lydia agreed, hoping they would catch sight of him to explain.

"Then it really is time for all good girls to go to bed. At least this Italian grandmother, that is."

Lydia peered at Ana closely, startled by the comment. Ana looked less like a grandmother than anyone she had ever known.

She has more energy than many women half her age, she thought admiringly.

Aloud she complimented her. "I hope I look half as good when I'm a grandmother, Ana."

Ana smiled, pleased by the tribute. For a minute they walked in companionable silence to their destination.

Santos shit, Rodolfo swore comically as he walked down the slope of the deserted side streets.

He'd arrived at Mr. Mike's only moments before to find that neither Ana nor Lydia were there.

What kind of game is this?

Now after walking three miles up the hill, he'd have to walk all the way down again. Taxis were as scarce as water in the desert on this night. Then he laughed at himself, his sense of humor getting the best of him at last.

That little blonde sure fooled me all right. Who'd have thought someone so innocent looking would be so devious?

He trudged down the road back to Coconuts wondering how he would get his revenge on her, his vivid imagination already in overdrive.

When Ana and Lydia rounded the corner of the street they were greeted with a hilarious sight as waiters for Coconut's spilled out of the doorway, whistling as the two of them drew closer. Lydia scanned the group quickly hoping that Rodolfo was among them but was disappointed to find him missing.

"Ana," one of the waiters known as Arturo called out. "Come to the party with us."

"Where?" Ana asked laughingly, from the center of the circle that had formed around her and Lydia.

"*A mi casa,*" announced the bartender Pauley, proudly.

Lydia met Ana's eyes questionably, unsure as to the wisdom of such a thing. She decided to let Ana make the call.

Ana conferred quietly with her while the men waited patiently, laughing and joking together as the two women talked.

"You go if you like Lydia, but I am much too tired myself. I think I will just go back to the Citlali."

Lydia hesitated. "I don't think I would feel comfortable going on my own Ana. I don't know any of these people. Besides my Spanish is marginal. I think I should go back to the hotel with you."

Lydia was disappointed. *It would be nice to see how Mexican families celebrate in their own homes,* she thought.

"But I would take care of you *Senorita,*" a low voice growled softly in her ear. She whirled quickly.

"Rodolfo!" Ana and Lydia chorused.

"Where were you two?" Rodolfo asked somewhat tersely, his pride still smarting from being stood up.

"I walked to Mr. Mike's and you weren't there."

Ana explained that they had gone to the club but on finding it nearly deserted had decided to go to another one instead.

"You were in the wrong part of the club, Ana. The actual party was held downstairs. They moved the club there last month." Rodolfo explained to them, patiently.

"It was packed with people. I thought you two were playing games with me," he growled to Lydia, placing both hands on her shoulders and shaking her playfully.

Lydia laughingly protested, placing her hands on his broad chest in an attempt to stave him off.

"We are so sorry Rodolfo. We really did go there."

Rodolfo eyed the pair thoughtfully. They seemed sincere. He decided to forgive them and, smiling, he placed an arm around each, giving them a gentle squeeze before releasing.

Lydia and Rodolfo stood grinning foolishly at each other while around them the waiters began to comment, smirking and elbowing each other in the ribs. Ana watched them quietly before speaking up.

"Goodnight my darlings. I'm going to sleep. Rodolfo I am so sorry about tonight."

With reluctance Lydia turned to follow her. "Wait Ana I'm coming with you."

But Ana waved her back.

"Go to the party Lydia. Rodolfo will take care of you."

She looked sternly at him now, waving a Sicilian finger at him in warning.

"You will take care of her won't you Rodolfo?"

"Of course Ana," he replied placing a hand over his heart and staring deeply into Lydia's eyes as he pledged.

"I will guard her with my life."

"See that you do," Ana warned. "I'm going to hold you to that promise."

As she walked away she looked over her shoulder one last time and called back to Lydia.

"You'll be safe with Rodolfo. Come to my room tomorrow and tell me all about the party. I want details." She laughed in that throaty chuckle of hers and swayed down the alleyway to the hotel.

Lydia looked up into Rodolfo's smiling face and asked anxiously, "You're sure it's ok for me to come?"

Rodolfo grabbed her hand firmly and pulled her into the back seat of the taxi where she found herself firmly wedged between him and Arturo.

"I'm sure," he declared sincerely with a smile.

*I must be crazy to get into a car in a foreign country with five strangers,* she thought. She shrugged her shoulders and returned the smile with a dazzling one of her own.

She just knew this was going to be a night to remember and she shivered with anticipation as the car roared down the street.

At a little after two in the morning, John parked the truck and walked into the house. He was inebriated to some extent but unless you looked very closely or knew him well, you would never be able to tell.

As he moved to the bar off the kitchen and made himself another scotch with just a splash of water, he reminded himself once more that he was a controlled drinker. Not one of those sloppy drunks he knew. He hated people who lost control. It was particularly repulsive to him when a woman had too much to drink, especially when they draped themselves all over you and looked at you with cow eyes expecting you to save them or something. It had been that way at the party tonight. He shuddered in remembrance.

One of his associate's wives had too much champagne and the effect had been far from attractive. As the evening wore on she became more and more belligerent, tottering unsteadily in high heels knocking over lamps and ornaments. Her husband, a young finance manager with the local Ford dealership, was embarrassed and finally had to take her home.

It had been another New Year's Eve like so many others and he vowed he would go somewhere warm next year. The old crowd was beginning to wear a little thin. Silently John toasted the air and downed his last shot of the warm liquid, the effects of which barely registered. Meet some new people maybe. Experience something different than the same old crowd he was used to.

At the party tonight he had found himself watching the crowd. He paid particular attention to the ones who had been married or together the longest. He caught the smiles they gave each other from time to time from across the crowded room. It had made him feel very lonely—a feeling he was neither used to nor comfortable with. He needed to make some changes in his personal life. His thoughts turned to Lydia.

He wondered how she was faring this evening, a little worried that he hadn't heard from her. She had made as many moves toward him as he had toward her. Rather than irritating him, he had been content to let it happen.

Glancing at his watch, he decided against calling her. It was two hours ahead and he doubted very much she would appreciate being woken up at this hour, too early to call if she had gotten in late.

Or maybe she's not in yet, he thought briefly then dismissed the idea as unlikely. *Not Lydia, she's too much in control for that. Besides, she doesn't know anyone there. Where would she go?*

Thinking about her alone in Mexico he frowned. He should have gone with her. It had been his suggestion in the first place, indirectly or not and he did need a holiday. The last few months with her had been happy ones. He could easily see her with him for a long time—maybe even on a more permanent basis?

It wasn't a bad idea. Lydia certainly wouldn't be a bad choice. He knew from firsthand experience that he could do a great deal worse. She was successful in her own right. As a businesswoman she understood the demands that a business made on a person. She never seemed to mind the long hours he put in or the late nights with his buddies.

Neither did Theresa, he reminded himself before rejecting the thought as unworthy.

Lydia is certainly nothing like that woman. She's no slouch in the looks department either. Or in his bed for that matter. Marriage to Lydia would not be out of the question.

She'd like that, he decided. He suddenly understood he'd been blind for far too long and realized he had to do something about it before it was too late.

With the idea swirling relentlessly around his brain, John placed his empty glass on the counter and carefully wound his way down the hallway to his empty bed.

# Chapter Eight

The party was already in full swing by the time the cab pulled up in front of the tiny adobe house. The children spilled out into the street, excited to see their father and greet their guests. With one arm around his pretty wife, and another around one of his many daughters, Pauley proudly introduced his family to Lydia. There were eleven children ranging in ages from five to thirty. The remaining guests crowding about were made up of spouses, friends, and neighbors.

Pauley's wife Gemma, a cheerful rotund woman, bustled about looking for clean glasses and chairs. Someone handed Lydia a glass of a golden liquid and urged her to sit on what appeared to be their finest chair. Preferring to stand, she leaned close to Rodolfo as he made introductions. Some of the revelers were curious about the pretty blonde stranger in their midst. Their open warm smiles enveloped her. She was somewhat bewildered by all the noisy activity around them but soon began to relax and enjoy herself.

The night sang with Spanish music and laughter and flowed as freely as the beer and tequila. Lydia cautiously sipped her drink. In a short time her head was swimming with the unaccustomed effects of the beverage. Glancing up at Rodolfo who had one warm arm protectively across the small of her back, she smiled gratefully, comforted by his presence.

Someone offered her a bowl of what appeared to be some sort of soup. Not wishing to be rude, she accepted with a smile. Peering uncertainly into the concoction she could see pieces of meat, and what looked like hominy floating in a rich broth.

At Lydia's questioning look Rodolfo leaned closer and spoke softly in her ear.

"It's *Pozole*," he informed her. "A very traditional dish here in Mexico and particularly here in the state of Guerrero. Try it. You'll like it," he encouraged as she hesitated.

She handed him her now nearly empty glass and tentatively lifted the spoon to her mouth.

Delicious!

Surprised, she pronounced it *"muy bueno,"* earning delighted smiles from her hosts. To Rodolfo's amusement she ate every bit of it.

Her glass was filled again and this time Lydia took a bigger sip.

"Careful *Chiquita,*" Rodolfo warned her with a smile. "That is the finest tequila, but if you are not careful it will kick you like a mule."

Lydia laughed and took another burning swallow, and turned her attention to the party.

The fiesta was being held in the tiny courtyard. As with most Mexican families, Rodolfo explained, a shrine to the *Guadalupe* stood among a profusion of garden flowers. Sensing Lydia's fascination with the beautiful display, Pauley directed his boys to fill the fountain with water from numerous buckets and turn on the Christmas floodlights. Lydia gasped in pleasure, spontaneously clapping her hands in delight as the water spilled from clay urns and over rocks to the flowers below.

"They do this because you are a special guest here tonight," Rodolfo told her.

Touched that they would go to so much trouble, Lydia thanked her hosts profusely, complimenting them on how beautiful their garden was. Pauley beamed with pride. Any lingering doubt Lydia had prior to being here was instantly swept away.

In the corner of the patio one of Pauley's daughters turned up the stereo. Several people got up to dance. The music was infectious—the unfamiliar beat soon had Lydia tapping her toes in time.

Taking the bowl from her and setting it aside, Rodolfo took Lydia's hand. As the guests looked on with interest, he led her to the center of the courtyard to the makeshift dance floor. The group parted until they surrounded the handsome couple. Three of Pauley's grown daughters and their husbands ringed the outside and shouted encouragement as Rodolfo placed his arms around her waist. His eyes never left her face.

Lydia was caught up in the music, the heat and the look in Rodolfo's eyes. Unconsciously she moved her body against the one pressed tightly to hers. The circle closed around them again as more and more couples joined in. They were swept along with the others in a tidal wave of music and laughter. On and on they danced until they were exhausted—sometimes close, sometimes apart, their hands always touching.

When the music stopped, Lydia quickly moved off the dance floor, suddenly flustered. The room was spinning dangerously around her.

Too much tequila, she thought promising herself to slow down a little.

"Something wrong Lydia?" Rodolfo asked anxiously concerned by her pale face.

"No, no Rodolfo," she assured him quickly. "I think I have had too much to drink and I'm so hot...." Her voice trailed off. He smiled at her knowingly and she blushed.

That wasn't too bright, the voice in her head admonished.

"Perhaps you would like to take a walk with me in the moonlight to ah...cool off?" he suggested with his ever-present smile.

She looked at him sharply. Seeing nothing untoward in his expression she agreed as primly as possible under the circumstances. Taking the outstretched hand he offered her she followed him as he led the way through the crowd of partygoers, through the wrought iron gates to the streets of the quaint looking neighborhood.

Knowing nudges and winks, which Rodolfo fully noted but carefully ignored, followed them as they made their way into the night.

Silvery and full, the moon shone above them, casting a pale glow over the city. Lydia sighed in happiness as she followed its trek across the sky.

This is romantic as hell, she thought with pleasure, only wishing that John was here to experience it with her.

On the other hand if he were, they would probably not be here at this party. It was one diversion she realized a little guiltily, she would have been sorry to miss.

A sense of the unreal washed over Lydia as they strolled through narrow cobblestone streets in silence, fingers loosely entwined. Beyond the realm of her usual experiences in the past, she had a feeling of déjà vu even while passing through an area she knew she had never been to before.

On occasion, Rodolfo would call out greetings to friends he knew who were hosting parties in their courtyards. Genuinely pleased to see him, they all stared with unabashed curiosity at the blonde *gringa* by his side, big smiles of welcome on their open faces. She smiled back as they greeted them.

The feeling of being here before grew stronger the longer they walked. She mentioned it to Rodolfo, trying to keep her tone as light as she could.

Surprising her with his intensiveness he responded.

"Sometimes it is like that Lydia. My ancestors believe that we have been born many times and lived many times. Who is to say you were not once a Mexican woman?"

Then he laughed and an arm snaked around her waist. He squeezed lightly.

"Maybe you were my woman in a past life," he teased her as he leered closer, a wolfish look on his face.

She swatted him away playfully much to the amusement of several passersby. Rodolfo laughed harder but dropped his arm.

Lydia stole a look from beneath lowered lashes, studying his proud charismatic face in the light of the moon. The shadows outlined a chiseled face, strong jaw and determined chin. All in all it was a handsome face without being a pretty one. She liked what she saw.

Sensing her scrutiny Rodolfo abruptly stopped walking. Gently placing his hands on her shoulder, he turned her toward him. She scarcely breathed, unsure as to his intent, afraid to find out but wanting to just the same.

*He's too handsome,* Lydia thought giddily, head tipped back, heart racing.

Dipping his head forward Rodolfo kissed her softly on the lips, then paused for a moment and leaned back as if to gauge her reaction. Barely moving, her eyes fluttered open and met his for a moment. A question in his eyes for which she had no answer.

He bent toward her and kissed her again, more firmly this time.

For a moment Lydia stood shock-still in the middle of the street. A sweetness she had never experienced before washed over her body, filling her.

As his lips moved over hers he teased her with his tongue. She felt her own part allowing him entry. She made no attempt to stop him.

Suddenly, almost abruptly he pulled back, smiling as she swayed against him, momentarily off-balance. Her eyes flew open and she pushed herself a safe distance away from him, but he grabbed her hand again and they resumed their walk silently.

Feeling the need to say something she cleared her throat and began.

"I think there is something you need to know Rodolfo," she blurted. "I have a boyfriend. I'm sorry, I shouldn't have kissed you."

He shrugged his shoulders nonchalantly. What did it matter to him if she had a boyfriend in Canada?

*The strong silent type I see.*

She began again. "He's coming here in a few days. I mean he is meeting me here so I don't think we should...." She let the words dangle in the air.

Rodolfo stopped walking and turned to her.

"Your boyfriend is coming here?" he repeated incredulously.

"Yes." She replied slowly. "Sometime around the 12$^{th}$ or so."

*I can't even give him an exact date*, she realized angrily. *I don't even know if or when myself.*

His next words stymied her train of thoughts.

"If you have a boyfriend, then why did you kiss me," he demanded, his face clearly showing his disbelief.

"I don't know why," she answered truthfully. "You just looked so cute and the moonlight and...well I guess I am attracted to you. I just wanted to see what it would be like. I'm sorry. I shouldn't have done that." She hung her head, embarrassed now.

Smiling at her honesty he placed his fingers below her chin and lifted it. Slowly, ever so slowly he kissed her again, this time even more purposefully than before and she felt her bones melt as she leaned into him almost against her will. Her heart began to race and soon all conscious thought flew out of her head. There was just her and this man and for a moment the world seemed to disappear. She moaned.

At the need in her voice she sprang away, suddenly mortified by her behavior.

"That one was your fault," she accused him, eyes flashing as a hearty laugh broke from him. Unwillingly her lips twitched and she joined him.

When they had finally stopped laughing, Rodolfo suggested they go back to the party.

"Good idea," Lydia agreed relieved, wondering why the idea gave her a pang of regret at the same time.

Confused by her contradictory thoughts she quietly allowed him to lead her once more back to where they started.

Rodolfo had no such mixed feelings – he was disappointed. Determined to hide it from the petite woman beside him he stole a quick look sideways, watching secretively as she picked her way daintily over the rough road on flimsy sandals.

To his eye she appeared to be an angel in her flowing chiffon-like dress, golden hair catching the moonbeams from the sky. It looked like a halo as it framed the delicate features of her face, illuminating it. His whimsical thoughts amused him and unconsciously he increased the pace as if to leave them behind.

It was then he remembered his father's prophesy of a blonde woman. He nearly stopped in his tracks as he stole another look.

Was it possible? Could she be the one?

He cast his mind back over the last few years since his father's death, rapidly doing an inventory of his past romances—and there had been many.

Aside from an occasional redhead and many brunettes, there hadn't been a blonde among them that he could recall. If there had been she certainly hadn't made much of an impression on him. Inwardly he laughed, wondering if his father, wherever he was, found this funny too.

Poppa, if you had to send me a blonde woman to make me happy could you not have sent someone without a boyfriend?

This time he laughed aloud.

Lydia was maneuvering carefully around a mud puddle on the road when she heard his chuckle and looked up, quizzically.

Well, she thought slightly miffed; *he appears to have gotten over that little episode easily enough. I must have imagined the romance bit after all.*

She straightened her shoulders with determination. Suddenly the knowledge that she was indispensable and perhaps even a source of amusement piqued her, and her next words although sweet were heavily laced in acid.

Hiding her feelings adeptly, she flashed her most brilliant smile in his direction.

"Thank you Rodolfo for being such a wonderful guide, but you really don't need to stay with me all night you know. I am sure there are other places you would much rather be. Especially since you know that I have a boyfriend. I don't want you to feel obligated or anything."

She realized suddenly she was starting to babble and quickly stopped, staring wide-eyed into his handsome face.

Rodolfo only laughed again and reclaimed the hand he had lost moments before.

"I promised Ana I would guard you with my life," he informed her firmly. "The night is not over yet. I am where I want to be."

Good answer, she thought unaccountably pleased.

Lydia squeezed his hand lightly but said not another word as they stepped back into the courtyard of Pauley's home where the fiesta was in full swing with no sign of letting up soon.

In unison a surprised greeting chorused from the partygoers and for a minute Lydia was bewildered. Slowly it dawned on her that none of them expected to see them again this night. She blushed remembering how close she had come to giving into her feelings and throwing caution and good sense to the wind. She vowed not to put herself into the same situation again.

One brave *caballero* risking the wrath of his good friend Rodolfo grabbed

Lydia's hand and pulled her onto the dance floor. Under Rodolfo's glare he whirled her laughing into the midst of the group where the crowd soon swallowed them.

Made bold by the tequila he had consumer earlier her dance partner whispered something in her ear. She couldn't understand what he was saying to her but judging from the look on his face it was not hard to ascertain. She pulled back from him but he pulled her closer, her body now molded to his. Firmly she pulled her hand from his protesting grasp and weaved her way back to the sidelines and relative safety.

Rodolfo was talking to one of his friends where she had left him and Lydia made a beeline in his direction, her *caballero* hot in pursuit.

Feeling a presence beside him he turned to smile down at her. Seeing her pale, wan face he looked over her head and quickly accessed the situation. In one smooth movement Rodolfo pulled her closer and slipped a possessive arm over her shoulder.

Her admirer stopped in his tracks a few feet away as Lydia stood huddled in her protector's arm. Then, with a tip of his sombrero he shrugged and smiled good-naturedly. He spun on his heel and returned back to the party.

"Thank you Rodolfo," she smiled up at him gratefully attempting to remove his arm from her shoulder but he pulled her tighter to him.

"I think for the time being Lydia you need to stay close to me. There are too many wolves at this party." He laughed.

Like you?

But she stayed close to him anyway; liking the feeling of his arm around her and the protection it afforded her.

The rest of the evening passed uneventfully, Lydia stayed close to Rodolfo as he translated for her so that she would understand all that was going on around her. People were beginning to take their leave and Lydia realized that it was already 5:00 in the morning. Saying a warm goodbye to their hosts they slowly wound their way down the streets that were beginning to lighten with the rising sun.

"My house is just over there," Rodolfo pointed eastward. "I live with my brother Roberto. We can go there and borrow his car and I can give you a ride home if you like? I don't think we are going to find a cab at this hour, at least not for a long time. Do you want to see where I live?"

Lydia followed him, considering his offer.

At least he lives with someone so I should be safe, she reasoned. *Besides he has taken good care of me all night. Why not?*

*THE JADE PENDANT*

Taking her silence for assent, Rodolfo led the way. Soon they stood in front of a four story, white apartment building; the outside was badly in need of paint. The charming flower and plant garden in the courtyard offset it.

"This is where I live," Rodolfo said quietly, as Lydia looked around her in the early dawn of the morning.

"The garden is beautiful," she complimented not knowing it was the one thing he was particularly proud of in this neighborhood—the bright spot in an otherwise depressing area of town.

He thanked her and indicated a spot she could sit on the low stone wall where she could wait while he went into his house to talk to his brother.

While he was gone, her eyes took in everything around her. Far from being appalled by the obvious poverty around her she found herself to be strangely excited. One part of her knew that she was privileged to see this part of Mexico – a part that most tourists never see. She could never imagine John ending up in this part of town. She wondered if she was in any danger. Her fears were proved groundless when Rodolfo returned a few minutes later. She shivered, partly with cold, partly with relief.

"My brother was sleeping but he said we could use his car." He hesitated.

"Would you like to see my house? We have to be quiet," he warned, taking her hand. He took her hand, assuming she would follow.

A tug on his arm stopped him. He looked back at her, and saw the uncertain look in her eyes.

"You'll be safe," he whispered. "I promise."

Lydia hesitated again until curiosity got the better of her. She nodded her head.

He opened the front door, and stepped inside, and pulled her in behind him.

After the glow of the early morning light, the dark of the house was hard to get accustomed to. Regretting her decision, Lydia moved as if to back out. Rodolfo pulled her along a corridor and she had no choice but to follow him. The die cast, it was with some relief that she stepped into a warmly lit bedroom a few feet away. She gazed around the room approvingly.

It was small, she noted, but neat and tidy. The bed loomed larger than life in one corner of the room. She watched uncomfortably while he moved some clothes to a low stool in the corner and cleared a spot for her to sit down.

Settling herself gingerly on the edge, Lydia felt ill at ease. Her eyes darted around the room like a trapped animal. She caught sight of a guitar propped up next to the bed she grabbed it. Grateful for the diversion she strummed a few chords while Rodolfo watched impassively, a slight smile on his face.

She noted it was an electric Fender Stratacaster, an expensive model preferred by some of the best rock musicians in the world. Her ex-husband had owned one and had been fiercely careful that no one went within three feet of it. Remembering, she put it down gently on the bed.

"You play?" she asked him inanely.

"*Si*." He nodded approvingly. "You too."

"No, not really," she explained modestly. "I mostly play a classical guitar or acoustic. I know just enough to get by."

More comfortable now, she slid the guitar over and moved deeper onto the bed, one small foot dangling off the floor, the other tucked under her.

Rodolfo thought again how small and compact she was as he sat down beside her. Careful not to move too quickly he leaned over and kissed her lightly on the lips. Startled, Lydia stiffened, then a soft sigh escaped her and she kissed him back, relieved that he had made the move. Of their own volition her hands wove trustingly around his neck and nestled there.

The sweetness of the movement undid him and he slid closer, pressing her down until he was on top of her. Lifting her legs and parting her thighs he stretched out his full length, cushioning the bulk of his weight with his elbows.

Somewhere deep within she could feel the heat engulf her. She moved her hips as his lips grew more insistent, demanding. She matched him kiss for kiss, equaling his passion as his tongue played with hers and the fire within her burned hotter. He became bolder, his hands roaming her body freely now, confidently touching her breasts, her belly and finally moving lower.

Panic set in as a multitude of sensations filled her, threatening her sanity and reason. She began to struggle against him even as he stroked her.

"I have condoms," he informed her, mistaking the reason for her resistance.

The effect was like ice water thrown over her. She pushed him away with strength she didn't know she had, as she slipped out from under him and off the bed. Moving to the other side of the room, her breath came in short heavy gasps.

Rodolfo propped himself on one elbow, his own breathing labored, and scowled at the woman across the room from him.

Oh oh, she thought as he rose and moved to where she stood plastered against the wall. *I really got myself into a mess this time.*

She held her hands in front of her as if warding off a blow and instantly he stopped, his head cocked sideways.

"I'm not going to hurt you Lydia," he promised softly, moving closer as her hands lowered.

She raised them again, touching his chest and holding him at arm's length as he pressed again.

"Stop," she commanded firmly. "I want to go home now."

His eyes narrowed, breath labored as she glared at him unflinchingly.

He tried again. "Lydia" a pleading note crept into his voice and he dared to step closer.

"I'll be careful. I have condoms," he coaxed.

Oh God.

Aloud, "Don't step any closer or I'll scream and wake your brother," she threatened, panicking now at the look of pure lust in his eyes.

At her words Rodolfo abruptly stopped his pursuit of her and shook his head as if to clear it. Muttering something unrecognizable in Spanish, he flung open the door of his bedroom and pulled her down the corridor and out into the courtyard after him.

Still cursing softly under his breath he opened the passenger door of the small car parked in the driveway. With elaborate courtesy he half helped, half pushed her into the passenger's side. In silence he crawled into the driver's side and started the engine. The little Volkswagen roared to life.

As the tension grew, Lydia sat huddled against the door as far away from him as she possibly could get. The ride back to the hotel was silent and uncomfortable. Already she was beginning to feel ashamed for leading him on and for her subsequent reaction to the situation.

*You handled that like a teenager,* she berated herself harshly, remembering belatedly the stern warnings her friends had given her about Latin men.

Searching desperately for a way to salvage the evening, Lydia broke the silence.

"Rodolfo," she tried placing a tentative hand on his arm.

He flinched.

She tried again.

"I'm sorry this happened Rodolfo. It is entirely my fault. Please forgive me."

No reply.

Daunted, she continued regardless.

"I had such a wonderful time tonight and now I've spoiled it. Please tell me you forgive me and we can be friends?"

Silence. Defeated, Lydia slumped deeper into her car seat sure she had completely blown it.

After a long moment Rodolfo spoke.

"*Si Senorita,*" he relented, directing a small smile at her. "We can be friends and it is I who should apologize to you. I should not have pushed you. I know you have a boyfriend and I should not have tried anything with you. But," he grinned wickedly at her, turning her earlier words against her, "you should not look so cute either."

Lydia laughed along with him, relieved that peace had been restored and they could put the past behind them.

Too soon, Lydia thought, as the car pulled across the street in front of the hotel. It was time to say goodbye.

She started to get out, but stopped when Rodolfo touched her arm to detain her.

"I'll take you fishing *Senorita,*" he offered, his dimples deepened attractively in his face.

"Do you like to fish?"

"I love it," Lydia enthused thinking back to the few times she had gone with her father, seeing them now as some of the only good times they had spent together.

Before he could say another word, Lydia leaned over and kissed him quickly on the cheek.

"Good night Rodolfo. Thank you for a wonderful time."

Lydia jumped out of the car before he could move toward her and dashed across the street to the sanctuary of the Citlali. Behind her she could hear him call her name but pretending not to hear she kept going until the door to her room was closed safely behind her.

Out maneuvered again, Rodolfo smiled admiringly at her retreating figure.

For a long time he looked up at the room where the lights had gone on momentarily after her disappearance. A soft glow spilled to the street below before they were extinguished. He instinctively felt it was her room. For a brief moment he toyed with the idea of climbing the balcony to see. In light of all that had happened he quickly discarded the idea.

Smiling to himself, he thought again of his father and his deathbed prophecy. He wondered if it was going to happen the way he had envisioned.

Only time and the fates would tell.

Sleepy now, Rodolfo yawned and shifted the car into gear. He drove thoughtfully toward the projects he called home.

# Chapter Nine

John woke with the beginnings of a headache. As it made its way toward his temples he reached for the Advil on his night table he kept there simply for this reason. He hated waking up this way – especially as he planned to go into work and catch up on some paperwork. He had promised his daughter he would drop by for dinner later. If he was lucky, he would get home at a decent hour for a goodnight's sleep.

Deciding he had lazed there long enough, John eased himself off crisp white sheets and headed for the bathroom. The harsh light hurt his eyes as he blinked blearily at his reflection in the mirror. He was stunned as always by the growing amount of gray hair at his temples. Lydia professed it gave him a distinguished look but, he thought it just made him look far older than his years. The deep circles under his eyes didn't help matters. Crowfeet at the corners and laugh lines around his mouth were hard won, he always told people, but unattractive next to the puffiness and blotchiness of his face and complexion.

I had better get a handle on the late nights and drinking, he realized as he gazed at himself critically. *I don't want to look like an old man before my time.*

His family, with the exception of his mother of course, consumed more than their share of booze. Partly, he supposed it was due to his Irish background; the other part because of the city he lived in. Prince George, with its many amenities and modern services was still a lumber town in nearly every aspect, filled with hard working blue-collar workers. Not like those sissies he had to deal with from Vancouver. These people were real. They played as hard as they worked. Most of that play involved alcohol. As a hard core "player" he had had lots of practice. He grinned as he remembered when he had taken his first drink.

His father had first initiated him into the brotherhood of drinkers. Jacob Mathews was known as a hardworking, straight-shooting man, respected by many, liked by all. Once a farmer in Saskatchewan, planting wheat crops and raising cattle before he died, he could outwork, outride and out drink the best of them. A person could always depend on him for a new joke and if it was a little off color – well, what did that matter? No one could tell a joke like Jacob.

Although not rich by any stretch of the imagination, the family always had plenty of clothes to wear, a roof over their heads and enough food to eat for a family that included three strapping boys.

John was twelve when Jacob really started to hit the bottle. Times were tough and the crops that year had been much sparser than in the last ten put together. Near drought like conditions had turned the usually fertile fields into dust and money was scarce. His usually cheerful mother walked about tightlipped and disapproving as his father became more surly and bitter. He began to spend more time in the local tavern than in the fields.

One evening Jacob arrived home after dinner. He was drunker than a skunk and looking for company. His mother and brothers were down at the neighbors farm helping birth a calf and John was home finishing up some homework he had neglected. Plopping the bottle of Jack Daniel's in front of him, his father invited John to join him in a "man's" drink and ordered him to take a swig. Eager to please and afraid to refuse, John did as he was told.

He never forgot the warm, burning sensation as the liquor slid down his throat. He began to cough, then choke and spit, but when it was offered again by his laughing father, he took another long pull of the liquor. Taking the bottle from him and still laughing, Jacob wove his way to the bedroom where he promptly passed out.

Eventually the rains came and the next year got better. His father's behavior improved, but for John, things were never the same again.

Maybe laying low on the booze this year should be my New Years' resolution, John thought as he reached for a towel and headed for the shower.

Tomorrow he'd phone Lynn at the travel agency and get her to book him a flight. He'd surprise Lydia, get some much-needed R&R and come back a new person in a new year.

With the notion now planted firmly and gaining ground in his mind rapidly, he stepped into the shower in an attempt to wake up and start his day.

Catlike, Lydia stretched luxuriously in her narrow bed and smiled at the memory of the previous evening. She relived the entire adventure as she lay in her bed. She allowed herself to touch on her encounters with Rodolfo. She blushed again, thinking how foolish she had been to put herself into such a horrible situation. Another man less honorable than Rodolfo could well have taken advantage. She was fortunate things had not gone too far. It would have been hard to face John when he finally decided to make an appearance.

It had been a night to remember and the best New Years' Eve she had ever had.

Letting the silk nightdress she wore slide unheeded to the floor, she stepped into the shower stall. As the tepid water coursed over her skin Lydia mentally contemplated the clothes in her wardrobe. She decided on a cheerful yellow sundress with matching yellow and brown sandals.

Just the color to match my mood, she thought happily—short and snappy!

As she lathered shampoo in her tangled hair, she thought maybe she would head to the beach after breakfast and work on her tan. While rinsing off she wondered lazily what Rodolfo was doing, then shrugged and turned her attention to finding a towel on the rack outside the shower door.

It was well past noon before Rodolfo stirred and faced the day. He groaned softly into his pillow as the sunlight hit his eyes. The neighborhood seemed more subdued than usual on this first day of the year. It was if the dogs and the roosters had hangovers. Certainly there wasn't the usual chorus of ruckus and barking or the usual sound of babies crying to be fed. He was thankful.

Hearing the subdued clatter of the family in the apartment, he decided it was time to get up. It was his day off and he had no plans other than to lie in a hammock, and maybe watch a soccer game on TV, and eat as much food as Yola cooked. Groaning slightly from the headache he could feel emerging, he dressed slowly and joined the family in the living room.

Roberto and Yola looked up from the couch where they sat watching one of the many new soap operas—TV novelas they called them here, and grinned sympathetically at the look on his face as he entered the room. It was plain to see that their roommate was not up to his usual chipper banter and they teased him lightly before offering him breakfast from the pan on the stove.

"¿Que pasa? ¿Estas infermo?" *(Are you sick?)*

Andrea, their daughter, smiled warmly at her favorite uncle from the floor where she was coloring. He smiled affectionately in return before taking his plate of eggs and beans from Yola's outstretched hand. He poured a glass of freshly squeezed orange juice with shaky hands and gulped the sweet nectar gratefully. He reached for a still warm roll that Roberto bought from the market without fail every morning.

Roberto, who was one year older than Rodolfo, was considered the more stable of the two. He had married his high school sweetheart weeks after they graduated, and had worked as head of maintenance at the prestigious Villa Del Sol Hotel ever since. Any lingering wildness he may have had disappeared rapidly with the birth of his daughter. He considered himself to be a happily settled family man.

He worried that his restless brother would never find the peace and contentment he had. He had watched him wade through one relationship after another. He knew that Rodolfo's divorce had hit him hard. Still in his mind it was time his brother picked up the pieces and settled down again. As he joined him at the table he kept his thoughts to himself and for a few minutes they talked about the previous night and the parties they had attended.

Roberto, Yola and Andrea had gone to a church celebration to be followed by a neighborhood party. Rodolfo briefly filled his brother in on the goings on at Coconuts the night before. He reached into his pocket and pulled out a few hundred pesos from his considerable earnings in tips to go toward feeding the family. As always, Roberto accepted gratefully.

Listening intently as Rodolfo related the party at Pauley's and told him about the blonde *gringa* he had taken with him, Roberto suspected there was much more to the story than Rodolfo was willing to reveal. Though secretly worried that once again his brother was about to be involved in another meaningless romance he kept his own counsel.

At that moment his daughter called him from the living room to come see the picture she had completed. As he examined the orange coconut tree with pride, he wondered what life had in store for his sometime wayward brother.

Rodolfo experienced no such pangs of regret other than that of a wolf who had lost his prey. He was sure that given another chance, the little blonde girl from Canada would not escape him so easily. Chewing slowly, and grinning inwardly he wondered what Lydia was doing and how she planned to spend her day.

Playa La Ropa was quieter than usual but Xotchel warned Lydia it would get packed by early afternoon. With that in mind she decided to head out earlier. Before she did, she knocked on Ana's door and invited her to come along. Delighted to have something to do, Ana readily accepted and made herself ready in record time. Ana had a becoming wide brimmed hat perched jauntily on her small head and now as they set off, Lydia complimented her on it.

A short taxi ride had them on the beach in less than fifteen minutes. They ordered two freshly squeezed orange juices and settled contentedly on the yellow padded lounge chairs at Patty's Restaurant.

Generously lathering sunscreen on her skin, Ana chose to sit completely in the shade of a tall palm tree. She told Lydia that she never ventured into the sun, preferring to keep her skin milky white.

"At my age it's important to keep those wrinkles at bay for as long as I can."

Lydia could see by the excellent condition of Ana's skin that is was good advise and she applied the lotion liberally to her exposed limbs. Lydia wore the strongest protection you could get, but still liked the warm honey glow her skin attained with a tan and the fact that her hair turned a blonder shade in the sun. Thankfully, no real harm had been done from falling asleep on the beach yesterday and she promised herself to be more careful today. She cringed whenever she saw young girls on the beach broiling in the tropical sun and it was hard for her to restrain herself from passing them her lotion.

In addition to how healthy she was beginning to look, Lydia was amazed by the condition of her sometime unruly hair.

Mexico agrees with me, she decided, wondering why she did not come to this country more often.

Her mind wandered to the last trip she had taken to Mexico many years before and she knew that was in part the answer.

It was shortly after her hurried marriage to Dennis. He decided that Mexico would be a perfect spot for a honeymoon. To surprise her he had booked passage on the Carnival Cruise Line for one week on the Mexican Riviera. The ship would stop in Puerto Vallharta, Mazatlan and Cabo San Lucas: That way he reasoned, they would get a taste of three different places instead of just one. At the time it was a perfect idea.

Once underway and promising to be back in an hour, Dennis explored the ship. Lydia chose to unpack their things, happily going about the tiny quarters rearranging and getting organized. One hour passed, then two and Lydia was worried at first and then, annoyed. She decided to go in search of her new husband.

She had no idea as to where he could be on such a vast ship. She tried the bars first. After an hour of searching she had still not found him. Dispirited, she headed back to the cabin, hoping he may have returned in her absence. She spotted the blinking neon sign of the casino, pushed open the double doors and went in.

It didn't take long to find him in front of the Craps table, a huge pile of chips before him, surrounded by people. A willowy brunette in a low cut dress hung over him. He quickly shook her off when he looked up and saw his new wife approaching.

"Look at this babe!" he exclaimed excitedly, indicating the chips before him.

Tight-lipped she nodded her head. She peered closer and saw that he had already downed one to many. She sighed.

"You promised to come get me for dinner," she leaned over to whisper in his ear.

"Cash in, ok? I'm hungry."

Dennis stared up at her blearily sure she had lost her mind.

"Are you nuts?" he asked. "I can't leave now. I'm on a roll, baby. Sit down; you can bring me luck. Better yet," he handed her some chips, "Why don't you go play the slots over there. I'll be along soon."

He gave her bottom a conciliatory pat and a gentle push toward the silver machines along the wall, and then callously turned his attention back to the game. Spinning on her heel she left the room.

"Earth to Lydia."

Startled, Lydia lifted her head and regarded her friend.

"What did you say? Sorry. My mind was a million miles away."

"I can see that," Ana replied, amusement in her voice. "I asked you how the party was last night. I want details remember."

Laughing, Lydia related the events of the night before, giving her friend insightful impressions of the people, the music and the customs she had witnessed.

"Everyone was so wonderful to me Ana and I felt almost as if I belonged there. They made such a fuss over me. I couldn't help but compare that to some of the boring parties I have attended back home."

"I'm glad you had such a good time," Ana acknowledged fondly. "But how was Rodolfo? Did he take good care of you like he promised? Did you kiss him? What was it like?"

This time Lydia burst into laughter that began somewhere deep in the pit of her stomach.

"How did you know I kissed him?" she asked incredulously.

"How could you not," Ana replied with a mischievous grin.

"So, tell me all?"

With some trepidation and not a little embarrassment Lydia related the incident with Rodolfo, downplaying as much as she could.

"I nearly blew it with Rodolfo I'm sorry to say. It's certainly not like me to put myself in those predicaments but thankfully it worked out in the end."

Ana leaned over and patted her hand.

"I've put myself in a few of those situations too. You have to keep in mind that these Latin men have hot blood running through their veins, not like most American men I know. Unless you're prepared to follow through, it's better not to light the fire, I always say."

Lydia regarded her friend with a small smile tugging at the corner of her mouth.

"I just bet you were some hell-raiser in your day," she teased her.

"Was?" Ana raised her eyebrows adroitly.

"Girlfriend, I still am! The stories I could tell you would make your toes curl if you pardon the expression."

With that pronouncement Ana pulled the brim of her hat lower on her forehead and closed her eyes.

Chuckling good humouredly, Lydia followed suit, content to lie here in the sun and daydream about Mexican fiestas, moonlight and Latin men. Lulled by the soft warm sun and gentle breeze, she had just closed her eyes when all too soon a soft voice in her ear brought her back to reality.

"*Hola Senorita*, you remember me? It's Felipe."

Lydia slowly opened her eyes and smiled.

"Hello Felipe. How are you?"

"*Muey Bien Senorita*. You want to go snorkeling with me today?"

Lydia looked over at Ana who was by now regarding them in amusement. She turned back to the handsome young man before her.

"Maybe, Felipe. How much?"

"Oh for you no charge," he smiled winningly at her and Lydia groaned inwardly, thinking it was time to set the record straight right away.

"Thank you Felipe that is very nice. You should know I have a boyfriend."

"Where is he?" Felipe asked looking around him.

"He's still in Canada," Lydia replied truthfully. "But he's coming here in a few days."

"Felipe shrugged. "No problem. He not here now. Let's go." He pulled playfully at her hand.

"*Vamanos*."

"Wait," she protested laughingly as he hauled her off the lounge chair. She looked at Ana who watched the by-play with real interest, a smile on her lips.

"What do you think Ana? Want to go snorkeling?"

"Where?" Ana asked their young would be guide.

"Today we go to Las Gatas? Felipe answered matter of factly. "We can take my boat," he offered sweeping his arm toward the beach where a small fishing boat anchored offshore.

For a minute Ana looked doubtful then her expression cleared and she lifted her shoulders in Lydia's direction.

"Why not? I won't snorkel myself but the trip over will give me a chance to tell you about the legend of Las Gatas and how Zihuatanejo came to be."

"That sounds wonderful," Lydia enthused. "Another story!"

She turned to Felipe who was grinning broadly.

"Okay Felipe we'll come. But I insist you let us pay, at least for the gas."

"Okay," Felipe agreed good-naturedly. "*Vamanos.*"

With Lydia and Ana on either side of him he led them to the beach where he waded into the water and pulled his small boat to shore so they could climb aboard. In a few short minutes they were on their way out of the gentle surf and heading toward open sea.

The ocean spray blowing in their faces cooled them and exhilarated Lydia on the short ride to the beach. Below lazy lashes Felipe watched her approvingly as she breathed in the salt air deeply. There was a smile on her lips and she stared wide-eyed at the beauty around her.

As they approached, Lydia could see that Las Gatas was in some ways very much like Playa La Ropa and Ixtapa Island with its restaurants and cabanas dotting the sand. To her right at the end of the point she noticed a large cabana and what looked like oversized straw huts. She asked Felipe about them.

In careful English he explained their origins. An American named Owen Lee, who had come here many, many years ago; owned them.

Ana supplied more information to the fascinated woman on the seat facing her.

"Owen is a thoroughly charming man," she enthused. "He's been here longer than anyone can remember. Years ago he dived with the very famous Jacques Cousteau and although he is well into his 70's, he still takes people out on diving excursions and tours, followed by lunch at the restaurant you can see from here. We should have lunch there later."

Lydia followed where Ana pointed and could indeed make out tables and chairs along what looked like a makeshift seawall. She nodded her agreement while Ana continued her tale.

"Years ago he hit on the idea of allowing people to rent his grass huts.

They're more luxurious than what the early natives lived in to be sure, but they are definitely huts nonetheless. The most interesting thing about Owen, though, is the book he's written about Ixtapa Zihuatanejo that you really should pick up. I'm sure the bookstore, Byblos, has copies."

"That's a good idea, Ana. Now tell me the story you promised," she pleaded as the boat drew close to the dock where they would be landing.

"As soon as we get settled," Ana told her. "And only if you let me start from the beginning. It may take awhile because it's very complicated and involved."

Lydia agreed. She was intrigued with what was to come.

They docked and Felipe helped Ana and Lydia out of the boat and onto the dock. He told them that he would meet them at Owen Lee's place once he had anchored the boat.

As they strolled along in the warm sand, waiters who tried to entice them into their restaurants followed them. Ana laughingly waved them away, indicating that they were heading to the far end of the beach.

Felipe was already there. He had anchored the boat securely and swam to the seawall; snorkeling equipment was next to the seats he had reserved for them near the beach.

As he bustled about putting fins and snorkels together, the pair settled down quietly and Ana began her tale.

"In 1531, when the story takes place, the natives knew Zihuatanejo as Blue Bay. It was a quiet cove like hundreds of others that dotted the Pacific coast and Central America. Its inhabitants were small tribes of Mahuatyl Indians who lived in the jungles and hills high above the sea.

At the same time the Spanish *conquistadors* were invading all across Mexico and down the Pacific coast, taking people into slavery wherever they landed. In what is now the state of Jalisco, they confiscated the area's precious woods and built Spanish ships to transfer the goods they had looted to more desirable climates along the Pacific coastline.

Renegades who escaped capture however, were becoming a tremendous problem for the Spanish by becoming pirates. It was reported that they murdered entire ships and kept only the most valuable cargo. Counted among the cargos of salvaged booty and valuables were women.

At this time, the Spanish ruler was King Felipe, (Ana smiled at their guide who puffed his chest out with pride). When he found out what was happening to his ships, he sent soldiers and well equipped ships to attempt to put a stop to the lootings and murder.

Once that happened the renegades were forced to escape inland. One such particularly despicable crew landed in what was then called Blue Bay, where they unloaded cargo, crew and women hostages. To avoid mutiny, the pirate Captain of the ship then burned his ships.

The crew wasted no time in delving into one of the ship's treasures—fine Spanish wine. The sailors immediately forced the women into slavery. Drunken and disorderly they squandered their loot, losing all track of time in the process. Only through the initiative and the hard work of the women hostages could they have survived."

"What a fascinating story," Lydia exclaimed as Felipe, listening alongside her nodded.

"Oh this is just the beginning," Ana assured them, secretly pleased to have such an avid audience. She resumed her tale as they leaned closer.

"Within this story there grew another legend and this legend to this day is passed down by village storytellers. Based on historical documentation, the story supports the theory of a matriarchy that was formed a few years following the landing of the pirates. This matriarchy flourished for over one hundred years and inspired the renaming of Blue Bay to Zihuatanejo, which translated means, 'The Place of the Sacred Women.'

"This part of the legend revolves around the appearance of a mysterious woman among the female hostages of the pirates. Her name was Cihuatyl. The story tells of Cihuatyl's escape from the pirates. She took with her twelve of the best women hostages to a hidden beach. There she taught them the ways of survival preparing them for the Matriarchy to come. Despite the close proximity of Cihuatyl and her disciples to the pirates, they were to remain undetected behind a huge wall of rocks that separated them. In this way they remained secluded and safe for several years."

"How do you know all this?" Ana only smiled mysteriously before continuing.

"One day, three large ships bearing the purple and gold sails of Spain sailed into the harbor and anchored at the tip of the land bordering the open sea. In need of laborers to build a winter palace for his queen, daughter, and their ladies in waiting, the man known as the Puppet King, Rey Calicinzon cast his eye upon the motley crew of Blue Bay and enlisted their services in the true conqueror's way – by force. In no time at all the men were taken hostage and dragged away while their woman who had remained with the pirates were abandoned and left to their own resources.

Now at last they were free of their captors. Soon after, Cihuatyl and her twelve disciples joined them to make the matriarchy she had prophesized years before.

Several years passed before Rey Calicinzon decided the projects he wanted commissioned were complete. These included the building of a bathing pool for the princess, which you see ahead of us."

Ana pointed to the rock formation a few feet off shore and noted it did indeed look like the enclosure of a swimming pool.

"It was designed to keep sharks and other large fish away from the women in Calicinzon's group," she explained more fully.

"By now, the former drunken pirates were sober, strong, and much less arrogant than they were before their capture. As reward for work well done, Calicinzon decreed they could return home to the hostage women—under his rule of course. Once there, he proposed a system of outrageous taxes upon the population, making unreasonable demands on natural resources. To make matters worse, in the absence of the former pirates, the women of the newly created society had become strong. They processed a new authority and sense of selfhood. They were not interested in their would-be conquerors.

"In order for the new civilization to comply with all the rules with which to make the King's coffers grow and expand, it was imperative that they obtain more laborers to do his bidding. In short—the pirates needed children.

"With this as a bargaining chip, the women spelled out their own conditions to the startled men. These included that they be treated with respect. Further, they would have equal say in the governing of the new village with all its rules and laws. Should the pirates not wish to comply, and then quite simply the women would not bear their children. If they became pregnant they would find a way that the child not be carried to term, thereby ending effectively the men's power over them.

"The men reluctantly agreed and from that time on pregnant women were highly esteemed, with Cihuatyl ruling as mother of the village for many years to come."

"That is an incredible story," Lydia clapped. "But what happened to Cihuatyl?"

"Oh that's where the supernatural element enters into the story," Ana answered with a smile.

"Many years later after a farewell to her women, legend has it that Cihuatyl ascended to the stars; her final wish to her followers was that her story be told for many generations to come. In this way she would never be forgotten and Zihuatanejo would always be the place of the sacred women."

Lydia reached over and gave Ana a hug.

"Thank you for another wonderful story Ana, it was beautiful."

"*De nada*," Ana waved the compliment away. She looked over at Felipe who was staring at the two of them, a bemused look on his face.

"Now you had better get into the water with this boy before he burns up."

Grinning, Lydia and the brown-skinned guide quickly donned their masks and flippers and dove in to the cool Pacific waters.

# Chapter Ten

John hung up the phone contentedly, feeling he had accomplished something momentous in regards to the rest of his life. In ten short days he would be on his way to Texas for an overnight stay and then onto Zihuatanejo to be with Lydia. He should probably arrive just in time to take her out for dinner. He almost wished he hadn't committed to overnight in Dallas first, preferring to fly direct, but his mother had asked him to say hello to the "Texas Connection" as she called them. Not wanting to refuse such a simple request he had reluctantly agreed.

*Besides, he reasoned, its just one extra night. What difference could one night make?*

Just as he was wondering how Lydia was faring in Mexico the phone rang momentarily distracting him. Turning his mind from the pleasant thoughts of the anticipated reunion, he gave full attention to the caller.

Lydia in fact was faring very well, she thought with some sense of pride. The last two days she had filled with sightseeing—sometimes to remote villages nearby to check out the lifestyles of the people there. As days drifted lazily she felt a growing sense of peace within her, the hustle and bustle of her life in Canada a million miles from her thoughts. Long walks had her re-examining her own life carefully and really looking at the smiles and simple happiness of the Mexican people as they went about theirs. She wondered frequently if her harried existence was worth the stress and toll it took on her.

What is life for if you're always too busy to enjoy it?

Questions to which she had no easy answers. She walked the long stretches of deserted beaches, knowing she needed to make some changes. If only she knew how.

Lydia plopped down on the beach to watch the final red and gold of the sun as it dipped below the horizon. The sheer beauty of it nearly took her breath away. Then dusting off the sand on her legs, she decided to drop by Coconuts later that evening to see who might be around.

You never know.

Hurrying to catch the bus she smiled inwardly. She was unwilling to admit the real reason for going there—even to herself.

Rodolfo put the finishing touches on his tables and hurried back for his flambé trays. Flambé were the specialty at Coconuts and he took pride in the way he prepared the various kinds for his customers. A good fire-show meant good tips for him, too.

You're getting as materialistic as a gringo; he chided himself with a grin as he placed the trays in the corner for easy access later.

The truth of the matter was that money meant very little to him. Something he still blamed on the failure of his marriage. Between the two of them they had made above average wages but his ex-wife was always casting around, looking to make more. Or perhaps someone who could provide her with more. When that "someone" failed to come through for her she had immediately regretted her decision.

Lately Beatrice had taken to coming by the restaurant to see him, or calling him at home. Rodolfo always instructed Yola to tell her he was out, or sleeping, or simply not able to come to the phone. Anything, as long as he didn't have to talk to her. When she showed up at Coconut's he ignored her completely. Piqued by his lack of interest in her she would then flirt with the *gringos* who frequented the bar hoping to make him jealous, making sure he saw her leave with one. Wise to her game, her behavior only hardened his heart against her.

Putting his wayward ex out of his mind, his thoughts turned to Lydia. Savoring the sound of it, he said the name aloud, liking the way it rolled off his tongue and earning himself an amused glance from Arturo, as he happened to pass by.

I'm behaving like a teenager, he realized, hoping she would make an appearance later that night.

At that moment, Tonita came forward to confer with him on the reservations she had made in his section that evening. Putting all thoughts of the alluring, Canadian woman aside, he bent closer and gave her his undivided attention.

Ana had just about given up on Lydia coming to the restaurant for a nightcap when, looking up from her usual chair, she saw her standing hesitantly in the doorway, eyes casing the place as if looking for someone. Spying her at about the same time, Lydia waved casually in her direction and started forward across the room.

"Sit down," Ana indicated the cushion on the bench beside her graciously. "Tell me what you've been up to these past few days."

"Mostly sightseeing," Lydia said noncommittally, "and a little shopping of course. Nothing too exciting really, but very relaxing. Just what the doctor ordered."

As she spoke Lydia's eyes darted around the room until she saw—she finally had to admit—the person she was looking for.

Smiling from the cashier's cage where he was waiting for change Rodolfo winked at her slowly, his wide smile lighting up at the sight of her.

Blushing, Lydia ducked her head and tried to concentrate on what Ana was saying to her.

"I think you've made a conquest," Ana teased her pointedly, watching as the red crept up her neck and over her friend's face.

"Oh that," Lydia laughed lightly. "We're just friends. That's all."

"Well your friend is heading this way and I think this is where I leave to powder my nose."

With that, Ana floated elegantly toward the rest rooms, her ever present scarves trailing behind her. Lydia fought to control herself as she glanced up to see Rodolfo heading toward her. Ducking her head quickly, she pretended not to notice him, realizing for the second time she was behaving like a schoolgirl.

Rodolfo stopped in front of her table and Lydia nonchalantly looked up, a noncommittal smile on her face. Rodolfo only grinned wider as if knowing the game she was playing. Placing his hands on the table he leaned over, liking the way she blushed so easily in his presence.

"*Buenos noches Senorita.*"

"*Buenos Noches* Rodolfo," she replied feeling the color recede, glad of the dimly lit room.

That's more like it, she thought, feeling more in control.

"Did you have a nice day off Rodolfo?" she asked carefully.

"How did you know it was my day off," he mocked her and laughed at the look on her face.

"Were you checking up on me?"

Lydia drew back stuttering, "Well I... I just..." Then her eyes met his and realizing he was only teasing, she laughed at herself and swatted his arm playfully.

"You are a brat," she said as primly as she could, her lips twitching as she tried to keep from laughing.

Dimples deepening, he leaned even closer.

"I have another day off tomorrow," he said invitingly. "Would you like to share it with me?"

It took her only a second to respond.

"Yes I would. Where are we going?"

Rodolfo grinned again at her eagerness. She reddened slightly but kept her eyes on his.

"That will be a secret," he replied. "I will pick you up at your hotel at 10:30 in the morning. OK?"

She nodded intrigued.

"Is there anything I need to bring?"

"Yes Lydia you could bring a swimsuit and sunscreen. If you like you can skip the suit." He teased her again and this time she laughed openly with him.

"See you *mañana*," he promised, moving away just as Ana headed toward them.

Lydia watched him retreat until Ana's amused voice spoke into her ear.

"Well?" she questioned curiously.

"What's going on? What did he say?"

Lydia smiled happily.

"We have a date tomorrow morning, that's all. He's going to take me somewhere but it's a secret. I am only supposed to bring a suit and screen."

"That's all huh? You must have made quite an impression for him to ask you out in the daytime."

Lydia stared at her curiously.

"What do you mean?"

"What I mean," Ana explained patiently, "is that most Mexican men around here will only ask you out for the evening, never for a whole day. Usually they will invite you to go dancing, and if you are real lucky, for dinner as well—then off to some cheap little hotel for a quick thrill if you let them."

"Really?" Lydia looked downcast.

"Oh, not you," Ana assured her with a tap on her arm.

"Obviously Rodolfo must respect you or he wouldn't invite you out in broad daylight. Like I said Lydia, you must have made an impression on him."

Lydia was relieved by her friend's words.

"I hope what you say is true Ana. After all John will be here in a few days and I can't get caught up in anything with anyone no matter how attractive I find them to be. And John really is a good man Ana," she reiterated earnestly.

"It just wouldn't be right for me to have a fling in the meantime now would it?"

*Maybe I should just cancel this date.*

Ana patted her arm again soothingly.

"Of course you won't have a fling Lydia, but you are here to have fun and fun is what you should have. I told you Rodolfo is an evolved man. You'll be safe with him. He is not a typical Mexican man and he will behave himself – if you want him to, that is," she laughed aloud.

"I will, won't I?" Lydia said with more confidence, hoping her gut instincts was right.

She laughed, realizing what she'd just said, and clarified for her amused friend.

"I mean I will trust him and yes I want him to behave."

Ana returned her smile with a secretive one of her own.

"You don't need to convince me," she protested, fanning her face quickly and batting her long lashes.

Lydia giggled as another waiter came to their table to take their drink order. They soon changed the subject to other things.

The next day arrived bright and sunny. Lydia sprang eagerly from her bed to greet the morning. The cool shower caressed her skin softly; nerve ends tingling as they came alive with feeling. Toweling off, she realized how much she was looking forward to her outing today. It wasn't everyone who got their own personal guide, and one who was native to the area. She was sure it would be a day she wouldn't easily forget.

*What if he doesn't show up?*

Her mind flicked back to last night, knowing she would be very disappointed if the day was canceled for one reason or another. But no, his parting glance had told her he was looking forward to this day as much as she. Maybe more.

With that she put all negative ideas from her mind and concentrated on what to wear for the day's excursion. Although she had no clue as to where he might be taking her, she finally settled on a sleeveless, full-length tie-dye dress that swirled saucily at the hem with each step she took, displaying the silver ankle bracelet she had purchased in the marketplace the other day. Pearl buttons from the low cut bodice gleamed brightly down the full length of the garment. Lydia strategically opened the last four at the bottom, showing her legs as she walked. Sticking a genuine panama hat on her head she viewed herself critically in the mirror. Its broad brim was the very thing for keeping the sun off her face while still looking stylish.

*It would help if I knew where we were going today,* she thought again, realizing at the same time that not knowing was half the fun and excitement.

At the last minute she threw in a pair of shorts alongside the towel and bathing suit she had packed. Declaring herself as ready as she would ever be, Lydia shouldered the bag she had picked up for a song at one of the little nearby shops and stepped onto the street under the watchful eye of Juan, the hotel's desk clerk.

Once outside, she blinked from the glare of the already hot sun and quickly donned her sunglasses. Glancing up and down for a sign of Rodolfo's brothers' red beetle she saw that the streets were entirely empty. Her heart plummeted. She was disappointed as she glanced at her watch to see that it was already five minutes past the appointed time. Ana had warned her last night that Mexican time was not Canadian time. She tried to keep her hopes up that Rodolfo would actually show. Sinking slowly, she sat dispiritedly on the steps of the hotel to wait.

*Still plenty of time,* she assured herself, shifting slightly on the stone steps to a more comfortable position.

Rodolfo stirred restlessly to the sound of someone tapping lightly on his bedroom door. He groaned and pulled the pillow over his head hoping to dissuade his visitor, whoever it may be. The sound persisted and he growled an answer.

"*Vete.*" Get lost.

"*Padrino?*" A sweet voice sounded through the door and he immediately softened.

"Are you asleep?" It was his niece.

Rodolfo smiled at her question.

"Not anymore," he replied in English knowing she wouldn't understand.

"*Si*, Mona," he amended, calling her by her pet name as he sat straight up in bed and invited her to enter.

Glancing at the alarm by the side of the bed he saw it was already 10:30.

*Shit,* he swore softly to himself as he leapt up, taking the proffered cup of coffee Andrea offered him, and headed directly to the shower.

He was late.

As he scrubbed his body vigorously in an effort to wake up he hoped she would wait for him. Then he relaxed. The look in her eyes last night told him she was just as interested in an outing today as he was, although maybe not for the same reasons. Still, it wouldn't do to make a bad impression. He knew from experience how funny people were north of the border about time and he had a feeling Lydia would not be an exception to the rule. Toweling off quickly he dressed with record speed and headed out the door, scooping up a breakfast tortilla stuffed with eggs from the pan on the counter. *No sense in going hungry, too,* he thought practically.

The sound of a horn and screeching tires caused Lydia to look up sharply from the book she had been reading. As the little red beetle careened recklessly to a stop in front of the hotel, she stood up quickly and grinned happily at the sight of its lone occupant. Noting that he was only fifteen minutes late she leaned in the passenger window to greet him, curiously assessing his attire.

She'd never seen him out of his waiter's uniform of crisp white shirt and carefully pressed black pants and she suppressed an urge to laugh aloud.

His long black hair, unusual for most Mexican men she had noted, now flowed freely and wildly past his shoulders, like one of Ana's fancy Spanish fans. At Coconuts he always wore it tightly slicked back in a ponytail, neatly away from his face. Deciding it suited him this way, she moved on.

As he got out of the car to open the door for her, she saw he had chosen a pair of cut-off shorts and she was glad she had chosen to pack a pair of her own. It was his T-shirt that caught her attention though, and caused her amusement. Like her dress it was tie-dyed too. His had wilder colors and featured a large picture of an elephant.

*He looks like Cheech & Chong,* she thought, biting the inside of her cheek to keep from laughing aloud.

Mistaking her amusement entirely on her pleasure at seeing him, Rodolfo grinned wider than ever, his open face smooth and relaxed as he took her shoulder bag from her and opened the passenger car door. As she got in, he leaned over her and placed her bag on the back seat then clinched the seatbelt around her with another smile, his face inches away from hers.

"Good," he spoke for the first time. "You're ready."

Nodding approvingly he didn't bother to apologize for his lateness. Lydia slowly let out the breath she had been unaware she had been holding, and tried to compose herself. As he started the car Lydia ventured to ask him where they were going.

"Fishing," came the prompt reply and for the second time in an hour Lydia was pleased she had brought along a pair of shorts to wear.

"Great," she replied happily. "Somewhere special?"

"Yes, to me it is," he acknowledged. "In fact *Barra de Potosi* is my favorite place in the whole area. Not too many tourists know about this place unless they know locals, so I hope that you will enjoy it as much as I do."

"I'm sure I will," Lydia said, pleased to be shown something new and different from the normal tourist treks.

The drive took nearly thirty minutes. Lydia drank in the scenery in amazement at the lush greenness around them. Coconut and mango trees lined the roadside, the thick jungle growth, stopping shy of the asphalt. As they turned down a dirt road, beautiful and exotic flowers spilled over fences and out of ditches, filling the air with their perfume. Here and there small homes, some little more than wooden stick shacks dotted the countryside. Naked, brown-skinned children waved happily at them as they drove slowly by and Lydia enthusiastically returned their waves from the open window of the car.

Now as they entered the quiet streets of a small *pueblo*, Lydia watched the villagers as they calmly went about their daily lives, feeling as if she had landed in another time. Women, backs straight and strong balanced heavy loads of food on their slender necks, while an occasional donkey carried a pile of wood across his back and ambled next to his owner down the dusty road. Ever present chickens and pigs darted in front of the vehicle and they laughed gleefully even as they narrowly missed them. Lydia settled back contentedly in her seat with a soft sigh.

John did tell me that to really see Mexico I had to get in there with the people, she thought as she slid a sidelong glance at her guide. *I'm not sure if he meant I should see it with someone as attractive as Rodolfo, but here I am.*

She giggled aloud, earning a puzzled smile from Rodolfo who smiled back but just kept driving, not feeling the need to respond in words.

He considered the woman beside him with approval, noticing that the tight, pinched look she had had when she first arrived had all but disappeared from her eyes and mouth. It softened her somehow; made her look younger and more relaxed. Mexico certainly seemed to agree with her and he smiled again at the face that shone in sheer pleasure at all she saw around her.

"Your country is so beautiful," she complimented him when she noticed his eyes on her.

"I wish I could live here forever."

"Maybe you will one day *Chiquita*," he said solemnly, taking her words at face value. The pronouncement sounded a little like a prophesy, even to him and for a minute they were both silent.

*THE JADE PENDANT*

The hot drive ended as Lydia saw a sign, which read Barra de Potosi. Rodolfo turned down a sandy driveway. Parking beneath the overhanging branches of a palm tree next to a ramshackle building, Rodolfo stopped the car and hurried to open her door. Not used to the chivalry, but enjoying it nevertheless, Lydia waited patiently before stepping out onto the hot sandy floor.

"This is it," he proclaimed proudly as a Mexican woman rushed forward to greet them.

Exchanging kisses on the cheek, Rodolfo placed a friendly arm around the pretty young woman and introduced them.

"This is Minga, the best cook in Mexico," he bragged proudly. "Next to my mother of course." he said reverently as Lydia burst out laughing.

Laughing, he translated to Minga who beamed affectionately at her friend before replying in rapid Spanish, her eyes on Lydia who looked on with a small, slightly jealous smile. Her words brought a curious look to Rodolfo's eyes. She smiled once more at the pair of them before returning to her kitchen.

"What did she say? Was she talking about me?" Lydia asked suspiciously, her curiosity getting the better of her.

Rodolfo chucked her playfully under her chin, and kissed the top of her head lightly.

"Yes *Nina*," he teased her. "She said it was about time I brought a girlfriend here with me. Even a jealous one."

Lydia blushed to the roots of her hair. She made protesting sounds but was unable to utter a word as she stared at Minga's retreating form.

Girlfriend? Jealous?

Turning, she glanced up at Rodolfo, flustered but pleased to see that he was a darker shade beneath his tan too and she relaxed under his amused grin.

Taking her hand and hefting the shoulder bag over his shoulders, Rodolfo led the way to the open-air restaurant. He stopped as he heard her sharp intake at the sight that lay before her.

Brightly colored hammocks were strung between smooth poles beneath the thatched roof of the eatery and plastic flags waved cheerily from every imaginable surface.

There must be at least 100 of them, she thought in amazement.

Delighted, she ran to the hammock closest to the edge of the restaurant and climbed in, her sharp eyes rapidly taking in everything around her. Her toes wiggled happily in the cool sand as she straddled her perch. For a minute she swung with satisfaction in her netted cradle, wondering why she had avoided taking a holiday before now.

Watching her childish delight, Rodolfo smiled.

Everything interests her, he saw at once, pleased by her reaction. *And everything about her interests me,* he realized on the heels of his previous thought.

Deciding it was time to prepare the tackle for their fishing trip, Rodolfo left Lydia idly swinging in the hammock while he went to find Minga. Choosing the bait from her outdoor freezer, he expertly strung up his line, wrapping the cord around two coca-cola cans and baited the hooks with bits of shrimp. The rest he placed in a plastic bag inside his knapsack for future use. He pulled out a large fish from the freezer, and, walking back to the kitchen he handed it to Minga who took it carefully.

"These look good," he said of the Red Snapper. "Can we have it Mexican style and with lots of garlic?"

Minga grinned at him slyly as she plunged the catch into a nearby bucket to thaw.

"I'll have it for the princess when you return, "she laughed at him openly this time.

Rodolfo joined in

"See that you do Minga," he commanded with humor. "We wouldn't want the princess to wait when she gets hungry."

Then seriously, "I think we should be back around 2:30. Would that be okay for you?"

"Yes that will be fine," Minga nodded already planning what other foods she would cook to accompany the fish.

"*Gracias* Minga," Rodolfo called over his shoulder as he walked back to where Lydia still lay rocking.

She smiled hugely at him and yawned mightily.

"I nearly fell asleep," she declared as he pulled her out of the hammock to stand close beside him. For a minute the two stared at each other, Lydia the first to look away.

"Where to now?" she asked gamely.

"Fishing." He replied promptly, pleased with her attitude.

"Then we come back here for a delicious fish dinner. How does that sound to you?"

"Perfect." Lydia looked around her.

"Where's our fishing gear?" she asked puzzled by the lack of rods and reels.

Rodolfo rummaged briefly in the knapsack until he produced the coke cans complete with fishing line, rusty hooks and the bag of shrimp.

"All we need here," he declared as Lydia looked doubtful but interested. "Come on. I'll show you. *Vamanos*."

Laughing, Lydia took up her knapsack and headed to the bathroom to change into her shorts while Rodolfo waited patiently in the hammock she had just vacated, still warm from her body.

When she returned to stand before him, he opened his eyes and stared at her approvingly taking in rapidly the denim shorts and tiny bikini top she had put on. It was certainly going to be a struggle to concentrate on fishing; he could already see that much as he took her outstretched hand and allowed her to heft him up.

Following his lead, Lydia walked behind him across the hot sand toward a small wooden boat pulled up onto the shore of the lagoon.

As she climbed in and Rodolfo pushed off the sand bar, Lydia was relieved to see that they would be fishing in the lagoon and not the ocean connected to it by a tiny peninsula nearby. She had an abnormal fear of the ocean, she knew, sure that in one lifetime she had drowned in its mighty embrace.

Sensing her fears, Rodolfo assured her.

"We're just going along the shoreline today Lydia. After small fish."

Visibly relaxing, Lydia leaned back as Rodolfo rowed, liking the way the muscles rippled on his bare arms, his lips pressed together in a small line as he concentrated on the movements. For a while they paddled on in companionable silence, each deep in their own thoughts surrounded by peace and quiet.

Rodolfo stopped rowing and pulled the small boat close to shore beneath the vines of the jungle. Lydia peered into the murky depth as Rodolfo readied the gear, handing a coke can and baited hook to outstretched fingers. Following his lead she threw her hook into the water, unsure as to what to do next.

"We're just going to jig," he showed her as he reeled in while at the same time pulling on the line in an up and down motion. Lydia did the same and soon the pair were happily throwing and reeling in their makeshift fishing rods with practiced skill, catching one small fish after another.

Sometimes Rodolfo would row further and stop at places around the lagoon where he thought fish would be lurking. All afternoon they caught yellowtail, red snapper and a laughable frogfish that puffed out its belly in indignation when it was caught, croaking loudly in protest. They always let the fish go back to their watery homes, much to Lydia's relief.

"The really big fish are in the ocean," Rodolfo explained, adding that maybe she would like to go deep-sea fishing with him sometime – in a bigger boat of course, he amended in light of her fear.

Lydia nodded her acceptance although knowing with John's arrival such a thing might not be possible. But she was unwilling to spoil the outing by bringing the subject up.

Several happy hours passed when the rumbling of Lydia's stomach reminded her that she had not eaten a thing all day. Rodolfo turned the boat around and headed home, teasing her about the volcano that she must have swallowed that morning. On the slow paddle back to shore, Lydia tried to thank her host.

"*De nada*," he shrugged off her thanks. "I am happy you liked it. It is nice to see you have such a good time. And," he said pointedly, "Such a good fisherman you are, too."

Lydia colored, as she laughed at his outrageous praise, pleased just the same. She *had* caught a lot of fish and some of them were big, too!

Once safely back on shore, Lydia helped Rodolfo pull the boat a safer distance up on the banks of the lagoon. Hand in hand they ran over the hot sand that threatened to burn the soles of their feet and ducked beneath the roof of the restaurant, laughing. Two ice-cold beers appeared as if by magic in the hands of one of Minga's young daughters and they greedily gulped them down, raising their hands in a request for two more. These they sipped at a more normal pace as they swung in a pair of hammocks strung out side by side.

While they waited for the food to arrive, Lydia lazily asked Rodolfo to tell her about his family.

"I was born in a cave in the mountains of Chihuahua," he told her, his face serious while he enjoyed the shocked look on hers.

"Really! I was born in the Copper Canyon. Do you know where that is?"

Lydia shook her head not knowing whether to believe him or not, but interested just the same.

"Then I'll have to take you there some time," he promised her before continuing his story.

"It was not an ordinary cave *Chiquita*," he teased her again.

"It was a luxury cave – two bedrooms. My mother gave birth to eight of us in that cave. When we were being born she would tie a rope around the trunk of a tree. She would pull on that rope and give birth to us standing up." He shrugged at her horrified expression.

"What else could a woman do?" he reasoned and she had to agree with him even as she shuddered at the thought of it.

Beyond anything she had ever known and would never in all likelihood experience, God willing, she tried to conjure the vision of a woman giving birth in that way and found she couldn't. Although her family had been poor in some ways, her mother had had each and every one of them in the sterile surroundings of the county hospital.

"Tell me more," she breathed, fascinated, and always ready for a new tale.

"Tell me about your parents. How did they meet?"

Rodolfo smiled at the excited curiosity in her voice.

"That, *Chiquita,* is a very romantic story. *Muy romantica!*" He smiled tenderly at her remembering the story his mother had told him so many years ago.

"Tell me," she begged him, a light shining eagerly in her green eyes, giving them a near translucent look.

Rodolfo settled deeper into his hammock before speaking.

"*Si, Senorita* Lydia. I will tell you a story."

# Chapter Eleven

"Angelina Perez was a young woman of extraordinary beauty and grace. At the age of seventeen, her parents decided to visit distant relatives in the mountainous regions of Chihuahua, far to the north of them. As a privileged child who had lived in a monstrous sized house in the outskirts of Guadalajara, "Angel" was born with the proverbial spoon in her mouth. The only daughter of a wealthy family of Spanish descent, Angelina was petted, cosseted and extremely well cared for. Unlike many of her peers, her family believed in the education of women so she was fortunate enough to have received hers in the best private school in the country. Even now plans were tentatively underway for her to be sent to Switzerland for "finishing", a prospect that for all its merit appealed little to her.

After her return in one year, it was expected that she would be ready for marriage to a suitably acceptable man as befitted her station. It was imperative to the family line that she produced heirs.

A lesser young woman would have been spoiled or snobbish but it was to Angel's credit that she was neither of those things, possessing a generous spirit and a wonderful sense of humor. All who knew her remarked on her charm, poise and sweetness, all qualities that would make it easy to find a good match for her as her parents hoped.

If Angel had also possessed a shy retiring personality, it would possibly have been better for those involved but the fact of the matter was, Angel was a headstrong, incurable romantic, whose one thought was to have adventures – as many of them as she could. She dreamed longingly of the days when she could travel and experience a little of the real life she saw or read about in movies and books, before she settled down to one man for the rest of her life. A dutiful daughter, she kept her feelings to herself even while suspecting that the trip her parents planned was for her to meet her future husband.

A week of visiting and an endless round of fiestas left Angel dissatisfied and restless. Although it was fun meeting new people, the crowd she was introduced to was similar to the group of friends she had left behind, right down to the things they said and the clothes they wore.

For this I might as well have stayed in Guadalajara, she groused uncharacteristically as she became more and more discontent.

As she had suspected, her possible future husband was among those whom she met—the dashing Miguel Alvarez Rodriguez, son and heir apparent of the president of the Sierra Tarahumara Railroad.

Angelica liked the affable Miguel well enough, and knew that most women would give their left arm for a man like that. She privately thought he was a bit of a bore, with not much to talk about except parties and the clothes people wore to them, but he was pleasant and kind and obviously smitten with his distant cousin from the south. When he invited her and all of her family to visit the offices at the site of the railway company to view the new construction, Angelica who was always looking for something new to do was delighted that her father had accepted. Anything to escape the monotony!

Miguel, on the other hand, was anxious to impress his wealth upon the aloof Angelica, wishing fervently she would treat him as more than the family pet. With the idea of somehow persuading her to look on him in a more romantic manner, he arranged that the two of them would ride to the site in a separate limousine, her family members following behind in another. This was the way they set out on their journey to the fabled Copper Canyon.

As they drove, Angelica gazed around in awe at the wondrous sights, fervently interested in all that Miguel had to tell her. The mountains, majestic in their red glory were indescribably beautiful to her and she was surprised to learn that the Copper Canyon was even bigger than the Grand Canyon north of the border. An unexplainable stirring grew in her breast unlike anything she had ever felt before.

"The railroad is being built right through the mountains," Miguel explained proudly. "Perhaps you will allow me to take you on the maiden run when it is completed."

Privately he thought, *perhaps on our honeymoon.*

Angelica rewarded him with a warm smile. Her face glowed with the excitement of traveling around heart-stopping cliffs, through tunnels with thousands of tons of rock above her. Miguel felt more hopeful than ever and leaning over, squeezed her hand.

At twenty-four, Joseph Perez was already the assistant explosives expert with the Sierra Tarahumara Railroad. A Tarahumara Indian himself, he was tall, lean and considered very, very handsome. Too handsome some of the grandmothers thought. Their female offspring twittered anytime he was within sight of them.

Although he knew that women flocked to him, he had up to now paid little attention, deciding years ago it was imperative for him to establish himself first, before he took on the added responsibility of a wife and children.

Born to the poorest of poor families in the mountains, Joseph's family was nevertheless considered to be that of royal blood and as such was revered throughout the state. His father, the Shaman of the Tarahumara, a now nearly extinct tribe, had instilled his beliefs and high morals on his family almost from the moment of their birth. As the eldest son, Joseph was expected to take over from his father when he passed on.

In the meantime, Joseph had clawed his way up the company ladder to the position he held today. He was admired and respected for the risks he took that no one else dared. Due to the dangerous nature of the business, his job paid well. Soon he felt he would be ready to start a family of his own.

Joseph walked wearily to the construction site office for his next instructions and more dynamite, just as two limousines pulled into the yard and came to a stop, nearly running him over in the process.

Curious, Joseph stepped back to watch as a slightly pudgy, but well dressed man about his own age, stepped out of the car held open for him by the uniformed chauffeur. Leaning forward slightly, he then turned and extended his hand to the cool interior.

Joseph stood rooted to the spot as a beautiful young woman emerged from her luxurious cocoon and moved gracefully out of the shadows and into the bright sunlight. For a moment she stood there blinking as she tried to adjust to the glare of the white-hot light. As he watched, she raised a graceful hand to her brow to shade her eyes. It was at that moment her gaze fell on the dusty man standing as if paralyzed by the side of the road.

All time receded into the distance as the two stared at each other, oblivious to everyone around them.

You've come, his mind reached across the void telepathically.

*I'm home,* she sent back wordlessly.

In the confusion of disembarking and greeting company officials, no one noticed the obvious fascination experienced by two people from different worlds on the clay packed, dusty road.

## THE JADE PENDANT

It was Miguel who realized his intended was still standing where he had left her and he moved to apologize for the oversight. It was only then that he noticed the young man staring at Angelica. He was handsome even covered with the red dirt that clung to him like a second skin. Sharply, he called out to him to move on, pleased to see the deep flush that darkened the underlings face. A final hard stare and Joseph slowly moved away.

Angelica took a step forward as if to follow, then seeing the look of sudden anger on Miguel's face she pulled herself upright and smiled radiantly at her host. Slightly mollified he pulled the reluctant woman toward the offices where, pretending an interest she no longer felt, she allowed him to lead the way.

Joseph stared bleakly at her, convinced he had seen the only Angel on earth. Then, at the last possible moment the vision before him turned her head and smiled sweetly at the stranger she'd fallen in love with at first sight."

"Love at first sight?" Lydia asked skeptically.

"Don't you believe in love at first sight, *Chiquita*?" Rodolfo parried back, amused.

Lydia paused.

"I guess so...after all...your parents..." Then eagerly, "What happened next?"

Rodolfo smiled now more amused than ever by this woman-child before him.

For the rest of the day Joseph struggled to banish the memory of the beautiful young woman from his mind.

She's too rich for you. Who are you trying to fool? He berated himself endlessly. *Better you forget her.*

But no matter how hard he tried, the sight of her heart shaped face and luminous eyes constantly intruded into his memories. Bereft and after several days he finally approached his father for advice.

"If you love her," his father reasoned, "There is nothing that you cannot do. And, if she loves you, there is nothing that will stand in your way."

Joseph knew that one day the position of Shaman would fall to him, and as he listened to his father's wisdom, he felt more unable than ever to fill his shoes.

"But how will I win her," he asked discouraged. "I have nothing to offer her."

"But you do, my son. You have your heart. You'll find the way. If it is meant to be, you will find the way."

Back then in a town the size of Chihuahua, it was easy for Joseph to ascertain who the mystery girl was and where she was staying. *Angelica Perez,* he smiled at the irony of their last names.

In Mexico when two people married their names became hyphenated, joined together as one. If he was successful their names would be Perez-Perez, a lucky omen he was sure. Not knowing how long she would be staying, he decided to hurry his suit.

That night Joseph hired a local Mariachi band to play for Angelica outside her window. Dressed in the finest clothes he owned, usually reserved for weddings and funerals, he led the musicians to what he hoped was the bedroom where she slept. He was right.

As the sound of the romantic music drifted through the night and reached her ears, Angelica rose quickly and flew to the window, throwing up the sash. There in the moonlight below was the earnest face of the man she was soon to know as Joseph Perez, smiling up at her.

Muy romantico, she thought delighted.

Her thoughts were soon interrupted however by her angry mother scolding her and pulling her away from the window and firmly locking it behind them. Not in the least amused, her father strode out onto the manicured lawn to confront the unwelcome suitor and chase him away. Elated by the glimpse of his "Angel's" face, he respectfully complied with her father's wishes and departed, strains of Mariachi music flowing in his wake until finally it was gone.

Angelica was heartbroken.

"What did you say to him Poppa?" she cried, dismayed.

"I told him you were engaged to be married and he was to stop this nonsense at once." Her father answered sternly.

And that was how Angelica Perez learned of her impending marriage to Miguel Alvarez Rodriquez.

I'll never see him again; she despaired lying in her bed, her body racked with sobs.

Even Angelica had no way of knowing the true depth of Joseph's love for her. Determined that she was the only woman for him, he put together a plan of action to woo her and perhaps her family, too, into accepting him. Although disheartened by his first attempt, but in no way defeated, he and his musical Marauders took up their positions outside Angelica's window the very next night, and every night after that.

"Every night?" Lydia interrupted incredulously.

"Of course," Rodolfo answered blandly, surprised by the question. "We Perez men take what we want."

Lydia shivered, a thrill flickering at the core of her as Rodolfo continued.

"Night after night Joseph's band played love songs to Angelica and night after night her father chased him away. Always respectful but never apologetic, he would simply smile at her father and leave.

One night after several weeks of this, Joseph showed up on cue outside his daughter's window, her father gave in and allowed him a few songs before shooing him from the premises. Encouraged by the small favor, Joseph continued his pursuit, sometimes rewarded by the face of his Angel in the window before she was pulled away.

For the rest of the month he faithfully showed up at the house, always playing the love songs of the country until her father allowed Angelica to go to the verandah to speak to him under the watchful eye of her mother.

At first it was only a few minutes, but gradually, as nights went, by he would allow them more time until it was almost a half hour. For the young lovers it was not enough, but still it was better than nothing. Her mother, always sitting close by would report back to her husband the chaste conversations the couple was able to have and it was in this way he was able to learn more about her daughter's suitor.

Eventually Angelica told him tearfully that they were to leave the Copper Canyon and go back to their home in the city. Joseph knew he had to move quickly or he would lose his beloved Angel forever. Mustering his courage, and with the support of Angel's mother, who had by now come to admire the goodness in the handsome young man, he asked permission of her father for his daughter's hand in marriage. Seeing the look of love in the young couple's eyes and with the gentle prodding of his wife, Angel's father capitulated."

"And so now, here I am," Rodolfo teased.

"Are you telling me your mother gave up everything to live in a cave?" Lydia blurted disbelievingly.

He answered her seriously.

"Not everything Lydia," he explained as if to a child.

"She didn't have his love before and without love, what else is there?"

Lydia remained silent for a moment contemplating his philosophy.

Was he right? She asked herself as she considered her current relationship with John.

Sure, their friendship was growing, their admiration for each other solid and real. But Love? No, she was sure they didn't have that. At least not the kind she wanted. But it didn't mean it couldn't still happen, did it? She sighed sadly caught up in her thoughts.

"Here comes lunch," Rodolfo said and interrupted her reverie.

At the sight of the scrumptious lunch Lydia immediately brightened and with real appetite they fell eagerly on the food, determined to do it full justice.

Siesta followed lunch.

"I could get used to this," Lydia groaned as Rodolfo helped her into a hammock, choosing another one nearby for him.

"This is the life," Rodolfo expounded. "What else more do you need? We have everything here before us. Good food, the ocean, sun, sand and," he winked across the sandy space between them, "good company. Now get some rest and I will wake you in a while."

With a final smile at her, he closed his eyes. Unnoticed, Lydia watched him as his breathing deepened and he fell into the untroubled sleep of the good and innocent. It was not long before her eyelids grew heavy and, sighing with deep contentment, she obediently closed her eyes and she too fell asleep.

She was wakened by the feathery touch of someone gently caressing her cheek. Eyes still locked shut she stretched lazily in the hammock, a smile on her lips.

Now that's the way to wake a person up, she thought, content.

When John wanted her "up and at 'em," as he called it, he merely pushed her to the edge of the bed with his foot until, protesting, she left the warmth of his down filled comforter.

Reluctant to end her nap, she opened her eyes to find Rodolfo gazing at her, an unreadable expression on his face.

"Come on," Rodolfo said kindly. "Let's take a walk on the beach. The sun is not so hot right now."

Lifting her head from the comfortable bed she could see the sun had indeed dipped low on the horizon. Quickly she stood up and stripped to the swimsuit she wore beneath her shorts, revealing her curvaceous body to Rodolfo's admiring gaze. She blushed hotly.

"I'm hot and sticky, too" she said to cover her confusion.

"I need a swim."

"That can be arranged *Chiquita,*" Rodolfo said gallantly, indicating the wide expanse of ocean before them.

"Follow me."

## THE JADE PENDANT

Running over the now slightly cooler sand, they ran into the ocean's waves. As they crashed into her body Lydia blindly reached for Rodolfo's hand. He squeezed it encouragingly, sensing her unspoken fear.

"You should not be afraid of the ocean Lydia. It can be your friend. There is no need to fear her as long as you respect her power. The sea almost took my life once," he continued, remembering. "But she gave it back to me. I have always felt that maybe there is a special reason she spared me."

"What happened?" Lydia asked curiously as they stood in the waves holding on tightly with both hands.

"I had a beautiful boat once," he relied sadly, looking directly at her now.

Sensing it was a sensitive point with him and not wanting to pry she kept silent. He continued of his own accord.

"One night I went fishing and a storm came up without warning. I could not tell how far out to sea I was. It was pitch black with no moon to guide me and the waves were over twenty-five feet high. My motor stopped and my boat...how you say? Capsized?"

"My God," Lydia breathed, eyes wide at the imagery that flashed through her mind as she saw him struggling in the waves.

"I thought I was going to die for sure," he reminisced.

"I started to pray to the "Creator" to save me. I asked him to let me live so that I could find the purpose of my life. In the distance I could hear the sound of the waves crashing against the rocks but I could not tell how far away they were or even in which direction. I was getting very tired from swimming when all of a sudden a paddle floated in front of me. I was able to grab it and with it I was able to float to shore on the crest of the waves. So you see the Creator did spare my life."

Lydia was silent for a long while as she contemplated what horror and fear the man before her must have felt. Then her humor got the best of her and she teased him.

"So? And have you found it? The purpose of your life, I mean?"

Rodolfo regarded her with a slow smile.

"*Si Senorita*," he answered her seriously.

"I think my purpose in life is to dump you in the water." He moved menacingly toward her.

Startled, Lydia squealed, and then heart pumping she splashed water in his face and screaming, ran to shore with him in hot pursuit. Catching her easily on the sand he tackled her to the ground successfully pinioning her as she lay panting and laughing into his face.

Breathless, she looked at the face looming above her, his head blocking the sun, eyes warming her with their own special glow. Her heart skipped a beat and then another as his head lowered. Bending ever so slightly he kissed her, the taste salty yet sweet on her lips.

Ahhhhhhhhhhhhhhhh. The sound came somewhere within her and echoed on the wind in a slow agonized drawl.

Feeling her compliance and welcoming it, he moved his body to cover hers. Their bodies shifted to accommodate each other. As his kiss deepened, arousing her, John's face appeared in her minds eye. She stiffened and tried to sit up.

What am I doing?

Seeing her withdrawal Rodolfo backed away immediately although her one small hand stayed clasped in his. As he waited for the beat of his heart to slow and return to normal again he broke the silence.

"Are you sure you have a boyfriend?" he asked half teasing again, half serious.

Glumly she nodded, then seeing the humor of the remark began to smile. Soon, they were both laughing at the absurdity of the situation.

Attempting to further lighten the mood. Lydia sprang up off the beach and challenged him to a race.

"Come on. Last one to that coconut tree over there," she pointed east, "is a rotten egg."

Giving him no time to let her dare fully register she sprinted off. Rodolfo watched her admiringly as she ran gracefully across the white sand for a full minute before slowly getting to his feet, unconcerned. Tarahumara Indians were known throughout the world for their running prowess. He decided to give her a head start. As he began a slow trot he saw her turn her head to look back at him and he grinned wider picking up his pace.

A Perez always gets what he wants, he reminded himself. *And like my father before me I will too.*

Later, on the drive home they exchanged few words, words no longer needed between them. A new understanding seemed to have sprung up between them and a friendship formed. Tired but content with time to think their own thoughts, they rode back to the village satisfied at the way the day ended.

# Chapter Twelve

On her way out to breakfast the next morning, Lydia checked her mail slot for messages. Still no word from John. She debated trying to call him and was already reaching for the phone when she changed her mind.

I'm always making the first move, she thought resentfully, deciding it was John's turn to show some initiative. *Let him do it for once!*

Her decision made, she gathered up her knapsack and headed to the Municipal beach in search of a hearty breakfast.

She liked having breakfast at the Arcadia Restaurant, which was only half a block from the hotel and right on the beach. It was to there that she decided she would go on this beautiful morning. From a table on the patio she could watch the sailboats and fishing boats as they came into the harbor and the birds as they dived for fish. Daniel, the waiter there, was always ready with a welcome smile and a hot cup of coffee. He chatted to her in excellent English about his wife Marvelis and their two young daughters.

Tired from the day at the beach yesterday she had gone straight to her room after Rodolfo dropped her off. She had not emerged until now, not even for a bite to eat. To say she was hungry was putting it mildly.

Strolling down the pathway she thought back fondly to her date, if you could call it that, with Rodolfo. She tried to think when she had last had so much fun doing something as simple as going to the beach and found that she couldn't. Even the 'Big Kiss' that had turned her body to jelly had not spoiled the day although Lydia dared not think about all the things that could have happened had she let them.

If only John were here, she thought again bitterly. *I wouldn't be seeing Rodolfo at all if he was, and we could spend some quality time together away from anyone and everyone we know.*

Unwilling to let depressing thoughts overcome her and spoil her day, Lydia firmly focused her mind on the quest for food. After that, a day of shopping was sure to clear up the cobwebs, she thought with a grin. She checked her bag once more to make sure she hadn't forgotten her wallet.

John placed the receiver on its cradle impatiently. No answer in Lydia's room again. He wanted to tell her when he would be arriving but if she was never there what was he supposed to do? The man who answered the phone could barely speak English so he couldn't even get a message to her. He decided to try later.

The funny thing was that now he had made up his mind about his future, it was all he seemed to think about. He found himself missing Lydia all the time.

Yeah pal, and what if she says no?

Good question, he thought unwilling to let the idea gain momentum.

A customer walked in, rubbing his hands together and complaining about the bitter cold. Wrapped up in conversation, John was able to put his personal life aside. Business was steady from that moment on, keeping both he and his assistant busy for the entire day. When he finally did remember to call Lydia again it was well past midnight and he was already in bed half asleep.

I'll try again first thing in the morning, he promised himself as he rolled over and promptly dozed off.

The Indian market was crowded with people shopping for their daily supplies. They jostled Lydia relentlessly as she moved down narrow aisles. Although locals mostly frequented these stalls, on occasion tourists, like her, could be seen wandering aimlessly in the midst of the confusion as they looked in fascinated confusion at the colorful scene before them.

Fruit and vegetable stalls, busiest at the moment ranked just ahead of the meat market for general hubbub. Stall after stall of whole carcasses of pigs and cows hung, heads intact, baleful eyes staring at nothing at all. Long narrow strips of beef hung by strings to be cured. The strings were attached to wooden poles that swung high above the butcher's heads. In a corner of the market, skinned chickens lay nakedly exposed on counters, waiting to be chopped to order by discerning customers looking to fill today's cook pot.

Small boys, clean, but usually shoeless darted between the stalls—hoping to earn a few pesos by carrying bags of groceries for anyone who needed it. When the smells of the fish market finally threatened to overcome her, Lydia placed a hand over her nose and made a mad dash to where she hoped the dry goods were located.

"Whoa there," an amused voice spoke as she collided with a male chest

*THE JADE PENDANT*

thrust directly in her path. "What's the hurry?"

"I'm sorry," Lydia laughed removing her hand. "I'm just trying to get away from all these smells."

She looked up into a pair of dancing blue eyes and laughed again.

"I know you."

"You do?" the man looked surprised, his brow furrowed as he tried to place her.

"Yes I do. You were my first kiss of the New Year," she informed him before continuing on her way.

He fell into step beside her, still looking puzzled. As Lydia watched gleefully from the corner of her eye, realization hit him and he turned a deep shade of red. Embarrassed, he tried to apologize.

"Look," he began. "If I was out of line that night I am sorry. I may have had too much to drink."

Lydia stopped walking to laugh at him again.

"You want to apologize for giving me the first kiss of the year?" she teased.

"No. I mean yes," he stopped and laughed with her.

"Mind if I tag along?"

Lydia scrutinized him for a minute. In the daytime he was even more appealing than she originally thought. Strong jaw and even white teeth, which shone in a nicely tanned face. It was the merry twinkle in his eyes that decided her.

"Sure, why not?" she shrugged.

He looks like a cop, she thought, choosing to trust her instincts.

"Thanks. Name's Jim," he introduced himself. "Jim Meyer of Que Pasa Tours."

"My name's Lydia Jordan. You live in Mexico?" she asked.

"No, I'm a fireman from Canada actually."

Close, Lydia thought, pleased with her earlier deduction.

"The tour business is a sideline of mine. Why don't we grab a beer someplace and I'll tell you all about it?"

A short time later while seated on tall bar-stools in a quiet bar sipping cold Coronas, Jim explained his business to her.

"I specialize in introducing Canadians to the wonders of Mexico. It gives me a little income and a great excuse to travel. Right now I have fifteen people from Alberta here and they're having the time of their lives. They're on their own when they get here, of course, but this time I decided to come along, too."

"And people pay you for this?" she asked in admiration.

He shrugged.

"Why not? I've been coming to Mexico for over twenty years. I can save people a lot of trouble by filling them in on the do's and don'ts of traveling in a foreign country. Not only that, I give them an outline of the best places to go, restaurants to eat at and things to do once they get here. The way I see it's a win-win situation for everyone."

His enthusiasm for what he did was contagious. Lydia had to agree with him.

I bet I could find something like that to do here, she thought. *All these years of marketing experience and contacts I have gathered would be useful.*

Jim's deep baritone interrupted her train of thought. She mentally filed the idea away to be considered at a later date.

"What about you, Lydia? What brings you to Mexico and how long are you here for?"

Briefly she gave him the capsule version of her recent discovery of Zihuatanejo, adding wistfully, "My boyfriend John will be joining me in a few days although I'm not sure what day exactly."

Jim regarded her thoughtfully. He noted the bleak look that had come into her eyes at the mention of her boyfriend.

If I had a woman who looked like that, he thought virtuously, *I sure wouldn't be letting her go off on a vacation to Mexico without me.*

Years of experience and conversations he had had with some of his female clients had taught him that a woman in Mexico was considered fair game by just about every Mexican man that breathed air.

Canadian men too, for that matter, he thought ruefully.

If she was pretty and blonde, as Lydia was, then it was even worse. *This guy John must be some kind of idiot,* Jim thought.

He decided that as far as he was concerned, all was fair in love and war. In his opinion Lydia was fair game, and he meant to make a play for her.

"What are you doing tonight?" He asked casually.

"Ana and I thought we might go dancing tonight."

"She's a wonderful woman from New York who has been coming here for the past fifteen years or so. Some others may join us too. You're welcome to tag-along if you like," Lydia offered; suddenly shy.

Jim considered the invitation for a minute. Not exactly the offer he had been looking for, but what the heck?

Accepting the suggestion as a good idea he asked what time and where and when would they be meeting?

*THE JADE PENDANT*

"Around ten? We're meeting at Coconuts Restaurant for drinks first. " She stood as if to leave.

"Thanks for the beer Jim. It was nice running into you. I hope I see you tonight."

Jim rose to stand and leaning over, he gently brushed his lips against her cheek, sending a tingle down her spine.

"I will definitely see you later, Lydia," he promised softly before dropping her hand. With a final wave, he strolled down the street.

Lydia stared after him, a bemused look on her face.

First Rodolfo and now Jim. All I can say is, John had better get here pretty darn fast or he'll find me married and living in a grass hut in the jungles of Mexico.

Smiling at the impossible picture the idea painted, she swung her shoulder bag to a comfortable position and traipsed off in the opposite direction to her hotel for a much-deserved siesta.

John picked up the phone at his office on the second ring, hoping it might be a call from Lydia. It wasn't.

"John this is Dee. Lydia's partner?" the voice said in a rush of words.

"Have you talked to Lydia lately? I can't get a hold of her."

As Lydia's best friend and business partner John knew Dee very well, but he was surprised to hear her voice and had no idea why she would be calling him.

"Neither can I," John told her ruefully. "I have tried calling her several times but she's never in and I don't think the desk clerk knows enough English to get my messages through to her. What's up?"

Silence.

"We have a problem John. Lydia and I, I mean. I need to reach her right away." An idea struck her. "Aren't you supposed to be joining her in Zihuatanejo?"

"Yes I am. What's happened Dee?" he asked, becoming alarmed now. "Can I help?"

John heard a sigh on the other end of the receiver and knew it must be serious for this cool, calm woman to sound so distraught.

"I guess I might as well tell you and then you can break the news to her when you get there. It would probably be better for her to hear it from you in person than for me to tell her over the phone, anyway. Soften the blow so to speak."

"Tell me," John told her with quiet authority.

"I'll do all that I can to help."

For the next twenty minutes or so John listened intently to Dee, sometimes jotting things down on the pad in front of him, sometimes firing off questions he knew Lydia would want answers to. This was definitely something she would need to hear in person. There would be no sense in calling and spoiling her holiday now. Especially since there wasn't a damn thing she could do to fix it anyway, whether she was here or not. He thought about his plans for them as a couple and he began to smile at the irony.

This may ruin Lydia but she was going to need him now, more than ever.

With a satisfied smile, John turned back to the stack of paperwork that he had been doing before Dee's call. He was confident now that there was a way he could be able to turn this mess into something good and advantageous. Especially for him.

## Chapter Thirteen

When Lydia arrived at Coconuts just before 10:0'clock, she could see the place was already filled to capacity with animated people either finishing dinner in the outdoor restaurant or lined three deep at the popular bar. Pausing in the doorway, she scoped the room, looking for a familiar face.

Face it, kiddo. You know who you're really hoping to find.

The sight of Rodolfo's smile as she spotted him on his way to a customer's table rewarded her casual search. Not wanting to interrupt him at his job, she decided to head over to the bar. Waving a fistful of dollars as he passed, he indicated the crowd with a shrug of his shoulders.

"Later?" He mouthed. She nodded her understanding.

A tap on her shoulder and she whirled to find a smiling Ana behind her.

"Well," she demanded. "How was the date?"Lydia protested with a laugh.

"It wasn't a date, per se, Ana. It was a…a….a…I'm not sure what it was, really. It was so much fun. Remember though, John is arriving any day and it would be pointless to…" her voice trailed off as Ana rolled her eyes, laughing at her discomfiture.

Tucking an arm into Lydia's she led her to their usual table next to the bar so that they could talk.

"Girlfriend, if that wasn't a date then I just don't know the meaning of the word. Tell me," she demanded again.

"Nothing to tell, really, "Lydia hedged. "But I had a wonderful time. He took me to Barra de Potosi. Do you know it?"

Ana smiled reminiscently, thinking back to her own heydays with local Mexican lovers.

"Nothing happened, Ana. We just had a great day fishing, eating, swimming, sleeping…"

Kissing, she thought privately knowing that wild horses wouldn't drag that tidbit from her lips.

Aloud, in an attempt to steer Ana's attention away from her and Rodolfo she remarked brightly, "You'll never guess who I ran into today at the market?"

Ana raised one eyebrow in a question.

"Remember that guy we met at Rocca Rocks on New Year's Eve? You know, the one who gave me my first kiss of the year?"

Ana laughed, remembering well the handsome young man with the impish grin.

"His name's Jim and he is from Canada. I hope you don't mind, but I invited him to join us tonight."

"Mind? Not at all. I'd never say no to another man to go dancing with," Ana grinned.

"He was kind of cute in a bold sassy way," she remarked. Ana appraised her friend.

"For a girl who has a boyfriend, you sure do get around," she teased her.

Lydia blushed. "I know, I know. It's all in fun, but I think I better cool it a little. After all, John…"

"Will be here any day now," Ana finished for her as they laughed.

They were still laughing when more of Ana's friends arrived at the table and Ana greeted them warmly.

"Hello you two. Lydia, you remember Carla and Michael? Sit down and join us."

As Carla and Michael pulled up chairs, Carla asked curiously.

"Care to let us into the joke?"

Ana and Lydia just laughed. The need to answer was interrupted by the other arrival of a waif-like woman who Lydia had noticed at the hotel.

"Darling," Ana enthused. "So glad you were able to make it."

Introducing the new arrival as Kelly White, she mentioned casually to the group that she was staying at the Citlali, too.

"I think I saw you there yesterday," Lydia enthused.

"Actually," the pretty American woman replied, "I noticed you on the way down here. We were on the same plane coming down from LA. What a coincidence we ended up staying in the same hotel. Not too many tourists know about the Citlali. Like Ana, I have been coming here for many years for a few weeks at a time. How did you find out about it?"

Lydia explained her discovery of both Zihuatanejo and the hotel to the interested group. It was then she discovered that Carla and Michael were from a town, which was only two hours by car from where she lived in Canada—

another coincidence.

Do you ever get down to Kelowna?" Carla inquired politely.

"Not as much as I'd like to anymore," she answered, "but when I did I would always stay at a charming little hotel there on the lake. Maybe you know it? It's The El Dorado?"

"My favorite hotel," Michael enthused, and for the next few minutes they chatted of familiar places and people they knew, finding many things in common.

Lydia found herself liking them very much and hoping that she would be able to get to know them better while she was here. It seemed likely, given the fact that they considered Coconuts as their favorite hangout, and Lydia was sure she that she would run into them many times over the course of her vacation.

She turned her attention to Kelly and asked her how she came to know Zihuatanejo.

"I work for a major tour company in the United States," she explained, "Sometimes we do tours through Mexico, particularly throughout the Copper Canyon in Chihuahua."

For a minute Lydia was startled, now having heard about that place twice in as many days. She said nothing as Kelly continued.

"Most of us come here for a rest between tours. They can be quite exhausting but very lucrative, too. The best part of my job is that I work May to December and get the winters off. It's great."

"Sounds wonderful," Lydia agreed. "I need to find a job like that."

"Lydia is trying to come up with ways to stay here at least six months of the year," Ana piped up.

"But really Lydia you told me that your business is only six months of the year. You could come here for the winter months after that, couldn't you?"

Kelly regarded her thoughtfully.

"I'll keep a look out with my company if you like." She offered generously.

"Thanks," Lydia answered, then explained the company she and her partner owned back home.

"As Ana said, there may be a way I could do this," she told them.

"It will depend on a couple things back home. One of them being my boyfriend."

Kelly looked intrigued, but since Lydia didn't look inclined to elaborate and she didn't want to pry, she changed the subject.

"So what's on the agenda tonight?"

"Well, we want to go dancing I think," Lydia replied. "I invited a fellow Canadian Jim Meyer to join us. Maybe we can persuade Rodolfo, too," she said innocently, as Ana hid a smile behind her fan.

Carla and Michael interrupted whatever Ana was about to say, standing up at the same time as if pre-arranged.

"Sorry to run out on you guys so early," Carla explained with a smile, "but we're going fishing first thing in the morning and I need to get my beauty sleep. It was nice to meet you Lydia. Ana, Kelly, I'm sure we will see you around. It is after all a small town."

Michael laughed as he shook hands all around.

"Have a good time tonight and be careful. There are a lot of wolves around."

As he and Carla linked hands and strolled away, Ana smiled fondly.

"Those two," she sighed. "I'm surprised they stayed as long as they did."

"What do you mean?" Lydia asked as Kelly nodded her agreement.

At the puzzled look on Lydia's face Ana explained.

"It's just that they stay pretty much to themselves. I don't think they socialize with anyone really. Although this year they do seem to be more outgoing."

"Maybe they only need each other," Lydia said thoughtfully. She was quiet as she watched the couple say good bye to a few more people before they left by the back door and were swallowed up by the night.

Just then a shadow fell across the table and the three looked up simultaneously to meet the flashing blue eyes of Jim Meyer.

"Hope I'm not interrupting anything?" he smiled, "mind if someone of the male persuasion sits down or is this an all-girl's night only?"

Before Lydia could reply, Kelly jumped up and scooted along the padded booth to make room.

"You must be Jim," she welcomed him, patting the seat beside her as Lydia and Ana looked on, amused.

"Sit here. Now you have three women to dance with tonight. Lucky you," she tapped his arm playfully.

Jim looked across the table at Lydia and smiled.

"Yes, lucky me," he echoed seriously.

Rodolfo appeared at the table and startled, Lydia looked up to find his eyes quizzically on her. Sizing up the situation in true New York fashion, Ana introduced the two men to each other, adding succinctly, "And of course you already know Kelly and Lydia."

Rodolfo smiled at the group, but his focus came back to rest on Lydia. Electricity crackled in the space between them.

The tension between the two did not go unnoticed by Jim and instinctively he knew it for what it was. Sighing good-naturedly, he realized when he was beaten. A phantom boyfriend was one thing, but this was something entirely different. With a good-natured grin he turned his attention to the attractive woman pressed in the small space beside him and quietly engaged her in small talk. Kelly responded happily, oblivious to everything going on while Ana watched it unfold with the interest of a true storyteller.

"Will you come dancing with us tonight?" Lydia invited Rodolfo warmly.

"*Si*," he replied readily. "I think you owe me a dance." He smiled easily causing her to color furiously.

What is it about this man that makes me blush like a kid, she wondered. *My friends would fall on the floor laughing if they saw me like this.*

Rodolfo turned to Ana and gallantly included her in his invitation, adding that he would be able to meet them after his shift ended. The arrangements were made to everyone's satisfaction before he left them alone. As he moved away he aimed a special smile in Lydia's direction.

Jim observed her closely and noted the receding color.

"I see you've made a conquest," he teased her.

"We're just friends," Lydia protested as Ana rolled her eyes heavenward in the background causing Kelly and Jim to burst into laughter and Lydia to grin despite her embarrassment.

Deciding for the moment to let the matter slide, Jim turned back to the conversation he was having with Kelly while Ana and Lydia ordered more margaritas from the waiter for all of them.

After another cocktail, by which time the four had become well acquainted, they decided to leave for the club. Rocca Rock was located only one block from the village church, a fact made even more interesting because of the transvestite show the club presented on occasion. Ana had caught many shows here over the years but decided to keep this news to herself for the time being. It always amused her to see the expressions on the faces of unsuspecting people as they witnessed the tasteful but somewhat bizarre performances.

Tonight, as usual, the bar was hot and overcrowded. A young door-attendant dressed in black from head to toe led them to ringside seats in front of the stage and dance floor. The low cave-like interior created the claustrophobic feeling Lydia remembered from the previous visit. She inhaled deeply in an effort to calm herself as she looked around.

A few adventurous couples were already dancing to the wild beat of the music – a combination of Latin and disco mamba rolled into one. It was exhilarating. When Jim grabbed Lydia's wrist and pulled her to the dance floor she eagerly followed.

Lydia allowed the music to take over, the sound reverberating in the very core of her being as she moved to the rhythm. Watching her sensuous movements, Jim could almost see her as a Latin woman dancing on the streets in years gone by. Shaking the image, he reached for her and pulled her close to his chest as they moved together fluidly, never missing a beat.

"What's with you and the Mexican guy?" He shouted into her ear in an effort to be heard over the din.

"I told you…we're just friends. Like you and me." She smiled saucily as she danced out of his reach. Laughing he chased her, knowing instinctively not to pursue the subject and they finished the dance holding hands. As he led her off the floor he kissed her cheek before settling her back on her low stool next to Ana. Then, he reached for Kelly, who followed him to the dance floor, winking at her friends over her shoulder as she left. The two women laughed.

"What was that all about?" Ana asked, indicating the pair on the dance floor.

"Nothing," Lydia grinned. She was relieved as she watched Jim and Kelly together.

"It seems to have worked itself out, don't you think?"

Ana smiled in agreement just as a handsome young *Muchacho* tapped her on the shoulder and asked her to dance. As she whirled away she fluttered her fan in Lydia's direction, causing Lydia to laugh out loud with pleasure.

Lydia remained at the table alone, content to watch her friends dancing from her front row seat. A form fitted into the seat next to her. Turning she was astonished to see who it was.

"You finished early?" she asked him delighted, a ready smile on her face.

"*Si*." Rodolfo answered as he ordered a beer from the hovering waiter.

"I tell them I have a pretty senorita waiting for me and they let me go early."

Lydia smiled wider, warmly pleased by his presence.

This is getting ridiculous, she told her inner voice even while acknowledging that there was nothing she could do about it at the moment.

She decided to relax and enjoy the moment and when he asked her to dance it didn't even cross her mind to refuse.

As they stepped out on the floor to the welcoming smiles of their companions, the tempo of the music changed to a slow waltz. Their bodies melded together tightly, it was as if they'd danced together for many years. Lydia cradled her head on Rodolfo's shoulder as she felt his hand slowly caressing her lower back sending currents of electricity up and down her spine. Tipping her head back slightly her eyes met his.

He bent his head and pressed her lips gently and briefly as he tightened his hold on her. Closing her eyes, peacefulness washed over her as they swayed to the sensuous music.

Twirling gracefully in the arms of her dance partner, Ana watched the pair as they moved oblivious to anything around them. She wistfully remembered another handsome Mexican man many years ago.

Without warning the music changed tempo and was replaced with a throbbing disco sound, which thudded throughout the club. Startled, Lydia and Rodolfo sprang apart self-consciously, laughing at the abrupt mood-swing of the DJ. Over the loud speaker a radio-wannabe voice boomed out an announcement in Spanish as searchlights swept the stage. Couples began to leave the dance floor, Rodolfo and Lydia included.

"What's happening?" Lydia asked excitedly.

"The show's about to start."

Rodolfo pressed his mouth close to her ear squeezing her hand before turning his attention to the floor.

Lydia could feel the tension mounting as everyone waited to see what would happen next. The music changed again and the crowd broke into wild applause. A huge spotlight shone on the floor-to-ceiling curtain, which parted dramatically to reveal a jeweled, sequined figure. The crowd went into frenzy as the entertainer strutted up the few stairs to take her place at center-stage.

Microphone in one elegantly gloved hand, she cradled the audience in the palm of the other. Charisma oozed out of every pore of the impeccably groomed woman as she launched into the words of a popular Spanish pop song. Swinging her hips seductively she sashayed her way across the stage as if born to it. Entranced, all eyes in the room stayed fastened to the performer.

A tingling at the back of her neck alerted Lydia to the fact that something was not quite right. Comprehension dawned and she tapped Ana on the arm and asked the question that had been troubling her.

"Is she lip-syncing?".

Trying hard not to laugh Ana nodded as Lydia continued triumphantly. "I knew it!"

This time the group she was with did laugh uncontrollably, as they tried to explain what was so funny to the bewildered Lydia.

Finally, wiping the tears from her eyes Ana, unable to contain her glee enlightened her.

"Not only that, Lydia, but she is a HE."

For a minute Lydia stared at her uncomprehendingly, then back to center stage as realization struck her and her jaw dropped open.

"No.?" she said, astonished, as her friends collapsed uproariously at the look on her face.

Many hours later outside the club in the cool fresh air, Lydia took their good-natured teasing in stride.

"You could have warned me Ana. You know we Canadian girls aren't as sophisticated as you New Yorkers." She laughed again at her folly.

"I really thought she, I mean he, was a real woman."

Rodolfo bent to whisper in her ear, one arm snaking around her waist.

"I think it is safe to say that you are a real woman," he told her.

Lydia playfully slapped him away and pretended to look shocked as Ana looked on, laughing at the two of them.

"You are too bold tonight, *See-nore!*" Lydia said in an outrageously bad Spanish accent.

Grinning, he took her hand decorously. "Better?"

We even fit together walking, Lydia thought, appreciating the way Rodolfo adjusted his steps to accommodate hers. No mean feat, given the difference in their size.

She and John did not fit. She remembered thinking back to the walks they had taken together in Cottonwood Park last summer. Complaining that his strides were too long for her, she found herself jogging next to him just to keep up.

I wonder how else we'd fit, she thought lecherously risking a sidelong glance at the man beside her.

It was with some relief that they reached the hotel and Lydia was able to get a hold on her emotions again. A few feet away she could hear Jim asking Kelly if he could take her out for lunch tomorrow. She was pleased when she heard her new friend accept his invitation.

Ana broke the tender moment.

"Ta ta, my darlings!" She wiggled her fingers in their direction, bound for the lobby with Kelly close on her heels.

"Goodnight Jim, goodnight you two," she sang out, giggling over some offhand remark Ana whispered to her as they made their way to their respective rooms.

After they'd gone, Jim turned to the pair standing before him on the sidewalk, hands linked loosely together. He decided that three was a crowd. With a swift hug to Lydia and a handshake for Rodolfo he bid them both a *buenos noches* and headed towards his hotel, whistling in the darkness of the deserted streets as he went.

Alone together for the first time that night Rodolfo and Lydia stood regarding each other as the moon spilled across their faces, casting all that it touched in a magical silver glow. For once the dogs had ceased their incessant barking and even the ever-present roosters had stopped crowing and gone to bed.

Which is where I should be, Lydia thought but was as reluctant as it appeared Rodolfo was to say goodnight.

It was Rodolfo who finally made the first moves to go. With a gentle gesture he brushed the silky hair from her face, an unreadable expression on his own. Without a word or a backward glance, he turned and left her standing bewildered at his retreating back. For a moment she was tempted to cry out and call him back to her.

For what? Ask him to come to your room?

No, it was better this way. Better to leave things as they were. After all…she left the thought unfinished and hurried alone to her own bed.

## Chapter Fourteen

Lydia woke the first thing next morning feeling tired. These late nights were catching up to her. As much as she enjoyed kicking up her heels from time to time, she wasn't used to going out so many nights in a row.

Tonight might be a good night to turn in early, she thought as she groped her way to the shower, hoping the cool water would wake her up.

The next thing she had to decide was how to spend the rest of the day. A quick glance at the clock on her night table told her it was already eleven in the morning. She showered and dressed, slipping on a flowered sundress over her swimsuit. She wasn't sure if her plans would indicate a swim somewhere or not.

She joined Ana on the rooftop table and they discussed her options.

"You could do a lot of things today, Lydia." Ana wore a huge pair of sunglasses that effectively hid the ravages of her late evening.

"There's snorkeling. Or you could play tennis over in Ixtapa. You could go horseback riding again if you like. Although all that," she amended with a grimace, "sounds like way too much activity for me."

Lydia silently agreed as she sat buttering a piece of toast and sipping the rich strong coffee from the china cup.

"I know, Lydia," Ana brightened considerably as she regarded her friend.

"I bet you haven't been to the museum have you? It's right next to the Arcadia Restaurant you like so much."

"I wondered what that building was," Lydia admitted. "I have been meaning to check it out but there just seems to be so many things to do around here I never found the time before. That's a good suggestion. I think I'll go right after breakfast. Later I might vegetate on La Ropa for the day, have a late lunch and have an early night."

"I think you will find it very interesting and it won't take up more than an hour or so. Are you at all interested in local history?"

"I certainly am," Lydia told her. "Especially after you whetted my appetite with that wonderful story. I don't even think Felipe had heard that particular version before."

"He was interested wasn't he?" Ana smiled in smug satisfaction.

"He was," Lydia agreed. She wiped her mouth with her napkin and stood up.

"Thanks again for the suggestion, Ana. I may not see you later. Perhaps we can catch up tomorrow. I'll be raring to go then."

She hugged her friend good bye and set off in the direction of the museum.

Finding the building she was looking for was easy. She paid the few pesos entrance fee to a bored looking young girl, pushed on the turnstile, and entered the cool stone building. The museum was made up of a series of rooms, placed side by side in a perfect square. Each room represented a particular era or regional story. One room explained in some detail the history of the Mayans and Incas. It was this room that drew Lydia's attention the most. Another portrayed the famous Tarahumara tribe, highlighting their legendary prowess at racing and extraordinary stamina. She smiled as she thought of her attempt to out run Rodolfo on the beach the other day. He must be still laughing to himself about it.

Impressed by the overall layout and design of the displays and the exquisiteness of the hand painted murals, Lydia passed leisurely from one room to another. After an hour she gave up trying to decipher the meanings of the Spanish, which described the contents of each room. She concentrated instead on the delicate beauty of the figurines and clay pottery, protected against decay and inquiring hands behind glass houses.

A lone security guard glanced her way every now and then as if to check her progress. Other than him and the young woman at the entrance, she was completely alone with the past.

After a couple hours the shrill cry of a seagull through the open portals of the building reminded her that another beautiful world filled with sunshine awaited her. Adding another five pesos to the donation box on her way out, she slipped from the cool building into the bright sunlight. Satisfied that she had done one remotely cultural thing this holiday she ambled leisurely toward the pier to admire the numerous sailboats anchored there.

She bought a sandwich and some water and packed it in her bag before continuing to the end of the dock where the water-taxis bobbed gently in the waves.

Approaching the taxi closest to her, she leaned over to catch the attention of the young captain aboard.

"*Hablas Ingles?*" she asked. She flashed him a brilliant smile when he said that he did.

"Can you take me to a quiet beach somewhere?"

"*Si,*" came the quick reply. "Which one?"

Lydia thought for a moment, uncertain.

"I don't know. You pick?" she said carelessly, and he grinned up at her from below.

The next few minutes were spent in negotiating what was to both of them a reasonable price. The young captain helped Lydia into the boat and they set off. He told her about a deserted beach past Las Gatas known as Manzanillo and Lydia thought that sounded like a perfect place to spend the day. She could swim a little, relax a little and think about her future with no one around to distract her. As they skimmed through the water tiny droplets sprayed Lydia's face. She sat in the prow—a refreshing place in the hot afternoon sun.

"You will come back for me?" she asked her guide anxiously, as he helped her onto shore.

"*Si Senorita.* I will be back at four o'clock," he confirmed before shoving his boat farther away from the shallow end. Reversing the engine, he zoomed out of the tiny sheltered bay.

Lydia watched him until he became a speck in the distance. She was relieved to have solitude and quiet for the first time since she had arrived. She had grown to love Zihuatanejo in the short time she had been here but she had to admit it was one of the noisiest places she had ever visited. Turning inland she decided to explore her surroundings.

Before her gaze stretched an expanse of virginal sand; this carpeted the small beach. Spreading the towel she carried tucked under her arm, Lydia prepared to stretch out when a small movement to the right caught her eye.

Lydia jerked back and waited, afraid that it might be a scorpion, not knowing what she would do if one attacked her. She waited.

There it was again. Then another and another until with a shriek of terror Lydia sprang up from her kneeling position and ran into the shallows of the water. Turning carefully so she wouldn't slip on the rocks, she regarded the beach once more. All movements had ceased. Inquisitive now, she edged cautiously forward.

Something ran over her foot and she let out a tiny scream before she realized what it was. The discovery caused her to laugh aloud in sheer relief.

Leaning closer to the creature she could see that it was a tiny crab, hunkered beneath its shell and moving at incredible speed across the sand. The moment it sensed her presence it would stop and hunch down into its encasement in an effort to camouflage its true identity.

For the better part of an hour Lydia childishly amused herself by chasing the little creatures over the beach, trying in vain to catch one unaware before it noticed her. No matter how hard she tried, she couldn't get one.

Hot and thirsty she cased around her for her knapsack. It was gone. After several minutes of frantic searching, comprehension set in. It wasn't there!

Dismayed, she guessed she had probably left it on the boat and berated herself for her carelessness. A quick glance at her watch told her it would be several hours before her guide returned for her. She knew she wouldn't starve in that time, but the lack of water given her current state of thirst, was concerning.

And what if he doesn't come back? She thought.

Panic swept over her and despite the heat she shivered.

*Get a grip,* she rebuked herself sharply. *This is no time to lose it.*

Her resolve strengthened, she picked up her towel again. She was relieved that she had that much at least and strode over to the only shade tree, which was a few feet away from her. Looking out over the ocean, she scanned the horizon for signs of another boat. There were none. Determined to survive the day, Lydia tried to ignore her growing thirst as she placed the towel in the shade and sat down. She decided it was as good a place as any to wait for the boat.

Pleased with the deal he had made with the blonde *gringa*, the captain steered his boat through the crashing waves back to Zihuatanejo. He was particularly happy because the extra money would go a long way in wooing Rosita. He thought about where he would take her that night to celebrate. As he shifted in his seat his eyes fell on the canvas knapsack in the stern. It could only belong to one person.

Debating whether he should turn back and give it to her now or wait till later, he quickly spilled the contents on the bottom of the boat. The usual woman things he saw with disdain, lipstick, perfume, sunscreen and hairbrush. Pulling out a soft leather wallet, he flipped it open and counted the bills in awe. Nearly five hundred pesos!

Along with what she had already paid him, another five hundred pesos would enable him to show Rosita a good time, he thought. His mind raced – what should he do now?

It would mean leaving the *gringa* on Manzanillo, he realized, then shrugged unconcerned.

Someone is bound to miss her. And besides these *gringas* are made of money.

As he strolled toward the pier in the late afternoon a couple hours before his shift, started, Rodolfo realized it had been a long time since he had been there – not since the days when he had owned his own fishing boat. It felt good to watch the hustle of the fisherman as they filleted their fish to take home for dinner, the majority of the day's rewards had long gone to market. Proud tourists swigging beers on the dock bragged proudly to anyone who would listen about the fight they had put up in order to reel in their catch – the fight became tougher with every sip they took.

As he walked, several fishermen nodded or waved in his direction. They were surprised to see him down here after such a lengthy absence. Most of them believed he had gone to the states years ago to stay. He passed them with a salute and walked to the edge of the dock and peered in. He was aware of the painful emotions coursing through him. He realized how much he had missed the camaraderie of the people. Although fishing was largely a solitary pursuit, fishermen, a breed all of their own, could be counted out to help whenever the need arose.

Deep in his thoughts, he barely registered the single boat until it pulled up directly beneath him, effectively shaking him from his daydreams. He automatically reached out a hand to grab the rope and assist the lone occupant in securing his launch, wrapping a simple sailor's knot around the rusty rings on the pier. As he did, his eye spied a pink, canvas knapsack lying under the Captain's chair. It looked like familiar.

"*Senor?* Where did you get that knapsack?" he asked nonchalantly, watching the boy closely.

Surprised by the question, he flushed guiltily.

"It's mine," he fired back in rapid Spanish.

Rodolfo didn't believe him for a minute.

"A man like you carries a pink knapsack?" he barked scornfully. He jumped down into the boat and scooped it out of the hiding place.

"You don't mind if I take a look, do you?" he asked, knowing he outweighed the terrified young man by many pounds and towered over him a good many inches.

Without waiting for permission, Rodolfo quickly searched the bag, noting the various feminine articles within and seeing immediately that, even if it wasn't Lydia's, there was no way the knapsack belonged to this boy. He recognized Lydia's wallet—he had seen her pay her bar tab with it at Coconuts. A glance at the ID confirmed that it was hers. Glaring at the Captain who knew he was caught, Rodolfo moved towards him as he tried to wiggle past. Anticipating his attempt to escape Rodolfo reached out with one hand and caught hold of his shirt. The boat rocked dangerously against the dock, threatening to spill them both into the water.

"Where is she?" Rodolfo asked menacingly, fear rushing through him at all the things that might have happened to her.

The Captain maintained his innocence.

"Where is who?"

Rodolfo shook him like a wet rat. A small circle of fishermen looked on, prepared to back him up if necessary. It wasn't.

"I left her at Manzanillo," the coward sputtered. "She left it behind when I dropped her there. I would have given it back to her. Honest."

Rodolfo doubted that but he had no way to prove it. He hauled the boy onto the dock and shoved the unfortunate thief into the crowd of awaiting fisherman. Terrified, he lay there cowering at their feet.

"Sure you would have," he said disdainfully, breathing heavily.

He spoke to the crowd.

"Which one of you will take me to Manzanillo beach?"

A grim faced man stepped forward immediately. A long-standing friend in his early twenties, he was often called "Negro" because of the bronze color of his skin. Rodolfo nodded his thanks. He scooped up the knapsack and followed him quickly to his boat. Behind them they could hear the sounds of the men as they meted out their own brand of punishment to the unfortunate sailor. Scrupulously honest in their dealings with others, they did not take theft lightly—especially from one of their own.

Lydia woke slowly, blinking drowsily in the sun. Disoriented, she sat up and peered around her trying to get her bearings. It took her a few minutes to remember the situation before the familiar feeling of dread overtook her. She checked her watch. Five 0'clock! Lydia's mouth felt even drier. Her stomach protested as hunger threatened to overwhelm her. Shading her eyes, she looked out over the water. Nothing! The certainty that she'd been abandoned here started to sink in.

For the next while she watched as the sun began it's descent into the ocean.

Soon she knew that she would be in complete darkness. Anxious to do something, anything, she stood up and looked around her. Maybe she could make a fire? She quickly discarded the idea as ridiculous having no inkling how to start one without matches..

Rub two boy scouts together, the old joke flit through her mind and she laughed aloud, startling one of the birds in the tree overhead. *I'm losing it.*

The unmistakable drone of an engine wafted across the water. She hurried to the surf straining her eyes to peer over the water. She couldn't see anything.

I must be hearing things. She was disheartened as she turned to go back to her towel on the beach.

Then she heard it again. Whirling back she could now see a black dot appearing on the horizon. Hopes raised, she stared hard at the vision as it seemed to be coming closer, hoping against all odds that someone was coming to rescue her.

Mentally urging the captain to go faster, Rodolfo sat as far forward in the boat as he could. Waves threatened to swamp them as they plowed into the sea. Nervously he looked at the sky. He didn't like the darkening clouds overhead, a sign of rougher waters to come and maybe even a storm later on. In a little while the sun would be down completely making rescue even harder. He prayed she was all right. He hoped the captain had told the truth as to where he'd left her. *No, I think I scared him enough that he told the truth,* he told himself.

Turning to the rear of the boat he urged Negro to go faster. The engine whined in protest as Negro pushed the throttle forward and they picked up more speed. Rodolfo pointed to the beach ahead, but Negro, born and raised here was already headed in the right direction. As the monstrous rocks of the coast loomed closer they caught the welcome sight of a human form frantically waving some sort of flag from shore. Pulling in to the inlet, Rodolfo saw that it was Lydia. He breathed a sigh of relief. Minutes later they were heading to shallow water where Lydia raced ankle deep to greet them.

Leaping out of the boat he rushed to meet her and soon they were in each other's arms, Lydia nearly sobbing with joy at the sight of him.

My hero, she thought wordlessly hugging his hard body as if she would never let him go.

"Are you okay Lydia," Rodolfo asked anxiously as he helped her into the boat and Negro once more cast away.

"I'm fine now that you're here. Just thirsty."

Rodolfo quickly produced the water from her canvas sack and handed it to her. Eagerly she gulped the tepid liquid thinking that nothing had ever tasted so sweet in her life.

"Where did you find my bag? How did you find me?" the questions came eagerly now that her immediate thirst was satisfied. Rodolfo handed her the sandwich. As she wolfed it down he explained what had happened with the captain.

Then it was Rodolfo's turn to find some things out and placing his hands on her shoulders he questioned her sternly.

"How did you happen to go out with him in the first place?"

Now that she was watered and fed Lydia was feeling much like her old self and she answered him with false bravado.

"It was silly, I know. But I had this idea that maybe I could be the female version of Robinson Crusoe…" her voice trailed off as she caught the look in Rodolfo's eye.

"You should be more careful who you go with Lydia," he spoke carefully, not wishing to scare her but at the same time knowing it was necessary to warn her about the dangers she could encounter if she wasn't more cautious.

"You can't be so trusting *Chiquita.* Not everyone you meet is going to be like me and Negro here." He waved at the brown-eyed native who smiled when she grinned in his direction.

"Thank you so much" she said to him as Rodolfo translated for her.

"*De nada!*" his quiet reply answered.

Turning her attention back to Rodolfo, Lydia assumed her most humble expression and apologized to her savior.

"I am so sorry Rodolfo. Thank heaven you were there at the right time or who knows what might have happened?" She kept her eyes lowered, knowing what she said was true. If it weren't for these two she would still be there on the beach in the dark.

Rodolfo hugged her tightly to him to let her know she was forgiven, while at the same time wondering what he was going to do with this impetuous woman. To say that she was getting to him would be putting it mildly and he had a feeling he was going to feel more than a little sad when her boyfriend arrived. Moments like this with her would be lost to him forever. Rodolfo held her closer as Lydia snuggled deeper into his arms and closed her eyes, exhaustion and exposure to the elements finally taking their toll.

Cuddled next to him similar emotions invaded her thoughts. She tried to rid them from her mind. Here she felt cared for and safe. It had been a long time since she had ever felt this way, and she found she liked it.

Part of the reason she was so misunderstood was she gave off such a confident air and that most people found her somewhat intimidating—especially in business. It was her confidence that John professed to like the most about her – that and her independent spirit. The truth was, she was tired of people always assuming she was in charge and in control.

Thinking about John while being in another man's arms made her feel guilty. She started to pull away from Rodolfo's rough embrace, but he only held on tighter until relaxing, she let him hold her close.

*So this is what it feels like to have someone watch out for you?*

A short while later the boat slowed and pulled up to the dock, surprising both of them. Watching as they gathered their belongings together, Negro shook his head at what he saw happening in front of him. He had never seen Rodolfo act like this with anyone before – not since the days of his marriage to Beatrice, certainly never with a white woman. Ducking to avoid hitting the beam, he grinned knowing that Rodolfo was obviously in over his head. He said nothing until Lydia was safely on dry land again. It was then that he latched onto Rodolfo's arm and pulled him back.

In a low voice he inquired, "This woman Rodolfo. She is important, no?"

Rodolfo regarded him thoughtfully, a small smile playing on his lips before answering.

"*Si*, my friend she is important," he allowed, "but her Canadian boyfriend is coming in a few days so our time will be over soon. For now, I just take the days as they come."

With that he jumped out of the boat and walked the few steps to where Lydia was purchasing gum from two little native girls in calico dresses. He watched her as she laughed and joked, feeling his facial features soften in the dying light of the day.

Her transaction finished, Lydia turned in his direction, a big smile lighting her features as she regarded her "knight in shining armor". She waved her thanks over her shoulder to Negro, who stood watching the pair with something akin to envy. Rodolfo turned also, grinning at his friend over the top of her head. In a characteristic manner he raised his shoulders in a way that told Negro he couldn't help himself even if he had wanted to. Soon the pair was out of sight, swallowed up by the evening crowd as they headed out to one of the numerous restaurants along the promenade for dinner.

Negro whistled softly. He laughed and shook at his friend as he commenced tying up the boat.

*If I rush home now,* he reasoned, *Maria's tortillas should be just starting to sizzle in the pan.*

Thoughts of his woman and hot food made his mouth water and he hurried to finish what he was doing.

# Chapter Fifteen

At breakfast the next morning Lydia had just finished regaling her friend with her castaway-on-the-island drama of the day before. The reaction she received was typical of the flamboyant woman and Lydia sat grinning at her as she cooed in delight.

"You're not serious?" Ana regarded her friend in astonishment. "That is so romantic, Lydia. Rodolfo actually rescued you? What a great story this will make to add to my collection of Zihuatanejo stories."

Lydia laughed.

"I have to agree with you there Ana. The man is my hero, there's no doubt about that. Rescuing a damsel in distress, in this case ME, is too funny and unreal. Nothing like this has ever happened to me before."

"Thank heavens he happened to walk the dock that day. You say he hardly ever goes down there?"

"No he doesn't," Lydia replied. "Rodolfo told me that it was a fluke that he happened to be there at all. He had some time to kill before his shift and so he decided to take a stroll. I hope he didn't get into any trouble with his bosses for being late."

"I'm sure that they will understand when he explains everything," Ana remarked. "Now, tell me, what are you going to do about John when he gets here?"

"Do?"

"Yes, do. You can't go on pretending there is nothing between you and Rodolfo."

Lydia was silent.

"I haven't given it much thought Ana," she replied slowly.

Liar!

"Of course I really like Rodolfo – he's wonderful. But nothing's going to change. John will be here soon and that will be that. What day is it anyway?

*THE JADE PENDANT*

I thought I would have heard from him by now. Maybe I should call him?"

She stood up as if to go but Ana pulled her back down onto her seat.

"Don't you dare!" she admonished firmly. "Let him call you. I don't know John at all, but I must tell you I am not very impressed by his actions, or rather his lack of them so far."

"You're right," Lydia agreed reluctantly. "I should wait for him. To tell you the truth Ana I am a little worried. John is a very dependable person and it is not like him to not get in touch with me. You could set your watch by him. It's one of the things I like about him so much. Please Ana, don't make up your mind about John yet. He is a wonderful man and I want you to like each other."

"As for Rodolfo, I do know what to do. Nothing. Nothing has happened so far, you know, except for a few kisses here and there. Fun, but not serious and certainly nothing that has any kind of future like I have with John."

Ana smiled but kept her own counsel as Lydia continued.

"It's funny though, I feel such a connection to him. Rodolfo I mean. It's not something I can explain—it's just there." She laughed.

"I sound like a teenager. Does this make any sense to you?"

Ana nodded.

"Of course it does Lydia. I think that there are reasons people meet each other and sometimes we have a very strong bond with them when we do. Look at us. I feel as if I have known you forever instead of for just a few short days."

"I know what you mean. I certainly feel the same way," Lydia smiled and continued her thoughts aloud.

"I once had a friend who told me that if you wanted to meet the ideal man in your life you should sit down and write out everything you are looking for. All the qualities he should have, what he should look like, everything. She told me to be very specific. So I did. And, guess what?"

"John came into your life," Ana finished for her somewhat doubtfully.

"Exactly!" Lydia exclaimed.

"He is exactly what I asked for."

"Next you'll be telling me he was destined by God for you Lydia," Ana swept her hand disdainfully as Lydia laughed at her foolishness.

"No one can tell you what to think Lydia but I do have one piece of advice for you. You have to follow your head but most of all you have to follow what is in your heart. Listen closely to both. Sometimes what we want is not what we should have. I know what I would do, but I am not you," she held up her hand as Lydia's mouth opened to ask. She refused to say anything more.

"I am not going to tell you what I would do. This is about you. It is something you will have to work out on your own. Just don't take too long," she warned.

Lydia pondered Ana's words as she helped herself to more coffee from the urn. Her mind was whirling at the unexpected turn her life seemed to be taking. She wondered how she was ever going to get things back to normal again.

Watching as she struggled with her dilemma, Ana wisely decided to change the subject. For the next few minutes they discussed the shopping excursion they had planned for that day. Ana suggested a full morning of pampering at Silhouette's Beauty Salon followed by lunch at one of the sidewalk cafés on the boulevard where they could people-watch. It was a plan that Ana responded to with real enthusiasm.

Roberto eyed his brother closely across the dining room table where he sat methodically chewing his food, eyes down on the plate unseeing. He could tell Rodolfo was a million miles away and wondered what the reason for it was. Several times he had tried to engage his brother in conversation only to be met with occasional grunts and blank stares. He tried again.

"Terrible earthquake we had last night, wasn't it?"

Yola looked up startled from across the table, then seeing the mischievous look in her husband's eyes smiled and kept silent.

"What? Oh. *Si*." Rodolfo spoke absently, not bothering to look up.

"They say it's supposed to rain today, too?" Robert winked at his wife as he waited for Rodolfo's reaction.

This time Yola laughed aloud, the sound having the effect of shaking her brother-in-law from his trance. Rodolfo glanced up. Seeing the grin on Roberto's face, he rudely gave him the finger, which made both he and Yola laugh harder.

"Sorry. I was thinking," he smiled ruefully.

"About what?" Yola asked him, speaking for the first time that day. A quiet woman, she nonetheless had a great sense of humor and cared a great deal about her husband's younger brother.

"I was thinking about yesterday," Rodolfo told her as he launched into the events that had happened the day before.

He's in love, Yola concluded, her women's intuition kicking into overdrive as she watched his face while he talked about the blonde *gringa* from Canada.

Roberto was thinking similar thoughts. He wondered if he was going to get a chance to meet this mystery woman from the north. He sighed worriedly knowing that whoever she was she would go back to Canada and leave his brother's broken heart behind.

At noon John picked up the phone and dialed the long distance operator. Giving her the number of the Citlali he leaned back in his plush leather chair to wait.

"*Bueno.*" A woman's pleasant voice sounded musically in his ear.

"Xotchel is that you," John sat forward surprised that he had gotten through so easily this time. Telephone service was not one of Mexico's stronger suits he decided.

"*Si*, this is Xotchel," the voice acknowledged. "And you are…?"

"This is John Mathews from Canada. Do you remember me?"

"*Si, Senor* Mathews," Xotchel replied, delighted to hear from one of her most frequent customers.

"*Como estas usted? Bien?*"

"*Si*, Xotchel," John replied, "I am fine."

"Listen Xotchel, I am coming down there in a few days. I know it is short notice but I wonder if you have a room for me. I have a friend there already. Lydia Johnson? "

"Ah *si*, Lydia! One moment Senor Mathews and I will check for you."

Xotchel carefully put the receiver down to go through her records. The line went quiet and John took the opportunity to light a Cuban cigar, puffing furiously to get it going.

Lydia hates these things. I really should quit. He grimaced as changing his mind abruptly he put it out in the ashtray before him.

He leaned back in his chair again. A customer walked into the reception area and stood before the service counter.

"I'll be there in just a minute," John called out to him, cupping the receiver with one hand while he explained.

"I'm on long distance."

The man nodded, clearly impatient but willing to wait a little while at least. The minutes ticked by slowly. Just when John was beginning to think he'd been cut-off, Xotchel's cheery voice sounded down the line.

"You are in luck, *Senor* Mathews. We have a room for you. It's not your usual one and it is quite small, but it is the only one we have left."

"That will be fine Xotchel," John interrupted her, anxious to get off the line before his customer who showed every intention of leaving walked out the door.

"See you on the fifteenth."

With that he quickly hung up and hurried to the front counter to serve his potential client.

It wasn't until much later that a nagging suspicion that he had forgotten something woke him from a deep sleep. Groaning, he realized that he hadn't left a message with Xotchel for Lydia that he had called. Lydia still didn't know the day of his arrival. John rolled over in bed, hoping that somehow Xotchel would mention it in passing. Promising himself to rectify the situation tomorrow he snuggled down into his covers and promptly fell asleep.

At the appointed hour Ana and Lydia walked into the modern-looking beauty salon and presented themselves to the pretty young receptionist at the tiny front desk. Just then an extremely attractive American woman spotted them and hurried forward.

"Ana," the woman cried happily.

"It's so nice to have you back again. How long are you here for this time?"Ana introduced Lydia to Kimberly, the owner of the salon before replying.

"I will be here until at least April," she told her holding out her hands for Kimberly's inspection.

"I need maintenance," she proclaimed comically, as both Kimberly and Lydia laughed.

"I do too," Lydia piped up holding forth her own hands ruefully.

"Ana tells me you can get these poor nails in shape in no time."

"Don't worry," Kimberly soothed as she led them both to two beautiful hand crafted bamboo chairs.

"I have seen much worse. Why don't I work on you, Ana, and let Roselba work on Lydia?"

"Yes," Ana put in, "but we would also both like pedicures, a massage and facials, too."

"I don't see a problem," Kimberly replied frowning slightly. "Make yourselves comfortable while I check the appointment book."

When she was gone, Ana turned to Lydia. "Kimberly lives here year round," she informed her.

"She married a Mexican man many years ago. They have two beautiful little girls together. I believe she finally received her dual citizenship, too.

At that moment Kimberly rejoined them, catching Ana's remark.

"Yes Ana I do have dual citizenship now," she answered. " Gonzalo and

I have been married for eight years now. It seems like just yesterday sometimes. I can fit you both in, ladies. Should we get started?"

Lydia and Ana settled themselves at separate worktables. Roselba shyly put Lydia's feet in the warm sudsy water and took one of her hands in her own small brown one to begin the manicure.

Lydia sighed in bliss, stress from the adventures of the day before seeming to melt under the expert ministrations of the Mexican woman's touch. She wondered what it would be like to live in a foreign country full time, not sure whether she could do it or not. Ana's way of living here a few months of the year and returning to the United States seemed to be a good one. On the other hand, if you actually married a Mexican, that option would not be available to you, would it? She decided to ask Ana about it later. For now she was determined to enjoy the pampering.

Several hours later, Lydia and Ana emerged from the salon looking and feeling like "new" women. Their freshly scrubbed faces glowed from the expert facials they had received. Kimberly herself had professionally made them up. Radiating good health, their perfectly manicured feet nearly floated on the courtyard outside the shop to a tiny restaurant tucked neatly behind the shopping center. Feeling the admiring eyes of curious onlookers they seated themselves confidently under a brightly colored umbrella at a cozy table for two.

"I can't believe how inexpensive that all was," Lydia exclaimed as they seated themselves.

As a long time patron Ana was afforded the local rate and Kimberly had kindly extended the same courtesy to her.

If only I really was a local woman, Lydia mused as she paid the bill. She made sure to leave a generous tip for the talented Roselba on the way out.

"I know," Ana agreed. "In New York the same services would be triple what they are here. Kimberly's shop is considered expensive for Mexico. In my opinion, though," she declared holding her hands in front of her admiringly, "She's worth every penny."

"She certainly is. I have more than enough money left over for a wonderful lunch and maybe even a new dress," Lydia crowed happily as the waiter hurried to their table to take their drink orders.

Ana smiled fondly at her enthusiasm. It was fun to have this new person in her life—very different from her in some ways, but a kindred spirit nevertheless. It had been a long time since she had met someone who took so much joy in living. She wondered now if John knew what he really had in her.

Somehow she didn't think so. At that moment Lydia broke into her introspection, leaning over the table to grin mischievously.

"Okay girlfriend," she ordered playfully.

"I know you're dying to tell me Kimberly's story, so out with it."

Ana laughed aloud.

Like she said – kindred spirit.

"You of course are not at all dying to hear it?"

Lydia smiled and conceded the point as Ana began her tale.

"Actually it's a very sweet story…"

"…That day Kimberly had decided she had enough of California, Hollywood, star-stuck bimbos, and traffic lights. Working in a successful hair salon on Rodeo Drive meant that she had to contend with all of that and more. Her life was made up of sleeping, eating on the run and work, work, work, with precious little of anything else thrown in. She hadn't been on a date in months, gone to a movie or out dancing in absolutely ages. For some reason, she was feeling more antsy and restless than usual and wondered if this was all there was to life. Kimberly decided she deserved to have more. In order to get more however, drastic measures were necessary.

Against the advice of family and friends, her eyes turned south of the border to Mexico. She sold her little red sports car admitting that she felt a twinge as she saw it driving away. After that came her antique furniture which dealers in the area quickly snapped up. Personal items like stereo, television and a few odds and ends went too. She netted close to $10,000. It was more than enough to start a new life until she could find a job.

Booking a flight to Mexico City she said a tearful goodbye to her family and set out on her own. Her idea was to travel a little and learn the language. Perhaps she would teach English when her finances ran low.

For six months she accomplished all that she had set out to do. She reveled in her new freedom feeling she had left behind her stress in the U.S. She was on the beaches of Zihuatanejo when she saw that she was running low on money. She decided to stay where she was. She set about finding a job and a place to live.

As an English-speaking woman with a working knowledge of Spanish, it didn't take her long to find her first job at the beautiful Villa del Sol on La Ropa beach, cutting hair for wealthy clients. Her job entailed many of the same duties as she was doing in California. This time though, she was in a tropical setting with none of the stress or responsibility that had weighed her down so much.

Every day after her shift ended, she would run the full length of the beach and back. Her senses filed with the lush beauty around her. A quick dip in the hotel pool would leave her exhausted but completely content in her new life.

Her self-imposed exercise program did not go unnoticed by a young Mexican man who watched her every day with interest. You could say he was a typical beach boy. He was also the proud owner of the successful parasailing and watercraft rental business in front of the hotel. Each day as she ran by him he would call out a greeting to her, as did nearly all of the Mexican boys she passed. Sometimes she would ignore him. Other times as she grew accustomed to seeing him, she would flash a brilliant smile in passing. Finally he decided it was time to approach her.

Initially Kimberly was surprised that the handsome Mexican she had noticed spoke such perfect English. He explained that he had picked it up from the tourists on the beach. The fact that they could communicate well made it natural for them to overcome the barriers people sometimes encounter when first meeting someone from another country. Since Kimberly had few friends at this point other than a couple of the snobby co-workers in the hotel, she gladly welcomed the advances of the young man she came to know as Gonzalo. Before long they were dating on a regular basis. Everyone who knew them considered them a "couple". His family had taken a liking to her, and wholly approved of the match. This was unusual in most Mexican families of their stature. They nonetheless saw that Kimberly had a calming influence on their oldest son and were already eager to welcome her into the family as a permanent member."

Lydia who had been listening intently sighed with pleasure.
"And so they got married?" she said thinking the story was over.
"Not quite," Ana spoke solemnly as Lydia's eyebrows shot up in surprise. "Things had to happen first." Ana shot her THAT look before continuing.
Lydia settled down eager to hear the rest of the story.

Kimberly and Gonzalo had been dating for nearly two years when he decided that perhaps things were too serious and he didn't want to settle down after all. His family had been putting a great deal of pressure on him to marry Kimberly and produce children. He rebelled. To the dismay of everyone concerned, he decided to break off the relationship.

Although they parted amicably enough and decided to stay friends, Kimberly was devastated.

Wisely however, she decided to let things be for the time being with the hope that perhaps he would come around. Having too much pride to beg him to stay, she decided the best course of action was to play it cool with him and give him lots of space if that was what he needed.

It was. Gonzalo missed the long conversations he used to have with her before their break up. He would often pop by the shop or her apartment just to make sure she was okay. In the meantime, she started to date a little. Although the sight of her with someone else upset him, they continued their friendship.

With that intact, it wasn't unusual in the least when Gonzalo invited her to his housewarming party at his new apartment. Kimberly decided it was time to put a few doubts in his mind about his decision to break up with her and agreed to attend. Dressing carefully that night she threatened to outshine the very stars with her pale beauty, hoping that perhaps this was the night she would win her errant boyfriend back.

Following the directions on the invitation the taxi driver made his way to the address on the card. As Kimberly paid the driver she gazed at the outside of the building, she was in awe of Gonzalo's new residence.

It was a new sub-division in Ixtapa on a cliff, which overlooked the ocean. It was quiet, discreet and prosperous looking. Gonzalo was obviously doing well for himself. Although she was happy for him, she questioned what that meant for their future together. With some trepidation she stepped inside where her heart sank to the terra cotta tiled floor.

As she crossed the threshold of the beautifully wrought oak door she could see that what she was entering was a bachelor apartment, decked out with comfort and seduction in mind. On her immediate right she noticed the modern kitchen with approval. Fine porcelain tile and stainless steel gleamed in the soft light. Moving forward as if mesmerized, she stepped down into the sunken living room. Brightly colored pillows were thrown over the soft pastel leather couch invitingly. A Spanish style dining room laden with food, awaited guests on her left, the massive ornate dining-room table dominated – its mahogany wood reflected the many candles placed strategically around the room. As she wandered, she smiled warmly at a few people she knew but didn't bother to stop as she continued her inspection. The sound of voices drifted over the night. She moved forward in the direction they were coming from. Passing through the French doors that led to the patio outside, her senses whirled with the sight before her.

Hundreds of Novena lights in purple glass holders arranged around an oval swimming pool greeted her. With that, her last hope for reconciliation was gone. Disheartened, she moved to the edge of the balcony overlooking the ocean far below.

Gonzalo had noticed Kimberly the moment she entered the house. Unseen he drank in the sight of her as she floated around his apartment, her pale beauty, as always took his breath away. Pouring two glasses of icy cold champagne he followed her outside and called her name. Startled, she whirled. Tears glistened on her cheek. She was embarrassed and reached up to dash them away and stepped back as Gonzalo hurried forward, concern written on every line in his face.

Kimberly leaned against the railing. She felt it give way. Before Gonzalo could reach her, she tumbled backward down the steep cliff to the rocks below. She called his name as her screams echoed. She fell seventy-five feet straight down. Then there was silence.

Without thinking, Gonzalo leaped over the broken railing and climbed down the treacherous cliff to where Kimberly lay unmoving, bleeding, and broken on the rocks. He was in shock when he reached her side. Careful not to move her he yelled up to the anxious faces above him to call an ambulance. As they waited for help to arrive, he talked to her, pouring all of his love and friendship into the sound of his voice. He hoped desperately that she would somehow sense he was with her. He cursed himself for his stupidity in ever letting her go.

The medical team arrived. Together they hoisted her inert body carefully up the cliff to a waiting ambulance. At the hospital a team of doctors quickly accessed the seriousness of her injuries. A cursory inspection was all it took before they air-lifted her to a private facility in Mexico City, only a forty-five minute flight away.

"Incredible," Lydia murmured.

"It was incredible," Ana, granted. "Kimberly had broken every bone in her body. She spent the next year in traction, six months of it in Mexico City, before they moved her back to a hospital in Zihuatanejo."

"How terrible," Lydia breathed, trying to imagine the pain that poor woman must have gone through on the road to recovery.

"Yes it was, but if you were to ask Kimberly she would tell you that it was worth every day of the pain."

"You've got to be kidding!" Lydia exclaimed, disbelief plainly visible on her face.

"I'm not." Ana smiled smugly. "Ask her. You see it was during her time in the hospital that Gonzalo proposed marriage. They've been together ever since. It was worth it to her." She snapped open her menu with a practiced flip of her wrist.

"Now, what are you going to have," she asked Lydia innocently.

Lydia's mind raced as she pretended to study the menu. Unaware of Ana's covert looks, she attempted to decipher the choices before her. She couldn't concentrate on anything but the story. She thought how romantic it all was and so typical of the many stories she had heard from her new friend so far. It certainly seemed to be the place where magical things could, and did, occur.

More practical things demanded her attention, however, as the waiter appeared by her side, anxious to take their order. Putting all romantic nonsense from her mind for the time being, she busied herself with ordering lunch in Spanish. Her attempts to speak the language garnered her occasional smiles and much praise from her host.

Later, as promised the pair went on a shopping spree. They bought anything that struck their fancy including a new dress for Lydia. Tired, but completely satisfied, the exhausted women made their way back to the hotel for a siesta before they headed out later that evening.

Lydia twirled happily in front of the full-length mirror in her room. She was pleased with the new dress she had purchased that day. It was a bright brilliant color. The skirts of the halter-styled chiffon dress floated above her knees gracefully.

It's a Marilyn Monroe dress, she thought when she tried it on in the store. Ana urged her to buy it. The saleslady beamed and told her that it was perfect for her.

The slinky sensuous material clung to her curves, hugged her body and accentuated her shape seductively. A zircon stone set in a silver brooch sparkled merrily. It glittered in the deep v-neckline of the dress as she moved from side to side

She wondered briefly if Rodolfo would like it.

What matters is that I like it, she determined firmly, pushing the previous thought out of her mind.

With a final gay twirl of her skirts, she pulled open the door of her room and departed for another night of fun in Zihuatanejo

Rodolfo stood near the bar at Coconuts restaurant, his eyes glued on the doorway in the hopes that Lydia would show up tonight. Sensing a presence behind him he turned swiftly and nearly collided with Arturo. Behind him grinning foolishly was his co-worker and friend Carlos, the famed restaurant's head chef.

"Looking for someone?" Carlos asked.

"No I'm not," Rodolfo lied, attempting to by pass his friends, but Arturo stepped neatly in front of him, effectively blocking his path.

"Maybe she's found another lover," Arturo teased him as Carlos guffawed in the background.

"Someone Mexican? Maybe she's not coming to see you tonight at all?"

For a full minute Rodolfo contemplated shoving his fist in his friends' face. Instead he counted to ten slowly and forced a smile.

"I am not her lover," he informed them steadily.

"She already has a boyfriend who is coming here in a few days or so. In fact, I wouldn't be surprised if he arrived tomorrow." He nearly laughed at the surprise on their faces and hoped they would finally leave him alone.

No such luck. Carlos was not quite ready to drop the matter.

"Then what will you do, *amigo*?" he asked, all sign of teasing replaced by concern for his old friend.

"We all see how you look at her, *amigo*."

"And how she looks at you, "Arturo muttered under his breath. He saw the manageress of the restaurant and hurried over to talk to her before the place started to get too busy.

Rodolfo watched his friend depart before turning back to the man who remained rooted to the floor before him.

"We're just friends Carlos," he insisted strenuously. "Nothing more than friends."

Carlos wasn't buying it.

"Bah," he spat the word contemptuously.

"Women are friends, men are friends. But women and men as friends? Never!"

Rodolfo had to chuckle at the venom in Carlos voice. He clapped him on the back and moved away from his watch at the door. He knew that Carlos was probably right.

Maybe its time to end this 'friendship' now, he decided, unable to finish the thought.

Looking up suddenly, he saw her, and all common sense flew from his mind.

Lady in red! Watching as her eyes locked with his he felt his resolve melt and knew at that moment he was lost.

Pulling into the snow-laden driveway was easy for the 4X4 truck. Still, John sighed with relief that he'd made it home safe and sound through the blinding snowstorm. Having lived here for over twenty-five years, he'd almost become immune to the unbelievable cold but on a night like this he was glad that he would soon be in a warmer climate.

He wished he had not committed to stopping off for one night in Texas where the weather was sure to be nearly as bitterly cold as it was here. He would have preferred instead to fly directly to his sunny destination and Lydia's waiting arms. He still hadn't reached her. Sighing, he wondered what she was going to say about that when he arrived. Then he shrugged. Lydia was easygoing. It was unlikely she would give him too hard a time about his lapse in manners, especially when she saw what he had bought for her earlier today. He fingered the small box safely tucked in his pocket and reminded himself that he must pack it in his carry-on bag tonight with all the other essentials he was taking.

As he looked out the window, he saw with concern that the snow wasn't letting up. He wondered if his flight would be delayed. The radio on the drive home said they were calling for even more snow. The temperature would drop to minus fifty with the wind chill factor. It was sure to clear up by late morning sometime. He hoped so.

As he pulled the TV dinner out of the freezer and preheated the oven his thoughts turned back to Lydia. When she had received the job offer to work in Vancouver he had thought that the separation would probably be the end of their relationship. It hadn't worked out that way. Their friendship somehow managed to survive. He made frequent business trips there and tried always to see Lydia when he was in town – if only for dinner before he returned to Prince George.

He had really surprised himself by telling her about Zihuatanejo—something he had never done before, with anyone. Not even his closest friend, Bill, knew exactly where he liked to vacation. He had guarded the destination of where he went in Mexico religiously, preferring the anonymity of not knowing a soul when he wanted to get away to relax. It clarified for him just how deep his feelings were for Lydia.

Another thing that occurred to John was how from the beginning he had felt comfortable with Lydia. She was easy to talk to and have around.

Like a comfortable pair of shoes, he grinned, knowing that Lydia probably wouldn't appreciate the unflattering sentiment, even if she had been the romantic type. Which, he was sure, she wasn't.

Alone here in his home on this stormy night he could see the relationship clearly. He realized it was a good friendship—in so many ways perfect for him. If it wasn't the earth shattering love affair of the century what did it matter? He thought of her as a good friend. Sometimes he felt that was better than romance any day. He thought again of the fiasco with Theresa. It had started out with so much promise but had quickly turned to ashes, leaving a bitter taste behind.

The timer on the oven sounded, reminding him that it was time to put in the frozen dinner. He peeled the foil back over the meat portion as the instructions told him to do and hoped that this would be his last TV dinner for a long, long while.

Across the crowded room two hearts quickened and skipped a beat as eyes held, unable to look away. From the corner of the bar a lone woman watched quietly, a small-satisfied smile on her face. Raising her glass slightly, Ana silently toasted the gods. She knew that she had just witnessed the exact moment when two people fall in love.

# Chapter Sixteen

It was late morning before Lydia ate her first meal of the day. Munching happily on the egg and cheese-filled tortilla Xotchel had rustled up for her, she felt guilty for the trouble she was causing at this late hour of the day. Her face still burned with shame at the long speculative look Juan had given her when she stepped into the lobby this morning wearing the same red dress she had left to go out in the night before. She knew her feelings of embarrassment was ridiculous – she was old enough to do as she pleased – but her strict Catholic upbringing often warred with the more relaxed morals of the day. No matter what she did she couldn't shake that part of her past. Knowing that other people might think she was easy didn't exactly thrill her either, even if it was only the night clerk.

Ravenously hungry as she blissfully bit into her tortilla, she savored every mouthful and wished she could order up another one. No, she had already wreaked enough havoc on the kitchen and she knew she was lucky to have gotten this. As she ate she allowed her mind to drift over last night, wondering why she didn't feel even the tiniest twinge of regret, yet knowing that she should. For now, she was only happy with the memory of the evening before.

When he first saw Lydia standing expectantly in the doorway, Rodolfo thought his heart would burst with the pleasure of seeing her. He hastened to her side and whispered in her ear, soft and low so nobody would hear him.

"*Eres muy guapa,* Lydia," he told her. At her questioning smile he translated.

"You are very beautiful."

Lydia blushed with pleasure.

"Thank you," she said shyly, smiling up at him, liking the way his dimples danced in his face.

"Are you here to meet Ana?" he asked, taking one of her hands. "I think she's waiting for you at the table over there." He pointed out the elegant form of a woman sitting in a dimly lit corner of the room where she could see everything but not be easily seen.

"Yes, I am Rodolfo, thank you."

They stood looking at each other, content to say nothing as the restaurant and its patrons rotated busily unnoticed around them.

"We're going dancing again tonight Rodolfo," she told him.

"Would you like to come with us?"

Inwardly Rodolfo groaned. He didn't know if he would be able to handle another night of her in his arms but unable to touch her the way he wanted to. Although he knew the smart thing would be for him to say no to the invitation, he said yes anyway, cursing at his weakness.

"I would like that," he told her as he escorted her over to Ana's table where he relinquished her into the chair Ana had saved for her.

"I'll see you both later," he told them before tending to his customers once again.

The night had been pure magic from beginning to end, Lydia thought now as she finished the last of her coffee.

At the last minute Ana had begged off, pleading a headache and insisting that the two of them go on without her. Not sure whether to believe her or not, Lydia waited for Rodolfo's shift to end and together under the knowing eyes of most of the staff they left the restaurant.

The evening was already late and Lydia knew that Rodolfo must be tired from his busy night and suggested they go for a walk along the beach instead of to the nightclub as originally planned. Relieved, but not for the reasons Lydia thought, Rodolfo readily accepted. Hand in hand they strolled down the sandy stretch near the pier.

The night was surprisingly chilly for this time of year. Lydia shivered in her flimsy dress. Rodolfo responded by wrapping one arm around her waist to ward off the cold. Hips wedged comfortably against each other as they moved, they walked the full length of the pier. From time to time they would stop at one of the benches to rest and talk.

Sometimes they would kiss—soft innocent kisses that served to whet their appetite for more. They talked about their lives, their feelings and what mattered to them most in life. Listening to his soft voice, husky from the smoke of the restaurant, Lydia felt she was a part of him. It was a strange realization to have but undeniably true.

"I almost forgot, *Chiquita*." Rodolfo dug deep into his pockets and produced a small velvet pouch.

"I have a present for you."

Lydia's eyes widened with surprise and delight.

Ducking his head he laid the soft bag in her hand. Then he lifted his eyes and watched intently as she eagerly opened it.

Lydia pulled open the drawstring and reached inside. Tugging carefully she withdrew an incredibly wrought necklace, its intricate design and beadwork beautifully crafted.

"It's beautiful," she breathed as she fingered the single stone. She held it up to the streetlight to watch it shine.

"I promised you a necklace Lydia, and here it is. I hope you like it." He went on to explain the piece while she stared in speechless wonder.

"The stone is jade from Mexico City. I added the silver wires that hold it together as well as the bamboo shoots and beads. The color and style are my own but my grandmother carved the head. It is the mate to this one," he told her pulling a nearly exact replica of the necklace he had made for her from under his shirt.

Lydia could barely see a difference until looking closer she could tell that his was slightly larger than her more delicate one.

"Mine is the male to your female one," he clarified for her as she commented on the dissimilarity, pleased she had noticed. "My grandmother told me that the two should never be separated."

Lydia caressed the smooth stone with her hand, feeling the power of two generations course through her before she handed the necklace back to Rodolfo.

"I can't accept this Rodolfo," she told him reluctantly.

"It is too valuable. You should give it to someone else someday. Someone who is special to you."

"You are special to me, Lydia," he insisted, taking the pendant from her outstretched fingers. He lifted her hair and gently fastened it around her neck.

Leaning back he to view the piece critically he said, "The color exactly matches your eyes Lydia. It's perfect for you," he pronounced almost to himself, satisfied with the result of his handiwork.

"My grandmother also said that the wearers of these necklaces will always be friends and never parted. That means you are stuck with me now," he teased her smiling deeply as she blushed.

"I hope so," she answered him shakily. Moved by the token she reached up and placed a soft kiss on his cheek.

"I will treasure this always," she breathed, tucking the jewelry in the bodice of her dress for safekeeping. It lay next to her heart.

In the wee hours of the morning Rodolfo finally turned to her, a questioning look in his eyes. Lydia knew what he was asking. With a nod, her heart hammering wildly in her breast, she wordlessly consented. They walked the nearly deserted streets and hailed a cab. Rapidly, Rodolfo instructed the sleepy driver to take them to a special destination, while Lydia sat quietly in the back seat beside him. Pressed close to each other his body heat mingled with hers in waves of desire.

I can still change my mind. She repeated the words like a litany over and over in an effort to keep calm

Deep inside she knew it was too late to turn back now even if she had wanted to. She spoke no words of protest that would break the spell. In a quiet neighborhood Lydia had never seen before, the taxi stopped and they got out in front of a charmingly rustic hotel. Lydia followed Rodolfo inside the dark lobby, glad of the shadows that hid her face from the curious eyes of the night clerk who had been sleeping in a hammock off to one side of the courtyard.

A swift conversation ensued between the two men and money changed hands from a surprisingly large wad Rodolfo carried in his pocket. Tips had been exceptionally good that night, a fact that made him doubly thankful given where he was at this moment. The would-be lovers made their way up the stone spiral staircase to their room as the night clerk peered after them in the gloom. He was sure they weren't married as the man had said but what did he care? He just wanted to go back to sleep.

Ill at ease, Lydia clung tightly to Rodolfo's hand as they wound their way up several floors to where their room was located. She had never done anything like this before and somehow it made her feel…

What? Cheap? Then, *at least it looks clean.*

Comforted by that thought she took a deep breath as Rodolfo unlocked the door and they stepped across the threshold.

Rodolfo crossed the room in the dark while Lydia fumbled for the light. Seeing the harsh glow of the bare bulb that flooded the sparsely furnished room she quickly flicked the switch off.

Don't these people believe in lampshades? She thought not for the first time since coming to Mexico.

In the glow of the moonlight, Lydia could see Rodolfo standing on the balcony with his back to her. She stayed where she was, feeling awkward and uncertain as to what to do next. She fought the urge to turn and flee. As if sensing her mood, Rodolfo turned and wordlessly held out his hand. For a moment, rooted to the spot, she debated her next move.

Should I go or should I stay?

He smiled and she found her feet moving of their own accord across the room to where he stood leaning casually against the stone railings. He pulled her gently toward him and placed one hand on the small of her back, the other in her hair. Pressing his lips to her forehead he murmured, soothing her with the sound of his voice.

"Angel hair. Soft like silk, like an angel's," he crooned as he gently stroked her.

Lydia swayed against him, lulled by his voice and caress. In a hypnotic voice he spoke to her softly, words of love—sometimes in English, sometimes in his own language. Her body tingled with desire. When he lifted her face to his, she met him with a hunger that matched his own.

"Don't stop me tonight, *Chiquita,*" Rodolfo whispered against her cheek when she pulled away. A splash of silver moonlight streaked his face and in his eyes she could see the question he was asking her, a quiet pleading in his tone.

Her answer to his request was to pull his lips down to meet hers.

"Mind if I join you?"

A deep voice spoke closely in her ear, interrupting Lydia's thoughts and momentarily startling her. She looked up and smiled at the face grinning down at her.

"What are you doing here Jim?" she asked, happily welcoming him.

"Sit down, sit down."

While he made himself comfortable she poured them both a cup of coffee from the urn on the table. One of the waitresses, Lupita, she thought, rushed over to the table to take his order.

Only a blonde, blue eyed man would get that kind of service in Mexico, she thought with amusement as the girl left to fill his request for orange juice.

Jim turned to her now, eyes sparkling as he regarded her thoughtfully.

"You're glowing," he stated matter-of-factly.

"Must be love."

Lydia flushed and started to protest but Jim waved it away good-naturedly.

"Believe me I know love when I see it girl and you are in love. Did your boyfriend show up last night?"

Lydia reddened even deeper not knowing what to say. The truth dawned on him and he laughed gleefully at her obvious discomfort.

"It's that Mexican isn't it? What's his name? Rodolfo?"

Jim regarded her closely, a sardonic half-smile on his face.

"Have you decided what to tell your boyfriend when he gets here?"

Lydia's face sobered as she struggled to find the words to explain.

"Forget it, Lydia. You don't have to explain anything to me. Don't you think things have gone far enough? I know it's none of my business, but you can't keep stringing this guy on forever."

"I know," she answered quietly.

"I mean Rodolfo is a great guy and everything but it just wouldn't work. We're so..."

"Rodolfo? I was talking about your boyfriend Lydia."

"John?" she asked stupidly.

"Yeah John. Its obvious you're in love, why would you want to go back to John?"

"Because...because it makes more sense...the thing is I really do care for John too. I'm just so confused. The last thing I want to do is hurt anyone."

"Hey girl, don't be so hard on yourself. I don't see a ring on your finger. Forget I said anything. You're on vacation. Enjoy it while you can," he laughed at the expression on her face.

Lydia smiled ruefully

"Thanks for the advice Jim, but you still haven't answered my question. "What are you doing here?"

"I came to say goodbye."

Her face fell

"Goodbye? I thought you were staying for at least two more weeks?"

"Gee I didn't know you cared?"

Lydia rolled her eyes as he continued.

"Seriously though, I have been offered an incredible opportunity."

Intrigued, she asked, "What is it?"

"First let me start from the beginning," he hedged.

"I was walking down by the pier. Being the outgoing person that I am I struck up a conversation with this guy from Texas. He has a sailboat anchored in the bay here. Let me tell you Lydia this is some sailboat. One thing led to another and he mentioned that his first mate was horribly sick from food poisoning. The doctor's say that there is no way he is going to be ready to set sail for at least another two weeks. This guy wants to set sail for Costa Rico now. He says he just doesn't want to wait that long."

"So?" she prompted, already fairly sure what his next words were going to be.

"So I offered him my services and he accepted. We leave first thing tomorrow morning."

Lydia sat back in her chair in amazement.

"You're going to sail all the way to Costa Rico? That sounds exciting. Are you sure you'll be safe? I mean you don't know this guy very well. What if he's…well you know…kinky?"

As her imagination ran rampant, Jim burst out laughing, amused by her concern.

"Look at me," he insisted.

"I'm a fireman, remember. Not exactly a weakling, you know. Besides, we guys from Canada are in pretty good shape."

Lydia pretended to give him the once over, not hiding her admiration for his muscular body. Jim's ruddy complexion turned a deeper shade of red, pleasing her no end.

"Careful girl," he warned her, "or I might stay and give both John and Rodolfo a run for their money."

This time it was Lydia's turn to look abashed. She quickly changed the subject.

"I wish you luck Jim. It sounds like the adventure of a lifetime. I think I'm jealous. I'd give anything to sail off into the sunset like you're going to do— especially now. Promise me you'll send me a postcard when you get back to Canada so I'll know you're safe. Let me give you my address."

As Lydia scrounged in her bag for a pen and paper, Jim chatted excitedly about his upcoming adventure. She wrote her address down and handed it to him. He stood up and quickly kissed her cheek.

"I better start packing and stock up on some supplies he said we're going to need. That's part of the job, apparently. If I don't see you before I go tomorrow take care, you hear?"

"Good bye Jim," she stood and kissed him on both cheeks before she let him go.

They regarded each other fondly. Without another word Jim sauntered casually away.

Lydia remained where she was, lost deep in her own thoughts. She realized that, despite his assurances that he would write, it was unlikely she would ever hear from him again. It made her feel sad. She wondered how she was going

## THE JADE PENDANT

to feel when the time came for her to say goodbye to everyone here.

Ana? Rodolfo?

As a child she had always hated saying goodbye to people, even to people she barely knew. The thought capitulated her rapidly back to her past.

"Hurry up Lydia or we're going to miss the bus," her mother yelled up the stairway.

Ten-year-old Lydia walked obediently to the door of her bedroom and yanked it open just as her mother met her on the stairwell. Impatiently she pulled her daughter's arm and dragged her out of the house to the car waiting in the driveway.

Swallowing back tears that threatened to spill over, Lydia hoisted her suitcase into the back seat. She got in the passenger side where her mother's best friend sat waiting behind the wheel, a sympathetic look on her face as she regarded the girl.

"Don't look so sad Lydia, this is a real adventure," Agnes tried to coax a smile from Lydia who looked sullenly away, refusing to be drawn in by the kindly woman at her side. Shrugging in the direction of Lydia's mother who was fighting back tears of her own, she turned the key in the engine and urged the red Ford to action. With a few chosen curses she twisted the wheel and drove to the Greyhound Bus stop.

It was a day Lydia would never forget. Shipped unceremoniously across the country to stay with relatives she had never met before for an undetermined period of time. Relatives she never knew existed.

Since her father's illness her mother had been unable to care for the family. Taking care of her husband placed many demands on her. What with daily visits to the hospital, housework and raising kids, she found she just couldn't cope any longer. With her husband's release from hospital his care would involve round-the-clock attention as he recuperated. Difficult as it had been to make, the decision to farm the children out for a while was the only solution that she could see to her problems. Lydia, angry and confused wasn't buying it.

"Let me stay with you, Mama," she had pleaded.

"I could help you with the kids and the housework and stay with Poppa sometimes, too."

But, her mother had made up her mind. She was going and that was that.

Lydia was the last one of her siblings to be placed.

*Like unwanted baggage,* she remembered thinking at the time.

Lydia shook her head to clear the memory. As a grown woman she realized how the experience carried over into other aspects of her life. She had refused to look back when she left Dennis—her only goodbye was a short note saying that she was leaving him. Not even a reason why, only that she was going.

The ironic thing was that her relatives had been very kind to her and had gone out of their way to make her feel at home. In hindsight she knew that her parents could not have done anything different, given the seriousness of her father's illness – so serious he almost didn't make it as she discovered many years later. Nevertheless, Lydia knew deep down that her insecurity stemmed from that single incident.

Time to let it go, she coached her inner voice.

Lydia stood and stretched her cramped body, the warm sun streaming down on her on the rooftop café. Dropping thirty pesos on the table she hurried to her room to grab her knapsack. Glancing at her watch she saw that it was 12:30. Rodolfo had told her he would be by in half an hour to take her to another beach. She didn't want to keep him waiting. Knowing what she did now about Mexican time, she thought there was little chance of that. Mexicans on the whole were very casual when it came to keeping accurate time. Their favorite expressions seemed to be either *Mañana* meaning tomorrow, or *mas tarde*, which meant later.

Despite this, Lydia found herself hurrying to her room for a last chance to freshen up and comb her hair before Rodolfo arrived.

Rodolfo roared up to the front of the hotel in his brother's car and loudly honked the horn, earning him disapproving looks from passerby on the streets. Grinning inwardly, he wasn't about to let anything or anyone spoil his good mood and he waved in response to their sour faces. Waiting patiently, he tapped his hands on the wheel to the beat of one of his all-time favorite musicians, Santana. His mind drifted back to last night as the sounds of the guitar blared in the background.

He had been amazed by how well the two of them had fit together, in and out of bed. Their bodies interwove so naturally, their rhythms matching perfectly.

She had been so nervous. The thought had endeared her to him all the more. He had felt protective—certainly not the way he felt about most of the women he'd been with. For a few minutes she had looked as if she was going to change her mind and run away, but she had stayed.

She had courage. He approved.

She was not what he had come to expect from a typical *gringa*. She had a combination of passion and restraint, combined with an air of innocence, which had both surprised and delighted him.

The reason I am here again today, he teased himself. A face appeared in the window opposite him, startling him momentarily.

He leaned over and rolled down the passenger window.

"You're early!" Lydia exclaimed, pleased.

"I seem to be the one on Mexican time. I just need to grab my camera and we'll go. I'll be right back," she said lightly and skipped away back inside the cool recesses of the hotel.

Rodolfo grinned wider, his heart foolishly light. He realized that in her enthusiasm he had not had a chance to get a word in edgewise. He had noted, too, the jade pendant around her neck. It pleased him.

Turning off the engine, Rodolfo slumped back down in his seat, as the strains of Santana wound down.

No sense in wasting gas, the practical side of him exerted itself once more.

Lydia climbed the stairs two at a time like a kid on her way to a party. The thought amused her. Just as she was rounding the first landing the familiar sound of Xotchel's voice called out from the lobby below. Eyes dancing, Lydia halted her progress and leaned over the railing.

"Yes Xotchel? You are calling me?"

"*Si* Lydia. I meant to tell you that your friend John Mathews from Canada called the other day."

Lydia paused, silent as the news sunk in.

"Let me just get my camera Xotchel and I'll be right back down," she said finally. She continued more slowly up the stairs.

A few minutes later Lydia faced the kindly proprietress of the hotel with an expression of foreboding on her face.

Seeing the gloomy look on a face where before there had been such happiness, Xotchel hastened to reassure her.

"Oh Lydia don't worry, it is good news. John said he is coming here on the 15th, which is a couple days from now. I know from talking to you that you have been waiting for word of him and so now you have it. *Es bueno, no?*"

"*Si*," Lydia answered slowly trying unsuccessfully to smile.

"Did he ask to speak to me?"

Xotchel shook her head reluctant to tell her.

"No Lydia he didn't. He sounded like he was in a hurry but I am sure he would want you to know he was coming. He is your boyfriend, *si*?"

Is he?

Aloud she assured the puzzled woman in front of her.

"*Si*, Xotchel he is my boyfriend. Thank you for the message. Did he tell you what time he was arriving?"

Again Xotchel shook her head.

"No, Lydia only that it would be the 15th."

She wondered if the rumors about Lydia and the waiter from Coconuts restaurant were true after all.

"Lydia? Are you alright?"

Feeling faint, Lydia mustered a careful smile.

"Yes Xotchel I am fine. Thank you again. Yes, it is good news."

Another false smile stretched her lips as she tried to convince herself.

Xotchel stared at her with sympathy before she shrugged and said briskly, "*Bueno* Lydia. Have a wonderful day, today."

"What? Oh yes, thank you Xotchel, you too, *gracias*."

Lydia stumbled her way through the door to the hot sidewalk.

Rodolfo glanced impatiently at the watch the Indian Chief had given him. It had been a gift for taking him fishing last year.

What is taking her so long? He worried afraid that maybe she had changed her mind. *No, there she is!*

His heart leapt, mesmerized by the sway of her hips as she walked slowly toward the car. He sensed that something was wrong, and he waited anxiously. Climbing into the car she flashed him a weak smile, unlike her usual wide-open ones, confirming his doubts.

"What's the matter Lydia?" he asked.

Lydia faced him. Eyes carefully neutral she searched his face as if to memorize his features. She made a quick decision, determined that nothing would spoil this day.

"Nothing's the matter Rodolfo," she smiled brightly, hoping to dispel the look of skepticism in his eyes.

Leaning over, she kissed him lightly on the cheek her fingers lingering along the length of his jaw line.

"Here I am on a beautiful sunny day in paradise with the most handsome man in Mexico at my side, going off to another wonderful beach. What is that word you say to me all the time? *Vamanos?*"

Rodolfo laughed, obviously relieved. She seemed to be her usual self again. He put his concern on hold for the time being.

"*Si*," he agreed. "*Vamanos!*"

The engine roared quickly back to life he as put it into gear and soon they were racing down the streets toward the countryside for yet another unexplored terrain.

Walking briskly down the trail at Cottonwood Park, John was determined to work off these excess winter pounds. An unseasonable Chinook wind had blown in overnight and so he decided to take advantage of the warmth. These winds usually only favored Alberta and occasionally the lower regions of British Columbia. This was a first for Prince George in over twenty years.

The trail seemed more crowded than usual as people of like mind took advantage of the incredible weather. John found himself nodding to more than a few acquaintances as he walked. They were obviously as happy as he was with the change of climate.

John was inordinately pleased with himself. He was looking forward to being in Mexico soon. His business was going extremely well. This month alone they had picked up yet another government contract from another branch of the forestry sector. That meant more trucks going out. More trucks meant more money.

He was even able to leave his assistant Curtis in charge for once. All outstanding contracts signed sealed and delivered. All Curtis had to do was maintain the status quo until his return.

If only I had better news for Lydia, he thought.

A furrow appeared on his brow as he thought about his conversation with Dee and what he had to tell Lydia. He wasn't looking forward to that conversation at all.

He thought back to his call to Xotchel and how remiss he had been in asking her to pass a message on to Lydia. He sighed, hoping that the hotel proprietress would take it upon herself to do so. If not, there was nothing he could do about it. He had decided to take the evening flight to Vancouver later tonight instead of tomorrow morning. That way he would be able call on a few of his contacts in the lower mainland before he boarded for Texas sometime tomorrow afternoon.

He wondered why Lydia hadn't bothered to call him since her arrival in Mexico nearly two weeks ago. He was after all, later than he had originally planned. Why hadn't she checked in and find out what was going on with him?

She must still be smarting over the fact I didn't get her a birthday or a Christmas present. He grimaced, wondering how he could have been so thoughtless.

He really hadn't had time. Christmas was the busiest time for them. It would slow down again in January. He had been amazed when a parcel from her had arrived Priority Post on Christmas Day. Inside was a beautiful limited print of a Robert Bateman painting—one of his favorite wildlife artists. He had called her, promising he would spoil her with a little something when he got down there. Although her tone of voice may have been a little cooler than usual, at the time he thought he had appeased her.

*Perhaps I was wrong.* He wanted to kick himself for his stupid blunder.

Hopefully the little something he had bought for her would clear up any misunderstanding or hurt feelings she may have. Convinced he had the situation firmly under control, John set aside any doubts he may have had and picked up the pace as he hurried home to finish packing.

Lydia rolled lazily in the matrimonial hammock, which was strung between two poles at the Burro Burracho Restaurant, which meant the Drunken Ass, at Tronçones Beach. From her swinging bed she could hear the pounding of the surf as it slammed into rocks nearby. The wide expanse of sand lay endlessly before her and was completely uninhabited. The sheer wildness of the place entranced her, lulling her with a sense of power and awe.

Beside her, Rodolfo stirred in his sleep. She moved her head slightly and watched him as he dozed. His handsome features were calm in repose. She tenderly traced his craggy face with one finger. Deep laugh lines played along his mouth.

Like a baby, she thought with a smile.

At the touch of her hand, his eyes sprang open, a childlike expression on his face as he tried to focus on where he was. As he became aware, he smiled at her. Reaching for and finding her hand he gently kissed her fingertips one by one then released them. A delicious shiver ran down her spine. She returned his smile with one of her own. Minutes passed as eyes locked they lay together, faces inches apart.

"Good afternoon *Senor* Lazybones," she mocked him.

Smiling he pulled her closer, the hammock swinging wildly with the movement. Locked in his tight embrace she pretended to struggle while he teasingly tickled her ribs.

"What did you call me? I think you'd better apologize, no?"

"No." She grinned vainly trying to capture his relentless fingers.

"Ok. Ok. I give up," she squealed and immediately he stopped torturing her.

Panting hard now, they stared as their passion for each other flared again. Lydia moved sensuously against him.

"Perhaps you should surrender now," she whispered as she felt him harden against her.

"I surrender," he murmured moments before his lips captured hers.

Much later the pair finally came up for air, hidden from sight from other customers in the outdoor restaurant by picnic tables. Rodolfo spoke first, his voice husky with desire.

"We'd better get out of this hammock before we do something the other guests may not wish to see—and while I still can," he joked half heartedly as her eyes followed his to the bulge of his shorts.

Lydia laughed shakily, embarrassed by the realization that she was quite content to do anything he wanted at that moment regardless of other patrons in the restaurant.

I am a wanton, she acknowledged.

To cover her confusion Lydia hauled herself out of the net, leaving him swinging uncontrollably. Laughing, she reached down to pull him up beside her. Her eyes darted around the room in the hopes no one had witnessed their interlude. If they did, no one seemed to notice or care, the clientele were engrossed as they were in their own conversations far on the other side of the outdoor café. Sighing with relief, her fingers combed her hair as she attempted to tidy her appearance.

A deep, slightly accented voice caught her by surprise. She jumped when it spoke behind her.

"Well look at that Ingrid. If it isn't Lydia Jordan."

At the sound of her name, Lydia whirled, Rodolfo pressed closely behind her. Amazed, she recognized the couple as Richard and Ingrid Gunther, clients of hers in Prince George. As owners of the famous Log House Restaurant there, they had bought advertising during her recent campaign.

"What are you doing here?" Lydia sputtered a greeting, conscious of Rodolfo's near naked body next to hers. Their curious glances flicked from her to him as Richard spoke.

"I could ask you the same thing," he laughed "but I can see what you're doing here. The question is how did you get here?"

Lydia laughed, pointing to the red Volkswagen in the parking lot.

"What a wonderful surprise to see you," she stepped forward and eagerly shook their hands.

"I had forgotten that you were coming here in January. What a coincidence."

They agreed it was unlikely they would both end up here at the same time. Rodolfo remained quietly in the background his eyes watching Lydia interact with the strangers. Lydia turned to him, dismayed by her lack of manners. Apologetically, she reached for his hand and pulled him forward to be introduced.

"Richard, Ingrid, I would like you to meet my…uh…Rodolfo Perez," she improvised.

"Rodolfo has kindly offered to guide me around while I'm here." Lydia laughed self-consciously as she saw Ingrid's eyebrows shoot up. She could only imagine what they must be thinking.

"Pleased to meet you Rodolfo." Richard shook his hand heartily as a pretty young girl of about twelve bounded up the stairs from the beach to stand beside him.

"And here is our daughter Katie. Katie, you may remember Lydia Jordan when she came to our restaurant? And this is her friend Rodolfo Perez."

"Hello." She smiled her eyes wide as she recognized the blonde woman.

"Aren't you from Prince George?" she asked, amazed.

"Sometimes." Lydia smiled in return.

"I've been to your restaurant many times and I am sure we saw each other then."

Rodolfo broke in, speaking for the first time to the group at large.

"Lydia and I were just about to order lunch. Would you care to join us?"

Richard accepted the invitation on behalf of his family and soon they were sitting at a long wooden table overlooking the beach. As they made themselves comfortable on the rattan chairs, Richard turned to Lydia, curiosity plainly written on his face.

"How long have you two been here? I didn't see you come in and we've been here all morning, haven't we Ingrid?" She nodded.

Rodolfo and Lydia shared a quick look then Lydia turned and pointed to the hammock in the far corner, her face coloring rosily.

"We've been hiding," she joked, turning back to Rodolfo who winked mischievously at her.

Richard and Ingrid shared a look and burst out laughing—much to the confusion of Katie who was puzzled by the hilarity.

Grownups, she thought. *Who can understand them?*

A waiter appeared at their elbow just then to take their drink order, negating any further need for comment on the subject. Richard ordered ice cold Coronas for everyone except Katie, of course, who wanted a lemonade.

"Are you from here?" Richard politely asked Rodolfo.

"And how did you meet Lydia?" he wanted to know, curious about the relationship.

Rodolfo shot Lydia a look before turning to face Richard. As he replied in his quiet voice, Lydia relaxed against the back of the chair, watching him as he interacted with her friends.

He can handle himself, she decided. She was relieved and turned away from their conversation to start one of her own with Ingrid.

"You know when Richard told me you come here every January I never really imagined we would run into each other. What a wonderful surprise."

Ingrid nodded, "I know. Not too many tourists know Tronçones because it is still relatively underdeveloped. We only just discovered it ourselves a few years ago and we have been vacationing here nearly every year for ten years. We love it."

"I can see why," Lydia remarked as she looked around her. The spray of the ocean reached her from the distance.

"How long will you be here for Lydia?"

"About another two weeks," Lydia replied suddenly aware that time was going by so quickly.

She glanced at Rodolfo who was engrossed in conversation with Richard who was listening intently to what he was saying.

Ingrid queried, "And how long have you known Rodolfo. He seems like a very nice man."

"Oh he is," Lydia replied enthusiastically tearing her eyes away to face her.

"I met him around New Year's. It seems longer though," she said brightly.

"John Mathews is coming too. You must know him from Prince George?"

At the familiar name, Richard looked up from the conversation with Rodolfo to answer.

"Of course we do. I remember you telling me that he was coming here around the same time as us. When is he due to arrive?"

Lydia cast an apologetic look at Rodolfo before answering, her lively face suddenly sober.

"I just heard today that he will be coming on the fifteenth," she admitted quietly.

"Two days from now."

Rodolfo looked sharply at Lydia before masking the expression on his face and lowering his gaze to the table.

So that was what was bothering her, he surmised correctly. He busied himself with the lime and salt for his beer.

Lydia avoided his eyes and concentrated on her friends instead.

"Yes, he left a message at the hotel this morning." She told them.

Ingrid watched the exchange between Rodolfo and Lydia with sharp eyes.

She's in love with him, she thought, surprised. *And, if I'm not mistaken he is love with her, too. Well, well, well. This is getting more interesting all the time.*

Richard's voice interrupted her musings. He was completely unaware of the tension around him.

"We'll have to all go out for dinner when John gets here," he suggested heartily.

"And you too, Rodolfo," he graciously included him in the invitation.

Rodolfo only smiled and nodded but said nothing.

Seeing the look of pain on Rodolfo's face, Ingrid wanted to kick her errant husband in the shins. When they were alone later she chided him gently.

"How was I to know, Ingrid?"

In the ensuing silence, Ingrid hastened to change the subject. She spoke about the beaches of Mexico they still wanted to visit and soon the group became absorbed in what were the best places to go. The afternoon sped by pleasantly over a delicious lunch of fresh seafood and more beers until they all were pleasantly filled and suitably drowsy. Despite the somewhat awkward beginning, Lydia could see that that the Günther's, Kate included, were very much taken with Rodolfo's charm and easy manner. She was proud of the way he handled their questions with ease and skill.

Lydia liked Ingrid's warmth and elegance and was impressed by how well mannered and behaved Katie was.

I wish I had a daughter like that, she thought wistfully.

As the waiter cleared the dishes from the table, Rodolfo pushed back his chair, stood, and reached for Lydia's hand.

"You will excuse us, I hope, but I promised Lydia a long walk on the beach and a swim before we have to leave. I'm on duty tonight at six."

The family nodded in unison. They stood to hug Lydia goodbye and to shake hands with Rodolfo.

"You can expect us at the restaurant for dinner later this week, "Richard promised him. "We'll make sure to ask for you."

"*Gracias Senor,*" Rodolfo shook his hand again.

Reaching across the table he shook Katie's hand too, pleasing her with the grown up gesture. They exchanged more promises to see each other soon then the two lovers set off across the hot sand.

For a long while they walked in silence, the waves lapping at their feet and erasing their footprints behind them. Unable to stand it any longer, Lydia broke the stillness. She stopped in her tracks and turned Rodolfo to face her. His look was unreadable.

"I wanted to tell you about John this morning, Rodolfo," she began.

"I just didn't want to spoil our day together."

"And when did you plan on telling me, Lydia?" he asked, curious as to what her answer would be.

"I don't know," Lydia hung her head, ashamed she that had kept it from him.

Impulsively, she wrapped her arms around his waist and placed her head on his chest. His back stayed rigid and unmoving for sometime but eventually she felt the comfort of his arms as they encircled her body. Lydia let out her breath as she felt him relax and conform to her body. In this way they stood swaying in the surf, feet planted firmly in the sand as the salt water rushed around their ankles, sometimes going as high as their knees.

Rodolfo placed his hand under Lydia's chin and forced her eyes up. There was a woebegone look on her face that touched him deeply. He felt his resolve melt and his anger fade.

"It's okay *Chiquita,*" he assured her.

"We still have some time together. Let us make the most of it while we can."

Sinking to his knees he wordlessly pulled her down beside him on the deserted beach and began to remove her bathing suit from her fevered skin.

Throwing his overnight bag on the bed John turned to the toiletry items on his dresser and packed them into the leather case. A small velvet box came last. He took one last look, admiring the sparkle of the gem inside. He hoped Lydia would like it! Opening a special compartment on the inside of the bag, he zipped it securely and closed the whole thing up.

Packing completed he hurried out to the truck, which was warming in the driveway for his drive to the airport. Tonight would find him at the Richmond Inn, close to the Vancouver Airport. He would probably be nursing a few scotches with some business acquaintances he knew there.

No sense letting an opportunity to do business go to waste, he thought, ever the businessman.

Sighing, he climbed into the truck and slowly backed up. His New Year's resolution to slow down on his drinking wasn't going so well, he realized. He had two weeks while he was on holiday to get it together. The last hurdle before relaxation would be his Texan cousins who enthusiastically lived the credo that not only were things bigger in Texas but they were better, too. His cousin Suzy, on his mother's side, had been ecstatic when he called.

"We're all so excited you're comin' hon," she drawled down the line in that twang he liked so much.

"We need an excuse for a party. Now what time ya'll getting here?"

John groaned aloud thinking back to the conversation. Sometimes it seemed like the very gods were against him, he thought, as he pulled into the Prince George Airport parking lot.

Rodolfo looked up expectantly toward the end of his shift to find Lydia sitting alone at one of the booths in the corner. She smiled in his direction. Shooting her a quick grin he hurried to complete his final clean up before punching his time card on the meter outside the office door. Finished in record time he presented himself before her table and captured a welcoming hand in his. He led her from the nearly deserted restaurant.

For a time they walked holding hands and talking about their night. After Rodolfo had dropped her off, he'd raced home. Lydia had taken a little siesta before going out for a light dinner along the beach alone. Rodolfo had only time to shower and change for work, beating the clock with only minutes to spare. He was tired he told her, until the sight of her had revived his flagging energy. Gratified, Lydia laughed and asked him just how much energy he had?

Rodolfo stopped walking and turned to her, head cocked to one side as if asking a question of his own. Lydia nodded and within minutes they hailed a cab to take them back to the hotel.

Riding in the back seat, Lydia laughed inwardly at the idea of going to a hotel for romance when she was paying perfectly good money to stay at the Citlali.

The fact was she knew that the owners of the small establishment would never approve of an unmarried woman bringing a lover back to her room. For that matter, although she relished what lay ahead, she didn't relish the thought of another scrutiny from the night desk clerk.

She needn't have worried. His face barely registered anything as they took the key he handed them and laughing raced each other up the stairs to the same room they had been given the night before.

A good omen, Lydia thought.

Once inside, door closed securely behind them, it was Lydia who made the first move and led the way. Having made the commitment for the second time there was no shyness and rising on her tiptoes she hungrily pulled his head down to meet hers. Impatiently, she unbuttoned his shirt; fingers fumbling in nervous anticipation as she pulled the tails from the confines of the waistband of his skintight black jeans.

Responding with a groan, as the material slid from him, he unzipped her simple black cocktail dress, sliding the straps slowly over her shoulders until it made a dark pool in a heap at her feet. Proudly she stood before him in her matching black bra and panties as he stepped back to look at her, eyes appraising before he removed those too.

The cool air tingled on her skin. Shivering she reached for him yet again. Eagerly he moved closer, murmuring soft words as their bodies pressed tightly together. Kissing her skin while his hands glided of their own volition, her legs weakened, threatening to give way with the sheer pleasure of his touch. As one they moved together his hand resting lightly on her taut nipple. She moaned softly. Excited by her response, he moved toward the bed. Sinking onto the mattress he drew her closer until she laid the full length of him. Feeling his hardness against her thigh, she slid her body deeper onto his maleness in welcome surrender.

# Chapter Seventeen

The plane took off without incident or fanfare. John breathed a sigh of relief when the Boeing 747 leveled and they reached their cruising altitude of 35,000 feet. He was not a particularly nervous flier but still he preferred to be sitting in a horizontal position as opposed to a vertical one.

From his window seat he watched the impressive Dallas skyline against the horizon until it disappeared under the clouds that rushed in to block it from view. John settled back into his seat to enjoy the five hours it would take to get to Zihuatanejo. He ordered a drink from the cart, which the pretty flight attendant offered.

If everything went according to plan, he figured he would arrive in Zihuatanejo by late afternoon, time enough to find Lydia, get cleaned up and go for a romantic dinner somewhere on the beach. Sipping on his scotch he stretched his long legs out, thankful that he had the row all to himself.

'A good omen, John' he could almost hear Lydia say, wishing she was here with him. *Soon,* he promised as he closed his eyes to try to get a few minutes shut-eye, worn out from the night he had just spent with his relatives.

The Texas Connection had immediately swarmed John as he cleared customs, stepping through the sliding glass doors and into the waiting area. Declaring loudly that he was the 'spittin' image of your daddy' they overwhelmed him with hugs from the women and hearty handshakes from the men. There were five of them in all. John struggled to keep them straight in his mind.

A tall, long legged redhead threw her arms around him last, her green eyes danced merrily.

"I'm Susie," she declared, "and this here is my husband Sam, my better half."

Sam merely shook hands and smiled a greeting, clearly the more reticent of the two. Susie continued the introductions.

"This here is your cousin Janice, my sister, your second cousins Lenore and

Jenny and Jenny's husband, David."

Seeing the confused look on his face she hastened to add, "Don't worry none about keeping us all straight hon, you'll figure it out. Basically we're all cousins," she said with a laugh linking an arm through one of his.

"Right now I think this calls for a celebration," she declared. She steered the group single handedly to the airport bar for a drink.

"Pleased to meet you all," John called over his shoulder at the group trailing closely behind.

Sam called forward, speaking for the first time.

"Susie has planned a real shindig for you tonight, haven't you Susie?"

She nodded with a grin as her husband continued, "Texas barbeque beef and all," he promised as John started to say that they shouldn't have gone to so much trouble. Susie cut him off.

"None of that now, you hear? How else are we to treat our Canadian cousin?"

John laughed and shut his mouth and meekly allowed her to lead the way.

"I can hardly wait," he grinned at the group while thinking inwardly there went his one opportunity to get a good night sleep before leaving for Mexico.

"You hear that?" Susie tipped her head over her shoulder.

"He can hardly wait."

At her words the group laughed uproariously as they walked into the bar and plopped themselves in front of the bartender. As he ordered up a round, David regarded his cousin-in-law with a sly grin.

"Are you sure you know what you're getting yourself into, John?" he teased.

Grinning, John thought, *if I had known this was the kind of welcome I was in for, I would have visited long ago.*

He was looking forward to a party. Leaning back in his chair he gulped the first of the many drinks the bartender was to bring him. He smiled at his long-lost, or newly-found, family depending on how you looked at it.

An hour later the group stumbled through the doorway of Susie and Sam's house, astonished to find the place packed with people, who were all shouting high-spirited greetings to the tall handsome Canadian.

The next day Susie drove him to the airport and insisted on waiting until his flight was called. After promising to visit again sometime soon, John made his way through the departure gate, his movements made slower by the king-sized hangover he sported.

As he dozed the headache subsided a little.

Turning her head in bed, Lydia woke to find Rodolfo watching her, a smile on his lips as he saw her eyes flutter open. She returned one of her own, stretching her limbs and snuggling closer to him beneath the covers.

"What am I going to do without you, *Chiquita*?" He murmured softly.

At his words tears sprang to her eyes and she pulled him closer to her.

And how can I give you up?

The words stuck in her throat, making it difficult to breathe as he squeezed her body hard against his.

You're just infatuated, a voice inside her mocked her. *John will show up and you will forget your little diversion.*

Abruptly, she moved out of Rodolfo's embrace. Confused, Rodolfo watched her as she slid out of bed. Unashamedly naked she placed her hands on her hips and facing her lover, taunted him as she swung her hips side by side.

"Well *Senor* Lazybones. Are you going to stay in bed all day or are you going to feed me? *Si* or *no*?"

Before she could react, he moved across the expanse of the bed, and, grabbing her wrist, pulled her roughly toward him, growling menacingly in her ear as she squirmed to get away. She began to laugh, her breath ragged as she attempted to catch her breath. Showing no mercy, he pinioned her beneath him, holding her wriggling body tightly intact.

"I will feed you *Senorita*," he smiled with an evil leer causing her to laugh harder than before.

"But first you have to work for your breakfast."

Holding her even tighter he pulled her head toward him and kissed her hard on the mouth. She pretended to struggle briefly. As his mouth softened and his kisses became sweeter she stopped, as he knew she would, and wound her hands behind his neck.

It was several hours before Rodolfo and Lydia dragged their spent bodies out of bed and hopped into the shower. Taking no notice of the icy water that cooled their sweat-soaked skin, they languorously soaped each other slowly, the heat of their passion threatening to rise and consume them yet again. As the goose bumps on Lydia's bare skin looked ready to pop off, Rodolfo reached behind her and tuned off the tap.

"I could warm you Lydia," he offered with a suggestive wink as she stared at him in awe of his stamina. Hurriedly she danced out of his reach.

"*No gracias senor*," she said primly, the rough towel wrapped protectively across her chest.

"I do have to get back to the hotel before they realize I didn't come back again last night."

Rodolfo laughed harshly as he stared incredulously at her from across the room.

"We're not teenagers anymore," he pointed out.

"What does it matter what the hotel owners think?"

Lydia considered the question for a few minutes before answering, picking her words carefully in order to make him understand.

"I guess it's just the way I was brought up," she finally told him ruefully, "Old habits die hard." Lydia shrugged.

"I know you must think that's silly but…"

"Silly?" Rodolfo interrupted her.

"What is silly?"

For a minute Lydia stared at him uncomprehending. When she realized he was serious, she threw back her head and laughed, delighted at the look of puzzlement on his face.

"It's when…when…" she groped for an explanation, stumped into silence. Then mischievously she picked up the pillow at her feet and aimed it at his head.

"That is silly," she told him triumphantly, ducking a foam missile that soared back at her.

One hour later, dressed and respectable they left the cool dark of the hotel to greet the midday sun. Disoriented, they stood blinking in the sudden glare, hands shielding their eyes to block out the bright light. There had been no one at the front desk as they were leaving so they'd simply left their key on the counter and slipped out, a fact, which pleased Lydia more than she could possibly say. All that was left now was to say goodbye. Lydia's heart turned over at the thought of it.

"I live over there," Rodolfo pointed behind her.

"I'll walk you to the corner and we can get you a cab."

Taking her elbow gently, Rodolfo steered her down the alleyway behind the hotel. Lydia wanted to have breakfast with him but seeing how late it was she decided it was probably not a good idea. Still, after such a night to remember, she was feeling let down in some indescribable way and her next words came out harsher than she intended.

"No problem Rodolfo," she told him as he walked her rapidly over the rough stones.

"I can take care of myself and you seem to be in a hurry to get home."

Amused, Rodolfo laughed and stopped walking to look at her.

"It is you who said you need to get back to the hotel to save your reputation, Lydia," he teased her until she had to smile.

Then he lifted her face in his hands and kissed away her doubts.

"I wish I could take care of you Lydia," he said seriously. "But a woman like you needs a rich man, I think."

Dropping his hands from her face he turned and raised an arm at a passing cab. Before she had time to protest both the remark and the suddenness of his action she found herself in the back seat of the car. Rodolfo leaned in the open window and planted a hard kiss on her lips before turning to give money and directions to the driver.

"I'll see you later," he mouthed from the side of the road. With a final slap on the roof of the vehicle he sent them on their way.

Craning her neck over her shoulder Lydia watched him become a speck in the distance. He stood not moving, standing where they'd left him on the side of the road. Sadly she faced the dashboard catching the eye of the driver in his rearview mirror.

Self-consciously, she raised her hand to pat down her hair, aware of the crude leer on his face. Flushed, she looked away, knowing how she must look to him in what was obviously last night's attire. Resolutely she straightened her shoulders and, meeting his eye in the mirror she shot him a hard, defiant glare. He looked away and for the rest of the drive concentrated on the road before him rather than on the passenger in the back seat.

As Lydia feared, Xotchel manned the front desk when she strolled into the lobby. She decided to brazen it out.

"*Buenos Dias*, Xotchel" she sang out as if it were perfectly normal for her to be wearing a cocktail dress at this hour of the day.

Behind her, Xotchel returned the greeting as she sailed up the stairs to her room, nearly colliding with Ana on the landing.

One knowing look from Ana as she eyed her clothes caused Lydia, to break out in a sheepish grin as Ana's hands flew to her face.

"My God Lydia," she exclaimed delighted.

"You're in love."

Lydia flushed, the silly grin plastered on her face.

"Don't be silly, Ana," she protested half-heartedly.

"John is coming here tomorrow. Xotchel told me yesterday."

Suddenly the full impact of what she said hit her. Abruptly she sat down on the stairwell, her face white.

Ana leaned over her concerned, "Are you okay Lydia?" she asked as she stroked her head soothingly.

"I'm fine," Lydia managed shakily.

"I thought I was going to pass out but I am ok now. Thank you Ana. I think what I need is to get something to eat and then I'll be alright."

She tried to stand but Ana held her back with a firm hand pressed to her back.

"Just sit there for a minute," she ordered before continuing.

"I know this is none of my business Lydia but I do feel responsible for this. After all it was I that introduced you to Rodolfo in the first place. What on earth are you going to do with him when John gets here?"

"I don't know," Lydia said quietly, her face bleak.

"All I know is that this is such a ridiculous situation and I have no idea how I got myself into this mess. I never meant for it to go so far. I mean, let's face it Ana…there is no way this could ever work with Rodolfo and yet I really do care about him."

"Well amen to that," Ana said in her litany.

"I was beginning to believe you had a lump of coal where your heart used to be. I am happy to see I was wrong about that."

"I wish I had," Lydia stood smoothing the wrinkles from her dress.

"It would sure make things much easier if I did, wouldn't it?"

Ana straightened, too.

"You still haven't answered my question Lydia. What are you going to do about Rodolfo and John?"

"I need to think about it Ana. Right now if I had to say, I believe that I should stay with John. At least I know who he is and what he is and where he comes from. What do I really know about Rodolfo? What if he isn't even serious about me at all? You told me yourself that Mexican men are notorious for playing with American women while on vacation and then when they leave that's all there is."

"Yes I did say that," Ana agreed with her, "but I also told you that Rodolfo was different. Am I right?"

Lydia nodded with a sigh.

"Yes you are right and I am inclined to agree with you – Rodolfo certainly is different. More different than anyone I have ever known."

Sadly she started up the stairway, her mind filled with many thoughts of the things she knew she would have to face eventually.

"Don't take too long to decide," Ana warned her unsmiling.

'Rodolfo is not a man you can play with for all that he is different and from the sounds of it, John is not either."

With that she turned and continued down the stairs on her way to do the errands she had planned for the day.

Lydia stared after her, feeling bad that her friend seemed displeased with her somehow but not knowing what she could do about it. She climbed the remaining steps to her room. The brightness of the day was already dimming. She decided a day at the beach may be just the thing she needed to get her thoughts together and discover what it really was that she wanted.

Wants and needs are not always the same thing, she reminded herself, recalling the lines of an old sales adage she had once heard.

Rodolfo clocked out at midnight, loitering as long as he could in the hopes that Lydia would walk in the door. Enduring the knowing winks and snide comments from his so-called friends and co-workers. Rodolfo lingered until the night watchman began locking up. He had to resign himself to the fact she wasn't coming. Dispirited, he left through the front door this time, his path taking him right in front of the Citlali. As he walked slowly past he glanced up at the balcony, startled to see a pale form looking down at him in the moonlight.

Lydia.

Slowly she raised her hand in a wave and then disappeared. He decided to wait.

Moments later Lydia glided out the front door of the hotel to stand beside him, nearly out of breath from her midnight flight down the stairs. Heart lighter at the mere sight of her he smiled a warm welcome and caught her close to him, kissing her softly on the lips.

"I looked for you tonight. Where were you?" he growled in mock anger and she smiled, knowing he was teasing.

Closing her eyes Lydia savored the moment of being in his arms again. She had promised herself earlier to spend the day thinking about what she had to do. It wasn't going to be easy but the decision she made was the only one that she could. All night she had debated whether to come to see him or not and had ended up going to bed early to avoid it.

Somewhere around midnight the moon streaming in her window had woken her. Panicking, she slipped out of bed and flew to the balcony outside her room. Looking down she saw Rodolfo standing there and her resolve had melted.

Stepping back now to see him smiling at her, waiting patiently for her answer, she was glad to be here.

"I almost didn't come," she whispered, "but I had to see you again, one last time."

At the full impact of her words his smile faded but remained on his face.

"Lydia," he breathed enjoying the foreign sound of her name on his tongue. "I am glad you came to say good-bye one last time."

With tears in her eyes, she leaned her head on his chest so he wouldn't see them.

"I only have one favor to ask you," he said pulling her face up to look at him. She nodded.

"Promise me you will not bring your boyfriend to Coconuts. Please Lydia. I understand you are going back with him. That is the way it should be. He can give you so much more than I can."

Lydia began to protest that that wasn't the reason but he placed a finger on her lips to silence her.

Wasn't it?

"Promise me Lydia. It would hurt me too much to see you together."

"I promise, Rodolfo," Lydia swore, her voice breaking with emotion and the unshed tears she had tried so hard to hold back began to fall.

Rodolfo kissed her then, first softly then more passionately before letting her go.

"You should go to bed now Lydia," he said seeing her bare feet and the flimsy wrap she had thrown over the sheer nightgown. Lydia nodded, head down.

With a final hard embrace Rodolfo turned and walked quickly away, his footsteps echoing on the cobblestones until they faded completely. Lydia lingered a little longer hoping that he would change his mind and come back.

Then what? The voice mocked her again knowing it would change nothing. Slowly, suddenly mindful of her attire, Lydia turned and moved toward her hotel and empty bed, this time allowing the tears to fall unheeded down her cheeks.

The next afternoon, from the desk in her lobby, Xotchel looked up just in time to see Lydia strolling through the door on her way to her room. Noting Lydia's tan approvingly but also seeing the bluish shadows beneath her eyes, she chose to ignore the latter.

"*Buenos tardes*," she greeted her warmly.

"Did you have a nice day at the beach Lydia?"

"*Buenos tardes* Xotchel. Yes I did thank you. I look much less like a white ghost now don't you think?"

"*Si* Lydia."

And much happier, too, she noted silently wondering once again if the rumors she had been hearing were true. *Stop it, you foolish woman,* she chided. *You have enough to worry about trying to keep this hotel running than worrying about the love life of your guests. Still...?"*

She shook her head as Lydia prepared to leave, her eyes falling on a piece of paper she had tucked into the folder on her desk.

"Wait a minute," she called out halting Lydia's progress across the small lobby.

"I almost forgot Lydia. There's a message for you from John Mathews. He is waiting for you down at Tatas Restaurant right now. Do you know where that is?"

Lydia stopped in her tracks and leaned over to take the proffered note from Xotchel's fingertips.

"Thank you Xotchel. Yes I know the place," she told her, having breakfasted there a couple times in the past two weeks. It had an unprecedented view of the bay and the food was consistently good. As she read the note, which simply told her what Xotchel had just said, her heart began to pound with some unknown emotion.

"Lydia?" Xotchel looked at her, worried by the look on her young guests face. Is everything alright?"

"Yes Xotchel," Lydia answered a bit too brightly, "everything is just fine. I'm just going to go to my room to change and then meet John at Tatas. If he comes back before I am down could you please tell him where he can find me?"

"Certainly Lydia," Xotchel told her as Lydia hurried up the stairs to escape the curious eyes of her host.

Interesting, Xotchel mused, eyes dancing at the drama that was unfolding before her, happy for the small diversion it afforded her no matter how brief.

Entering her room Lydia closed the door behind her and leaned back against it in an attempt to calm and catch her ragged breath.

*Breathe, breathe,* she coached until she was able to slow down sufficiently.

Sinking down on the snowy, white coverlet on her bed she waited until completely composed and relaxed before moving to the bathroom to ready herself for the meeting with John. She stripped off her beach cover-up and bathing suit and turned on the shower before immersing herself in the warm spray. Later, dressed and impeccably groomed, she critically surveyed her reflection in the mirror. At the last minute she slipped the jade necklace over her neck. Somehow comforted by the cool stone on her skin, its bamboo shoots and beads swinging seductively against her breast, Lydia took a deep breath and left the relative security of her room.

An ice-cold beer on the patio table before him, John surveyed the beautiful bay of Zihuatanejo with a contented sigh of pleasure. Tata himself, an old friend from years ago sat next to him, sipping lemonade while he talked about all the changes in his life since the last time they met. Having just regaled John with the story of his wedding to a Swiss woman he had met while she was on vacation in Mexico last year, he proudly informed him he was already the father of a beautiful little girl. Although John did not normally approve of "mixed marriages" he congratulated his friend on his happiness. A waiter came to the table to inform Tata that his brother and business partner needed him in the office. He excused himself from the table leaving John once more alone in blissful solitude.

Drinking in the scenery John could feel the stress leave his body with every wave that washed to shore. Waiting for Lydia to arrive, which he hoped would be soon, he recalled the first time he had come here years ago and the circumstances that had surrounded it.

It had been shortly after the breakup of his marriage. He knew that he had to get away from it all for a while. His ex wife, a raven haired beauty, was made bitter by her marriage to him and made sure the divorce proceedings were as unpleasant for him as they possibly could be, citing mental cruelty as her reason for leaving him. Mostly it was her pride and the fact that she had enjoyed the status that marriage to him had given her. Her ensuing actions had greatly shown him the full extent of her wrath and disappointment.

John felt terrible about the break up, a fact that his ex-wife would not believe, no matter what he said. Although not the sort of man to wear his heart on his sleeve, he had loved his wife deeply in his own undemonstrative way. Unfortunately for them both, she could never understand this facet of his personality and his seeming coldness made it impossible for her to accept him for what he was.

When a travel agent friend suggested to him that a vacation would be just the thing to get his mind off things, he had eagerly jumped at the chance. He asked her to pick the destination and she had chosen Zihuatanejo, a long time favorite place of hers. He had been hooked ever since.

John sighed again and taking a deep pull of his beer he drained it. He was content with the fact that although there were certainly changes to the fishing village since his last visit, the real charm of the place had not been touched or tainted in any way. Looking back over his shoulder for the waiter to bring him another, he spotted Lydia on the path coming his way. Hand shading her eyes against the sun, he watched her sashay between the tables, calling out greetings to Mexican waiters along the way, laughing at the outrageous flirtatious things they said to her but never stopping her stride for a minute. Knowing she was looking for him, John drew himself out of his chair to catch her attention.

"Lydia over here," he called as he moved forward to greet her. At her smiling approach he hugged her to him.

"There you are," he said unnecessarily to cover the joy he felt at her arrival.

"I was wondering if you got my message or not. Sit down," he led her to his table, his eyes raking her body in a way that left no doubt what he was thinking..

"My God Lydia you look wonderful."

Lydia laughed, despite her turmoil at seeing him, and spoke for the first time.

"Thank you John, so do you. It's good to see you," she added, surprised to find she really meant it.

"I mean it Lydia, you look great. Mexico certainly seems to agree with you. You look like you found your Hollywood."

Again Lydia laughed. The sound rang out across the beach and caused a few heads to turn in amusement.

"What does that mean, my Hollywood?" she asked smiling wider.

John looked rueful, "I'm not really sure" he admitted, "It's just that you look so…so…well wonderful," he said again at a loss for words.

"I don't think I have ever seen you look better," he complimented wholeheartedly.

Lydia was touched, not only by the words but also with the obvious sincerity with which John said them. Never before had he been so complimentary. Surprised, she found herself relaxing under his warming praise. Leaning over impulsively she kissed the cheek of the normally reticent man across from her and squeezed his hand fondly. When she pulled back she was surprised when he didn't let hers go.

"Thank you John" she told him again. "The truth is. I do think Mexico agrees with me. This place is absolutely wonderful."

"I knew you'd like it here," he said with no small satisfaction. "That's why I suggested it to you. Of all the people I know, I was sure that you would like it the most."

*THE JADE PENDANT*

Choosing not to ask why that was, she agreed with him instead.

"Well you were right," she said leaning toward him and peering closer. "You look a little tired John. Have you been working too hard?"

"A minute ago you said I looked great," John bantered jovially. "The truth is the relatives from Texas kept me up late last night and I had had a busy schedule in Vancouver the night before that, too. No matter though, a couple days of sun and relaxation and I will be as good as new. Although I'm not that tired," he winked at her suggestively, his meaning obvious.

A dull heat that surprised both of them started up her neck until it infused her face. She ducked her head to hide her confusion. John was merely amused.

"Don't tell me you've gone shy on me Lydia? Obviously I've let too much grass grow beneath my feet. Don't you worry we can take care of that later."

Unconsciously, he patted the small package in his pocket as if to assure himself it was still there. Lydia forced a smile to her face and changed the subject.

"Tell me about your cousins. I didn't know you had cousins in Texas," she remarked realizing that there were many things she probably didn't know about him.

As he relayed to her the details of the last couple of days she allowed her mind to wander until a silence told her he was finished and looking at her with a puzzled look on his face.

She smiled at him so that he would think she had been paying attention, when in reality her mind was a million miles away.

John responded, his perceptive eyes honing in on hers to ask, "So, tell me Lydia. Is Zihuatanejo everything I said it was?"

For a moment she stayed quiet and looked over the water as she pondered his words, wondering how she was going to answer him.

"More than I could have imagined John," she spoke so softly he had to strain to hear over the waves.

"Zihuatanejo is everything you said it would be and much more." She looked up at him with a sad smile.

"You might think this is strange but from the minute I stepped off the plane I felt that I was home, that I actually belonged somewhere. I think I told you that when I was married to Dennis we traveled so much I never seemed to know where I was half the time. I didn't put down roots. As a kid growing up I felt like I was an alien!" She laughed and waved her hand in front of her.

"I feel like I belong here. I really do. I wish I could live here—maybe not all year long but just in the winter months."

At his surprised look, she laughed again in an attempt to lighten the mood. Although he returned her smile, he stayed quiet while she continued, leaning eagerly forward in her chair.

"I've been thinking about something, John. You know my business in Canada is only for six months a year and the rest of the time…" She stopped, as she noticed the look on his face.

"John what is it? You're not having problems with your business are you?" she asked, concerned.

John sighed and shifted in his chair. His movements alarmed her. He squared his shoulders and faced her fully.

"I guess we might as well deal with this now Lydia so I'm just going to come out with it." He held up his hand as she tried to interrupt him. She fell silent.

"There are problems with business but they are not mine Lydia. Dee called me the other day just before I left. I did try to call you several times," he said defensively as her eyes suddenly flared.

She hadn't known.

"It appears that the Franchisor of your company has disappeared with all your funds Lydia. It looks like he took off in the night. They're investigating right now but it seems that he was going bankrupt. He cleaned out all of the accounts and took off. I'm sorry Lydia."

"That's impossible John," Lydia cried. Her eyes wild in her face as the impact of his news hit her with full force.

"We paid the Franchisor over two months ago. He must have paid the manufacturer out of that. So that means he's still got our units. They should be ready by now to deliver."

John shook his head.

"Dee thought so too. She called the manufacturer and it seems that the head office never did pay the manufacturer for your units. They paid for another one of the franchisees instead."

At her puzzled look he tried to explain.

"They were robbing Peter to pay Paul, Lydia. By the time it came to pay the manufacturer for your units, the money was already spent and there was no more. It's a tricky way to do business. It usually it happens to companies that are under-financed to begin with. I assume that was the case here?"

Lydia shook her head to indicate she that she didn't know. John felt pity stir in his heart for the defeated looking woman before him.

"Look, if it's any consolation to you the Franchisor didn't have much money to clean out of the account – only enough to get back to Australia. I hate being the one to tell you this Lydia," he took her hand again in a feeble attempt to comfort her, "but Dee thought it would be better for you to hear it from me in person than over the phone. Everything's gone."

Lydia sat back in shock. The bright sun dimmed as the world went black and started to swim. When she revived John was leaning over her anxiously.

"Come on," he said briskly as he assisted her from the chair and threw some pesos on the table.

"Lets get you back to the room and you can lie down. We'll finish discussing it there."

He supported her with an arm around her waist as they took the short walk back to the hotel. They walked past both Ana and Xotchel without a word as they climbed the stairs to her room. John pulled the drapes to shield her face from the sun. Lydia lay across the bed, her body numb with shock. John eased his body next to her and pulled her to his chest. He spoke quiet words of comfort as she asked her questions.

Eventually she sat straight up in bed and pulled herself together. John was proud of her. Seeing the resolve harden in her face, he let her be.

"Thank you John for telling me. This is just such a shock. I think I need some time alone to digest this. Maybe I should call Dee?"

"Dee knew you would want to do that Lydia, and she said to tell you 'absolutely not!' She made me promise to tie you up if you went anywhere near the phone, which by the way," he grinned evilly, "does hold some promise, don't you think?"

Despite her distress, Lydia grinned weakly, and then quickly sobered.

"It just doesn't seem right for me to sit here and do nothing," she complained.

"Don't worry Lydia, Dee told me to tell you that everything is under control and there is nothing you could do anyway. When you get back you can both call on your advertisers and explain what happened."

At the thought of that task Lydia groaned and laid back again pulling the pillow over her face.

John laughed. He took the pillows away, leaned over and kissed her on the cheek, then heaved his body off the bed.

"I'm going to catch a little shut-eye and leave you alone for a while. I'll collect you in a couple of hours and we can grab a bite to eat somewhere."

Lydia looked at him as if she was seeing him the first time, amazed by his staunch support of her.

He is handsome, strong, steady and reliable. A woman could do a lot worse.

"Thank you. You are a good friend to me," she told him gratefully.

"I will always be there for you Lydia," he promised, aware for the first time how much he really meant the words.

Leaning over her for a last kiss, he noticed the necklace around her neck and reached out to fondle it, his fingers running over the carved surface.

"That's a pretty trinket Lydia. You'll have to show me where you got it and I'll get one for my daughter too. I think she'd really like it." With a quick peck, he straightened and opened the door to her room, and closed it softly behind him.

Lydia sat perfectly still in the middle of her bed, her hand around the stone, which was still warm from John's brief touch. Her mind moving in a million directions as she tried to assimilate everything as well as analyze her feelings toward him. It only succeeded in making her tired. Her head began to ache from the stress of the day. She took off her necklace and reaching over, placed it on her dresser. Unnoticed by her it slipped behind the bureau and nestled between cracks in the floor.

Lying down, she decided to follow John's lead and take a nap before dinner. She hoped that when she woke she would find this was nothing more than a bad dream.

Ana and Kelly left the restaurant laughing at some silly remark the owner had made to them. They were headed to Coconuts for a nightcap before turning in. The sound of their laughter was contagious and delighted smiles accompanied them as they wove their way along the cobblestone streets in the direction of their favorite bar. Ana was the first one to sober, remembering what she had seen in the lobby earlier on.

"Lydia's boyfriend arrived today. I saw them together in the lobby. She walked right past us without saying a word. I sure wouldn't want to be in her position right now."

"I don't know about that," Kelly said struggling to hold back her laughter, which threatened to overtake her once again.

"I'd be happy with just one man. She has two fighting for her. Too bad Jim had to sail off into the wide blue yonder. I've been dumped before, but never quite this drastically."

Ana giggled as she threw an arm around her friend's shoulder, "You goose. He didn't dump you. He just went…sailing."

Giddily the pair broke into laughter again and rounded the last corner before the Coconuts.

Ana looked up just in time to avoid running into Lydia and the tall handsome man she presumed to be John Mathews on her arm.

"Lydia!" Ana exclaimed holding out her hands to her.

"We were just talking about you," she said, ignoring Kelly's snicker.

"Really?" Lydia smiled wanly as she tried to imagine what that conversation would have been like.

"John, I'd like you to meet two good friends of mine, Ana and Kelly."

John smiled and said hello. He watched as the three women chatted about their day.

"Why don't we go find ourselves a comfortable place to sit down? He suggested.

"I'm sure you all have a lot to say to each other, and I could use a drink."

"Good idea," Kelly asserted.

"We were just going to Coconuts for a nightcap Lydia. Would you like to join us?"

"Coconuts!" Ana and Lydia said in unison, their eyes aimed at their friend incredulously.

"What a great idea," John said.

"That has always been my favorite place. Are Pauley and Tonita still there?"

"Good," he said at Ana's reluctant nod, "and if I remember correctly this is the back way in isn't it?"

"Yes it is" Lydia said, trying to stall now, "but it's going to be pretty crowded tonight. Why don't we go someplace quieter instead?"

"Nonsense," John said as he took charge.

He tucked one hand under Ana's elbow and offered his other arm to Kelly.

"Coconuts is perfect."

While Kelly chatted amicably to John, unaware of the tension around her, Ana shot Lydia, an apologetic look over her shoulder. Trailing miserably behind, Lydia shrugged, resigned to her fate. They entered the bar and easily commandeered four stools side by side.

"It's not too crowded in here," John told her triumphantly. He sat next to her and looked around with satisfaction.

"I see nothings changed," he observed. "Place looks exactly the way I remembered it."

"Yes," Lydia agreed, head down to keep from being noticed by the staff,

"it is very nice here but a little noisy. Why don't we go next door to JJ's instead?"

John turned to her, his smile broad.

"This is a first," he teased. "Since when have you ever wanted a quiet place?"

Her need to answer was interrupted by the timely arrival of Tonita who greeted the group warmly before turning her attention to the Canadian man on the stool before her.

"So you're the John that Lydia has told us all about. I would never have guessed. Welcome back, John. It's been what? Two years now since I last saw you? How are you?"

John looked pleased that she had remembered him. "Yes its' been two years and you haven't changed a bit, Tonita. You look as wonderful as ever," he complimented her warmly.

"Where's Pauley tonight?" he asked looking around to see if he could spot him.

"Day off," Isabel informed him before casting a catty smile in Lydia's direction.

"You should come back tomorrow. I know he'd love to see you again." She smiled, remembering the excellent tips that John always left behind.

Not if I can help it, Lydia vowed as she cast her eyes frantically about the room frantically.

While John and Tonita chatted, Ana leaned over and whispered in her ear, "I'm so sorry Lydia. Kelly thinks you and Rodolfo are only friends, nothing more. If she had known she would never have suggested coming here."

"I know," Lydia whispered back. "It's just that I promised him I wouldn't bring John here and now look at us. He will be very upset. Have you seen him yet? Maybe he's left already?" she asked hopefully.

"There he is," Ana nudged her in the ribs waving her fan nonchalantly in the direction of the far wall on the other side of the room. Lydia spotted him almost immediately. He was leaning into the cashier's cage and talking to Debra who was sitting behind the desk.

He hasn't seen me yet, she thought in relief. She attempted to hide behind John's broad shoulders.

John then did something completely uncharacteristic. He leaned over and draped one arm over Lydia's shoulder, nearly knocking her off her precarious perch and exposing her to view of the whole room. Pulling her firmly toward him, he placed a fierce kiss on her lips, just as Lydia, eyes wide with surprise, saw Rodolfo turn to look straight at them.

Their eyes locked in a fixed stare from across the room. He looked as if he was going to smile at her until he took in what his eyes saw. Unable to move from John's firm embrace, she watched him visibly blanch. His eyes grew narrow and cold.

*I asked you not to bring him here they accused,* speaking volumes from across the room.

He started toward them as Lydia watched in horror. He brushed past her chair, face carved in stone.

Ashamed and knowing she had hurt him she pushed away from John. Breath seemed to leave her body and for the second time that day she felt her world spin and the floor reach up to meet her.

"What's the matter Lydia?" John asked. "Are you sick?"

He leaned closer to pull her back to him, thinking to comfort her.

"Are you still thinking about your business?"

Feeling faint, Lydia shook her head woodenly.

"Excuse me," she mumbled as she slipped off her chair and made a dash for the washroom.

Ana watched the whole exchange with the horrified fascination of a true storyteller.

"I better go see how she's doing," she suggested to the helpless looking man before her.

"Please do Ana. I gave her some bad news earlier and it must be what is making her feel so sick."

Ana shot him a strange look but held her tongue as she slipped off her stool to follow her friend. She entered the bathroom just as Lydia was splashing her face with cold water from the hand-painted porcelain basin. Handing her a paper towel to dry herself with, Ana asked her if she was all right.

"Oh Ana I am such a fool," Lydia said as she futilely tried to stem the tears falling down her face.

"Did you see the look on Rodolfo's face when he left?" Ana nodded. She certainly had.

"Please tell him it wasn't my idea to come here, Ana." Pause. "Kelly should never have suggested this," she finished accusingly, looking for, and finding her scapegoat.

Momentarily caught off guard Ana stared at her, her loyalty to Kelly warring with her new friendship with Lydia. Loyalty won. She spoke bluntly to the woman crying before her.

"I'm sorry things turned out this way, Lydia but you brought this on yourself."

Lydia raised her head to stare at her friend. Ana continued, this time in a gentler tone.

"Zihuatanejo is a very small place, Lydia. You were bound to run into each other at some point, sooner or later. If not at Coconuts, then certainly somewhere else."

Lydia sagged against the basin.

"You're right. I only have myself to blame. I should never have accused Kelly. After all it's not her fault that I am such an idiot," she smiled weakly.

"John told me you had some bad news today. Does it have anything to do with your business?"

Lydia nodded again miserably.

"Care to tell me about it?"

Lydia filled her friend in on the some of the details John had imparted to her earlier.

"Somehow this pales in light of this thing with Rodolfo though," she said, then laughed ruefully.

"I must be going nuts. My professional life is in a shambles and I'm more worried about a Mexican I've known for less than three weeks than I am about my business."

Ana soothed her with a light hand on her back.

"Don't worry about Rodolfo, Lydia. He's a big boy and he can take care of himself. It's you I'm worried about. I think you need to fix your make-up and rejoin that poor man. He is sitting at the bar wondering what in heaven's name is going on."

Lydia laughed shakily as she saw her reflection in the mirror.

"You're right. Go ahead and keep John company while I repair the damage here. I'll be there in a few minutes."

She hugged her friend. "Thank you for everything."

"No problem." Ana waved her fan airily and left Lydia to put on a new face.

Rodolfo strode angrily down the street in the direction of home, hoping that the night would work its usual magic on him. The minute he had seen Lydia his heart had given a leap of joy. Then he had seen the man draped all over her. He realized it was her boyfriend from Canada and immediately it angered him that she had gone back on her promise to him. He had pretended not to notice or care about the anguished look on her face. He'd done the only thing he could think of to do, and that was to leave.

Carlos had stopped him on his way out with a sympathetic hand on his arm, but Rodolfo had shaken it off. He was not in the least bit interested in seeing the look of pity in his eyes or hearing the "I told you so." He had somehow remembered to punch out on the time clock before he had fled into the streets.

Before he reached the canal, he paused at Madera Beach and breathed deeply, allowing the sea air to fill his lungs and soothe him as it always did. He watched the waves as they softly lapped to shore and felt his anger fade to be replaced with something else.

He's too old for her, he thought disdainfully. A moment of satisfaction filled him briefly until it, too, faded.

He realized it didn't matter what he thought about his rival. Lydia was the one who had made the decision and obviously it didn't include him.

She didn't look happy with him though – a glimmer of hope at the words before he dashed it away. *Good!* He thought childishly, the sentiment not bringing him the gratification he craved.

Angry again, he turned toward the *barrio* and strode purposefully into the lonely night.

# Chapter Eighteen

"Have you given any thought as to what you'd like to do today?" Lydia asked peeking her head around the bathroom door to address the man sitting in her bed, bare chest visible over the coverlet.

John had booked his own room, but, as far as he was concerned, there was never a question of where he would be spending the night. Initially reluctant, Lydia had discreetly let him in her room and into her bed.

Despite her mixed emotions, last night with John had been better than good. After some initial awkwardness, which John thankfully attributed to the length of time they had been apart, they had fallen easily into each other's arms. They came together in a rhythm that felt natural. In the morning she woke more confused than ever.

What kind of woman are you that you can hop from one man's bed to another? The inner voice she'd come to dread berated her.

Unable to sleep, Lydia had leapt out of bed and dressed quickly. Leaving the sleeping John behind, she went in search of coffee and croissants. He had been awake when she returned and was now happily munching flaky pastry, a cup of hot coffee in the other hand. With a mouth full of the delicacy he watched her dry her naked body at the foot of the bed before responding to her question.

"Whatever you want to do is fine with me. You've been here nearly three weeks. Why don't you be my tour guide today and I'll just follow you around? Just don't ask me to go shopping," he added hastily at the last moment.

Yes, shopping is not one of your strong suits; she remembered, biting her tongue on a retort as she remembered her forgotten birthday and Christmas presents.

She ducked back into the bathroom for a minute to retrieve her brush. When she returned, the towel was draped modestly around her.

Sitting on the bed while brushing her hair she suggested, "Why don't we go to La Ropa Beach today? I hate to say it John, but that lily-white body of yours needs a tan."

John laughed and peered down at his pale form.

"You're right," he agreed ruefully, "Playa La Ropa it is then."

Lydia stopped brushing to look at him.

"You still look tired John," she noted worriedly. "I think you work too hard. We need to get you rested up."

Unconsciously assuming the role she had played with him in Canada she took the cup from his hand and set it aside, and began to rub his shoulders with hard strokes. John responded to her ministrations, groaning as her fingers bit deep into his aching muscle, the tension beginning to leave him.

Pulling her down to lie beside him, he removed the towel from her body and whispered in her ear.

"I'm in your hands."

By mid morning they were both showered – Lydia for the second time – and dressed for the beach. *Silly to wash your hair just to get it full of seawater,* Lydia smiled to herself as they crossed the lobby.

She had searched her room in vain for the pendant Rodolfo had given her sure she had placed it on her dresser the last time. Remembering Rodolfo's comment about lifelong friendship, her heart plummeted. She decided to check with Xotchel later to see if one of the maids had found it.

Xotchel manned the front desk, noting their appearance with approval. Stopping by her desk, Lydia questioned the woman about the jade pendant. Xotchel promised she would mention it to the cleaning woman. Feeling sick about the possible loss, Lydia followed John to the street.

They make an attractive couple, Xotchel thought. Both of them radiated obvious power and success. *A much better match for Lydia than a poor Mexican would be.*

A twinge of sadness washed over her, surprising her with its intensity. She impatiently dismissed it.

"*Buenos dias,*" she called after them, watching from the window as they left the lobby in search of a cab.

The taxi deposited the pair at Patty's Restaurant, the place Lydia liked to frequent and suntan when at La Ropa Beach. Eager to please, the waiters rushed over to assist them with their lounge chairs, recognizing her from her previous visits.

"I see you've made friends, Lydia." John teased her as they welcomed her by name.

Lydia winked at him and shrugged Mexican style, as if to say she had no idea what he was talking about.

"Yes I have," she agreed flippantly.

"You'd better watch out or some Mexican lover will steal me away." She stopped, appalled by what she had just said, but John, applying lotion to his chest, didn't appear to notice anything amiss.

"This is the life," he commented as he handed the sunscreen to her and asked her to do his back. Lydia grimaced slightly at the body she had enjoyed only a short while ago, comparing it unwillingly to a leaner, brawnier one.

*That didn't stop you though did it?* She admonished herself before turning to bestow a brilliant smile in John's direction.

"You know John…this is a beautiful place," she began hesitantly.

"I've been thinking I'd like to live here."

She saw his mouth twist sardonically. She spoke quickly, holding up her hand to prevent him from interrupting.

"Let me finish, please. The idea isn't really so far fetched. After all, if I still had my business back in Canada it would be very easy for me to work it seven months of the year and come back here for five."

"But you don't have your business anymore," he reminded her gently.

"How would you support yourself?"

"I know that, but I am sure I could find something like it."

Still a little cross with him she continued.

"In spite of what you may think, I am not entirely without means and I happen to be very good at what I do."

"I know that Lydia," he allowed generously. "You sold me and I'm not an easy sell."

Slightly mollified, she expanded on her idea.

"I think I could take on consulting jobs, like my friend Denise does. Short-term projects that pay a lot of money but are only for a few months at a time. What do you think?" she asked him, seeking his advice for the first time.

As an astute businessman his opinion was important to her even though she didn't always show it. This time she found she was anxious for his approval. She was to be disappointed.

John began slowly, not wanting to burst her bubble in light of her enthusiasm. At the same time he felt it was important he give her an honest answer.

"First of all, I have every confidence that you would succeed in whatever you do. That is beside the point. Have you really thought this through, Lydia? It would mean job-hunting, apartment hunting and starting over whenever you returned to Canada. What kind of life is that? What about your future? Investments? Retirement? Have you given any thought to any of that at all?"

Slipping the glasses over her face to hide the anger and disappointment she felt at his remarks, she nevertheless had to concede that he was right in many ways.

"I'm not over the hill, yet John." She felt the need to defend herself. He chuckled rather than take offense.

"Of course how would you know? You missed my last birthday party," the words slid sweetly poisonous from her lips before she could take them back.

"And here I thought you forgave me for that, Lydia," he chuckled again and patted her arm patronizingly as he thought about the little box tucked away in his carry-on bag.

"Listen, why don't we talk about this later, Lydia? I know you're a determined woman but you never know what the future will hold," he said, infuriating her by what she perceived to be his total unwillingness to take her seriously.

Silently she fumed on the chair beside him as he closed his eyes and promptly fell asleep. A half-baked idea began to take root and she latched onto it, turning the pros and cons over in her mind and mulling the future possibilities—a future John had so bleakly tried to paint. He was right about one thing. She was determined, and if there was any way she could make the concept of living here, at least part-time, she was going to find it.

In the taxi on the way back to the hotel John tried to make it up to her, holding her hand lightly as he pointed out points of interest along the way. In spite of herself she relaxed against him and enjoyed the impromptu tour.

"I knew you would forgive me," he gloated smugly when she kissed his cheek after the ride and favored him with a smile.

"Trust me Lydia. You'd never be happy living here with little money, struggling to save when you came home just to come back here. That's no way to build a bank account, believe me. If you want my advice…"

I don't, she thought, forgetting that hours earlier she had indeed asked for it.

"…Go back to Canada, buy another business and work really hard for the next few years building it up. Then maybe you can take a few weeks off here and there. I promise you, you won't regret it."

Inwardly seething in frustration but unwilling to show her true feelings, Lydia thanked him, and told him she would take what he said under advisement. Sighing at the look on her stubborn face, John easily saw through her façade, but decided to let it go for now, not wanting to spoil their first day together. He suggested he take her to Bogart's, a favorite restaurant of his in Ixtapa for dinner that night. Eager to put the conversation with John behind her, Lydia readily accepted. She decided to concentrate instead on what to wear to the most expensive restaurant in the luxury resort.

Rodolfo walked aimlessly through the streets near the pier before he had to clock in for work. He had seldom felt less like serving rich, spoiled *gringos*. He'd rather cut off his arms at the elbows. The night stretched before him endlessly as he thought what was ahead. Deep in his thoughts, he collided with Ana as she stepped out of Byblos, the only bookstore in town. Head down, and intent on her purchases she hadn't noticed him either. Her parcels flew through the air as she looked down at the man who hurriedly bent to pick them up for her.

"Rodolfo," she exclaimed. 'I'm so sorry. I wasn't watching where I was going,"

"Me neither Ana," he admitted with a smile as he handed over the bags to her outstretched hands.

"Are you alright Rodolfo?"

"*Si*, Ana, you didn't hurt me," he teased the petite woman. He knew that wasn't what she meant.

"I am so very sorry about last night," she went on. "Kelly felt just terrible."

"Kelly?" Rodolfo asked, confused "Why?"

"For suggesting to Lydia that we all go to Coconuts for a drink, silly. We had no way of knowing Lydia had promised you she wouldn't go there and I just wasn't thinking. Lydia tried to stop her but…"

Rodolfo interrupted her carefully, "You mean it was Kelly's idea to come in last night, not Lydia's?"

"Oh God no, Rodolfo. I thought Lydia would die when Kelly suggested it, but there was no way she could get John to change his mind. She certainly tried hard enough. It seems Coconuts is a favorite haunt of his and he knows Tonita and Pauley from years back. Surely you noticed how upset Lydia was?"

"I was a little upset myself," he admitted dryly before smiling at her. His heart was lighter with the knowledge that, although Lydia had not kept her promise as she said she would, it hadn't been her fault. Knowing that made him feel better than he had all day.

"Don't worry Ana," he told her. "It's all in the past. We have to look forward to the future now."

Observing him shrewdly Ana remarked, "Yes Rodolfo we do. But you're in love with her, aren't you?"

"Yes I am," he acknowledged for the first time even to himself.

"But it's over now," he proclaimed firmly, sounding harsher than he had intended.

"I knew this day would come, there are no surprises here Ana." He was silent for a moment.

"I just didn't realize it would feel like this."

With that sad comment he touched Ana's hand in farewell and hurried away. Tears glistening, Ana watched him until he was far down the street before she too headed back to her room.

What have I done? She thought sadly as she remembered the glimpse of the heartache in her old friend's eyes.

She had almost reached the hotel just as Lydia and John pulled up in the cab. Spotting her in the distance, John pointed.

"Isn't that your friend Ana coming this way?" he asked.

Lydia turned to look. "Yes, that's her. Why don't you go ahead and shower and I'll meet you on the balcony for a cocktail before dinner."

"Sounds like a good idea," John agreed, as he waved a greeting to Ana, and disappeared inside the hotel.

As Lydia waited for Ana to catch up she reflected on the hotel. One of the most charming aspects of the Citlali she felt was the two-tiered balcony that overlooked the street. Filled with hundreds of plants crammed into the spacious area, it also had comfortable handmade chairs and a plush sofa. Traditionally, it was here the guests of the hotel met at the end of the day for drinks before going out to dinner.

It had become a special spot where Lydia could watch for Rodolfo as he arrived for work. The balcony afforded a clear view of the front entranceway to Coconuts. After her shower at the end of the day she had made it a habit to grab a novel from the selection provided by the hotel, then settle comfortably on one of the rattan chairs. She would pass an hour or two until the light faded from the sky and it became too dark to read.

As she read she would listen for the sound of Rodolfo's distinctive whistle from the street below. When it came, like a teenager she would fly to the edge of the balcony to flirt with him for a few minutes until it was time for him to go inside. It had become something of a romantic ritual with them—one they both looked forward to. Tonight, she glanced up and noticed the balcony was unoccupied.

By the time Ana had arrived on the doorstep next to her, she was trying to catch her breath from hurrying.

"I just saw Rodolfo, Lydia, and I can tell you that he looks miserable."

At the mention of his name, Lydia's heart beat faster.

"I'm sorry to hear that Ana" she told her quietly, "I'm feeling a little miserable myself. But I am sure he'll get over it."

"Yes, I'm sure he will too," Ana granted, a little taken aback by the callousness of the remark. "The question is, will you?"

With that parting comment Ana swept away, her fan fluttering furiously, a sure sign she was agitated about something.

Lydia stared at her retreating back, uncertainly.

Will you get over it? The question burned in her brain as she started up the stairs to her room.

Entering her sanctuary, Lydia was relieved to see that John had chosen to get ready in his own room. That gave her some time to prepare herself for the evening in solitude and privacy. Stripping off her sand-covered beach clothes and bathing suit she caught her reflection in the mirror. Pausing, she critically assessed her attributes. On the whole she was satisfied with what she saw. Running her hands across the soft, supple skin, she was thankful for the genes her mother had passed on to her, knowing that most people took her for years younger than she really was. A strict exercise regime kept her muscles hard and taut. Although she never dieted she was careful to eat well-balanced healthy meals. Her inspection was interrupted just then by a sharp knock at the door followed by the sound of John's voice.

"Lydia, it's me. Can I come in?"

"Actually John, I want to get ready. Why don't you let me shower and dress and I'll be out in fifteen minutes. Meet me on the balcony okay?"

A brief silence, then, "Sure thing, Lydia. See you in a bit."

His footsteps faded down the hall. She was relieved but knew that she had upset him for the second time that day. She hurried to the shower and let the cool water flow over her feverish body.

John dropped the ice cubes into the Martini shaker from the travel kit he always carried with him on trips and poured vodka over it. A half capful of

## THE JADE PENDANT

Vermouth, a twist of lemon for him and he had the makings of a perfect drink.

Shaken not stirred, he thought as he poured the icy concoction into a glass.

Dropping three olives after them he watched as they swam their way to the bottom before he took his first sip.

*Perfect,* he congratulated, *and just the way Lydia likes them,* he remembered as he bit into his first olive.

Lydia's behavior puzzled him. He went over the last two days trying to identify what the problem was. He knew something was wrong but he was unable to put his finger on it. One thing he did know for sure was her attitude toward him had changed. She was usually warmer, more exuberant…more passionate.

Not that there was anything to complain about last night, he hastened to assure himself. *It was just that she seemed changed - different somehow.*

Further speculation ended as Lydia appeared magically in the doorway. He was so deep in thought he hadn't even heard her approach.

"Penny for your thoughts," she said. She looked beautiful in an off the shoulder, white cocktail dress. She floated to his side.

"Wow," he breathed, pursing his lips in a long wolf whistle.

"You look delicious."

Lydia flushed a little at his obvious approval, smiling at his choice of adjective.

"Thank you, so do you. Well maybe not delicious exactly, but certainly very handsome. And I mean it this time." She laughed remembering her earlier comment about the color of his skin.

In actual fact he already had quite a bit of tan considering it was his first day out. He hadn't burned as most people did. His tan was already beginning to deepen to an attractive gold. It made his blue eyes look bluer and his even white teeth whiter than ever. Dark, slightly wavy hair tinged with gray along the sides made him look exactly what he was – a rich businessman on holiday.

John acknowledged the compliment by handing Lydia a freshly made martini. Raising his glass, he toasted her before taking a sip of his own.

"To a wonderful vacation with you in Zihuatanejo."

"To Zihuatanejo," she echoed. "And to a perfect martini," she added, taking her first sip and favoring him with a wide smile.

They chatted about the day and their plans for tomorrow. Listening to him outline some ideas he had, she took another sip. Something glinted in the bottom and she stared into her glass. Puzzled, she glanced up at John to find him grinning foolishly at her. She took two manicured fingers and dipping she fished out the perfectly cut diamond solitaire ring.

Holding it to the light, her breath caught at the exquisite setting and she slowly turned her attention to the man who had given it to her.

"Will you marry me, Lydia?" he asked formally.

Taking the diamond from her trembling right hand he placed it on the third finger of her left. Stunned, clearly unable to speak, for the moment she stared at him, a thousand emotions and thoughts whirling around her head—some joyful, some sad, all of them confusing.

*This is what I wanted, isn't it?*

John's smile faltered as he watched her, and she knew she had to say something.

"I don't know what to say," was all she could manage. "This is so sudden."

Relieved, John smiled in the dim light.

At least she hadn't said no!

"I know, Lydia. For me too. I guess I just realized how much you meant to me when you were gone. How much I want you in my life. How much I need you to be there."

"You need me?" she asked.

Incredulously she stared at him, surprised by his eloquence.

"Yes Lydia I do. And now, with your failed business, you need me too. I can help you get back on your feet again Lydia. We've never really discussed it, but I'm a rich man in my own right. If ever you need anything I'll be there to help you in any way I can."

*What about love?* Her romantic nature asserted itself, but her pride kept her silent as she heard him out.

"We'll make a great team Lydia. You can be anyone you want, do anything you want, whenever you want," he laughed a little knowing he was getting carried away and probably scaring her.

"Let's just do it," he said, confident now she would say yes.

Instead she murmured, "Can I think about it, John?"

At his surprised and disappointed look she hastened to explain.

"I just need some time John. This is all so sudden," she repeated lamely, wondering why she was hesitating at all.

John smiled down at her from his great height, placing his large, strong hands on her shoulders and drawing her to him.

"Of course you can, Lydia. Just please don't make me wait too long."

"I won't," she promised as she started to take the ring off her finger.

John stopped her.

"Keep it on Lydia. I like to see it on your hand and I think we both know it's just a matter of time don't we?"

Head down, he was unaware of the look she gave him as he slid the ring down once again. Still unbelieving, she held out her hand in front of her to better admire the bauble on her finger.

"It's so beautiful John," she breathed. "I don't think I have ever seen a lovelier ring."

"It's only beautiful because you're wearing it," John told her, surprising them both.

"I promise I will give you my answer in a few days," Lydia told him earnestly, kissing him on the cheek.

"A few days?" he joked, then rapidly sobered.

"Very well. Let's drink to a few days then. "May they go by quickly!"

With the toast made, he clinked her glass with his and kissed her softly on the lips before lifting it to his mouth.

Neither of them noticed a lone figure staring up at them on the balcony from the street below. Hidden by shadows, the man turned and walked dejectedly into the open doorway behind him.

# Chapter Nineteen

From the bedroom Yola winced as the sound of dishes shattered in the porcelain sink of her kitchen. She rolled her eyes at her husband who responded with a helpless look of his own.

A string of curses emanated from the room beyond followed by the sound of Rodolfo attempting to clean up the mess. Yola, thankful that her daughter had already left for school, told her husband to go talk to him.

As Roberto leaned against the doorway watching his brother, he changed his mind about talking to him. Rodolfo was usually the most even-tempered person in the world. Roberto hadn't seen him like this since Beatrice left him.

It must be a woman and probably the *gringa*. A glass shattered on the kitchen floor. Rodolfo turned with a sheepish expression on his face, looking defeated. Moving forward to ease his brother out of the kitchen before any more damage could be done, Roberto found himself disliking this mystery woman intensely.

The next few days flew by in a whirl of activity while Lydia and John did the typical tourist things. They even went deep-sea fishing, catching not just one but two good-sized marlins. John caught the first – "just to show you how it's done," he told her laughingly. He said it was her turn and she found the thrill of reeling in a hundred-and-ten-pound fish was incredibly exciting. When she saw a third one make a series of consecutive jumps next to the fish she was reeling in, she was even more excited – until the captain told her that it was the mate to the one she'd caught.

"Cut the line," she ordered him, to the amusement of John and the young Mexican crew.

"For God's sake Lydia, it's only a fish," John chided her. "There are lots of fish in the ocean."

Lydia sat there in shock, the day spoiled for her as she contemplated the fate of her catch. Not wanting to appear even more foolish than she already did, she remained silent for most of the remaining day.

Other days they spent exploring nearby islands, Lydia relating her adventure of being stranded on Manzanillo, without going into full details about her rescue. One morning they rented motor scooters to take them around town and into the surrounding countryside. They stopped at little out of the way places to purchase trinkets and drink ice-cold beers.

John's tan quickly turned mahogany in color as he said it would and she noticed more than one female eye turned to look at him with approval.

Why are you so surprised? She asked herself knowing he was as good a catch in Canada as he was here – maybe even better.

At the back of her mind was John's proposal. A few days later she was no closer to giving an answer than when John had first popped the question. She felt restless and out of sorts when she knew she should be feeling on top of the world. She knew that time was running out and John would be expecting an answer soon. It only served to make her feel more miserable than before.

After one particularly sleepless night, she rose before the sun and headed to the fish market on the beach to watch the fishermen come in with their night's catch. She had left John snoring softly behind in her bed. The flurry of activity lightened her mood as Mexican ranchero music drifted out over the calm sea and people milled in close groups near the boats. She grabbed a cup of coffee and sweet roll from one of the vendors and sat on the dock till the sun rose high over the horizon. After a long while of sitting in self-absorbed silence she rose and eased her stiff muscles before she hurried to the offices of Mexican Airlines down the street.

When Lydia returned, her face flushed and eyes dancing, John was already up and dressed for the day.

"There you are," he greeted her heartily, noting with approval the color in her cheeks. It was good to see her looking so happy despite the unacknowledged new tension in their relationship.

Feeling a little guilty for her behavior over the last few days, she crossed the bedroom floor to kiss him hello.

"Thought you might like to go to Las Gatas today?" she offered smiling.

"I went with Ana a while ago and absolutely loved it."

John, relieved to see her in a better mood than she had been in days happily fell into her plans.

"Fine by me Lydia. You're the tour guide, remember? Do we still catch a boat at the pier?"

"Yes we do," she replied glancing at her watch. "If I'm not mistaken they leave every ten minutes or so. Anytime they want to actually," she said with a laugh in reference to Mexican time.

Joining in, John quipped flippantly, "Probably why Mexico will always be a third-world country."

At Lydia's quick frown he knew he had said something wrong.

"Let's go," he said hastily before she could berate him and they got into yet another argument. Gathering up her knapsack he offered her his hand and they left the room together.

The pier they would catch the boat at was filled with tourists and the odd vendor, most of them headed to Las Gatas. Small, half-dressed Mexican children darted nimbly in and out of the crowds, some carrying bags belonging to tourists for a few pesos change. Holding tightly onto the knapsack John declined firmly each time they were approached. Lydia, however, smiled at a particularly precocious boy of about five and dug deep into her pockets for a couple pesos and handed them to him.

"You shouldn't encourage them," John growled. "You're just teaching him to beg."

"He wasn't begging," Lydia protested vehemently.

"At least he wouldn't have been if you had just allowed him to carry our bag to the pier. Besides, what's a couple of pesos to us when it can mean so much to them?"

"That's not what I mean Lydia," he began. "I just think…"

"Let's just get on the boat," she snapped waspishly and stepped into the nearest one lined up on the dock.

For a minute John debated following her, already anticipating the way the day was going with dread. Lately she'd been snapping at him every time he opened his mouth, and it was getting so that he was afraid to say anything at all to her.

*Especially if,* he thought as he stepped down into the boat, *he made any remarks at all about Mexicans. It was almost as if she felt she had a proprietary monopoly on them.*

Last night at dinner was a good example. Everything had been going smoothly – the food was wonderful, the music soft and sweet, and the décor itself was first class. At one point John even considered asking her if she had made a decision about his proposal. Then he made an offhand remark about the inattentiveness of some of the staff serving them, commenting that he found them to be under motivated and particularly true of most Mexican people. She had nearly bitten his head off.

"Just because people don't have a lot of money John doesn't mean they are unmotivated. Maybe they're happy just the way they are."

Since she had chosen to misinterpret his observation, he had changed the subject, but the rest of the evening had ended in an awkwardly cold silence. Later at the door to the room, she had pleaded a headache and suggested he might want to stay in his room that night. He'd had just about all he could take from her and had stubbornly insisted he join her in hers. Her response had been to keep her back to him all night and leave early this morning before he even woke up. On rising he found she had already gone and he couldn't help but wonder what she could possibly be doing at that time of the day.

Puzzled as he was at her behavior, he was nevertheless determined that the gulf between them would get no wider. Sitting beside her in the boat as the Captain guided the small craft out of the harbor to open sea he reached over and gave her a hug.

Sitting across from his best friend Ralph on his cool, front porch, Rodolfo could almost make believe that nothing in his life had changed. The knowledge that he was probably wrong filled him with a restlessness he seldom ever experienced.

*There is no such thing as a restless Mexican,* he chuckled softly to himself. *We're way too laid back for that!*

To help combat whatever it was that he was feeling, he had left his apartment, to the relief of Yola and Roberto. He wanted to try and burn off some of his excessive energy. Ralph, an English teacher at a private school in Ixtapa, looked up from the guitar he was stringing when he heard his friend's laughter.

"Well I see you still know how to smile," he remarked. "What's so funny?"

Rodolfo shrugged his shoulders, grabbing two beers from the cooler beside him. He handed one to Ralph, who took a sip before setting it down at his feet to complete his task.

"I was just thinking how jumpy I feel lately. Like something is about to happen. But nothing ever does here does it? Life pretty much stays the same day in and day out. We go to work, eat, wake up again and go back to work. That's all there is."

Ralph, who had a pretty young wife named Julia, and was the proud father of two very active, small children under the age of five, laughed heartily.

"That may be all there is for you buddy, but let me tell you my life is a little livelier than that," he nodded his head in the direction of his children playing at his feet.

"Especially with my two munchkins."

At the sound of his father's voice his youngest, a boy named Ricki, crawled over and grabbed him by the pant leg, begging for his father's attention. Ralph responded immediately by laying aside the guitar and picking his son up off the dirt to bounce him on his knee. Soon, his daughter too, not wanting to be left out toddled over and crawled up on the other knee. Cuddling close to her father she regarded Rodolfo with a wide-eyed stare.

"See what I mean?" Ralph said ruefully. "The problem with you Rodolfo, he went on to explain, "Is that you have too much time on your hands. What you need is a wife and some babies. You're alone too much – you think too much. Find yourself a girlfriend and marry her."

"No thanks," Rodolfo grimaced. "You know the women around here don't appeal to me and with my long hair I don't appeal too much to them either. Besides, they're boring. All they want to do is find a man to take care of them, give them some babies and then they let themselves get fat."

"You'd better not let Julia hear that," Ralph laughed, imagining what his shapely wife's reaction to his friend's words would be.

"Julia is different, Ralph we both know that. Besides she's not even from here, she's from Mexico City. You married the last good woman in town."

"Then go to Mexico City," Ralph suggested, only half-joking.

Rodolfo shuddered, thinking of the pollution and high crime rate of the largest city in the world.

"Thanks for the advice buddy but I think I'll stay where I am." Abruptly he switched topics.

"Let's play some music. I always feel better with a little Led Zeppelin or Santana."

Gingerly, Ralph stood, placing both children on Rodolfo's lap while he complied.

"You hang on to these guys for a little while and I'll go set up," he said as he turned to go into the house where the amplifiers were stashed. Ricki looked up at his father's best friend and gurgled happily, liking the kind look on his face, while little Claudia scrambled off his lap to toddle after her father. Seeing the contented wide gap-toothed grin on the little boy's face, Rodolfo's heart turned over. As he breathed in the clean baby smell he hugged him closer. He felt his restlessness ease from his body to be replaced with a

softening somewhere near his heart.
*Maybe...*

A silky breeze blew off the Pacific Ocean and wafted gently over the bodies of the two people tanning side by side on Las Gatas Beach. Almost immediately on arrival on shore, waiters all vying for their business had besieged them. They finally settled on one, which was mid-way down the row of restaurants. Eager to prove they had made a good choice, the waiters hurried to take their order and returned quickly with their drinks, a Pina Colada for him, a Coconut *Au Natural* for her.

The speediness of the service caused Lydia to turn to her companion and lazily remark, "Service is always better when you're around John. Why is that?"

"Probably because these guys know the boss when they see him," he joked back without thinking.

He saw the sudden flare of anger in her eyes and realized that he had once again said the wrong thing.

"Jeez Lydia...I didn't mean..."

"What? That you're the great white hunter and these poor Mexicans are your flunkies?"

Without waiting for his reply she lifted her body off her lounge chair and stalked angrily to the waters edge, effectively ignoring John who was calling out her name in exasperation behind her.

Sighing, John closed his eyes, thinking he might as well take a siesta. Lord knows he hadn't had much sleep last night what with Lydia tossing and turning all the time. He should have just gone to his own room as she had suggested but, as always, he had wanted to make a point. What that point was he had no idea, since in hindsight he would have been better off in his own room after all. Lydia had perversely kept to her side of the bed, clinging carefully to the edge and staying as far away from him as possible. Usually she slept spooned tightly against him, curled up in his arms like a kitten napping in the sun. Who could understand women?

Feeling foolish by her uncalled-for outburst, Lydia dipped her toes in the sea and turned back to look at John. Hat pulled low over his face she could see he was probably going to nap. She was relieved further conversation was not going to be necessary, at least for a while. She knew she was behaving badly. For some reason she either no longer cared or didn't know how to go about stopping it. She wasn't sure which. Deciding she might as well get some exercise, she was about to lope off down the beach when a tap on the shoulder stopped her. She turned around, a sudden smile on her face, as she recognized the person in front of her.

"Hello. What are you doing here?"

Carla smiled back at her brightly, her eyes expressively warm and friendly, "I thought that was you. Why don't you join me? Unless of course you're busy?" she added hastily following Lydia's eyes to the sleeping form on the beach."

"Not at all," Lydia assured her, grateful for the distraction as she followed her lead to another table a few restaurants away from the one they had chosen. "I think John is down for the count anyway."

*A link to Rodolfo*, she remembered, strangely comforted by the thought before she pushed it quickly away.

"Where's Michael?" she asked her host curiously.

She almost never saw one without the other and now she looked around the beach for a glimpse of him.

"Out there," Carla pointed out to sea.

"We have a small fishing boat and Michael goes out every morning while I write. Then, later in the afternoon we meet on one of the beaches for lunch. It works for me." She smiled, stretching her arms wide, contentment in every line of her body.

"Sounds perfect," Lydia agreed enviously, as a waiter came by to take their drink order.

Lydia belatedly remembered the one she had left next to her chair. Not wanting to return to where John was just yet, the waiter graciously offered to fetch it for her. For a few minutes they drank in companionable silence, each lost in their own thoughts, the cool liquid sliding refreshingly down their throats. Carla broke the silence first.

"I ran into Rodolfo the other night at Coconuts," she began, looking into the eyes of the startled woman in front of her and watching her carefully.

"He told me your boyfriend finally arrived. I take it that's him?" She fluttered a thin hand in the direction behind her.

"Yes that's him. That's John." Trying to appear nonchalant, she pursued the topic.

"What did Rodolfo have to say?"

Carla regarded her thoughtfully, wondering how much she should say without giving up the trust of an old friend of theirs. She decided to trust her instincts.

"To tell you the truth Lydia, Rodolfo didn't look too happy and I think maybe that has something to do with you, am I right?"

Lydia nodded slowly.

"You have to understand that we have known Rodolfo a very long time. He even came to Kelowna one summer to spend some time with us in our house last year. Rodolfo is like the brother I never had. I hate to see him so sad."

Lydia felt tears well up in her eyes. She tried hurriedly to blink them back before they could fall.

"This is crazy." She choked on the words as they spilled from her lips in a rush under the concerned gaze of the woman in front of her.

"Here I am with a wonderful man, sitting on one of the most beautiful beaches I have ever seen and I feel like crying over a Mexican man I haven't known for more than a month. I must be out of my mind," she said with a disparaging laugh as she wiped her face, embarrassed by her outburst.

The diamond on her finger glittered in the sunlight catching Carla's eye, "I'm sorry," Lydia apologized," I never cry and now look at me?"

Carla leaned over and touched her hand gently.

"You should never apologize for having feelings Lydia. I have to tell you that after yesterday I was worried about Rodolfo and to be perfectly honest with you. I was a little angry with you, too." At Lydia's surprised look she explained.

"I thought you were using him, but I can see you have genuine feelings for him, too. So, now what are you going to do?"

She picked up Lydia's hand and regarded the ring on the third finger.

"Does this mean you're engaged?" she asked bluntly. Lydia shook her head, "John proposed, but I haven't given my answer yet. I really thought I had this all worked out but now I'm just so confused, I don't know what to do."\

Carla thought for a minute before answering her, "I can't tell you what to do Lydia, only you and your heart can do that. But here is something to consider. Whenever I am faced with a problem I have no answer for I always ask myself this question. If today were the last sunset I would ever see, what would I do differently? Ask yourself that Lydia, then really listen for the answer and you will know what to do."

Lydia let a few tears fall before she dashed them away and stood up.

"Thank you Carla for listening, and for your advice. I will think about what you said. I see that John seems to be stirring over there and I should really get back to him."

"Not a problem," Carla smiled at her. "Listen, if you ever feel the need to talk again I'm always around."

Lydia thanked her again and headed back to John, leaving Carla to stare thoughtfully after her.

*Is there anything more complicated than love?* She wondered, remembering her struggle before she and Michael finally got togeth-er.

Michael! He should be here any time now. She stood and walked toward the surf, shading her eyes against the glare of the sun in the hopes for a glimpse of his boat. All at once she couldn't wait to see him.

As Lydia walked back to where John was, she knew without a shadow of a doubt that she had to see Rodolfo again before she left. The thought of leaving Mexico and never seeing him again overwhelmed her with a sense of loss and seemed almost unbearable to fathom.

Just one more time, she vowed, *and then I'll go.*

With that decision made, she felt a huge weight lift from her heart. For the first time that day felt happy again. Sinking into her chair beside John she kissed him on the cheek. He eyed her warily and held himself stiff. Knowing she was the reason for his cool manner, she took one large hand in hers and leaned closer. If he noticed the red rimmed eyes or tear stained cheeks he did not mention them.

"Friend of yours?" he asked carefully, unwilling to set her off again.

Feeling guilty for leaving him on his own for so long, she smiled apologetically, "Yes she is. As a matter of fact she and Michael live in Kelowna and come here every winter for a few months. They met in Zihuatanejo a few years ago and have been together ever since."

That's nice," John commented casually. "What does he do in Canada that he can swing that?"

"They" she emphasized, "have a construction company that they run together."

John remained silent, preferring to keep the tentative peace that was forming rather than stick his foot in his mouth as he had been doing so often it lately seemed.

Relieved that they were speaking to each other, Lydia suggested they rent snorkeling gear from the dive shop on the beach and head to the reefs for a swim.

"On the way I'll tell you the legend of Las Gatas and Zihuatanejo as told to me by Ana," she offered amiably.

"Sounds great," John complied dryly, hauling his bulk out of the chair to follow her curvaceous form down the beach.

## THE JADE PENDANT

The next two hours passed happily as they swam or floated as the mood took them in the crystal-clear water. Teeming with life, the blues, deep yellows and occasionally a bright red snapper darted in among the corals elusively.

Moving effortlessly in the gentle waves, clutching hands, a more confident Lydia glided John through the surf, pointing out various species of fish as they came into their line of vision. Their bodies darkened by the sun reflecting off the water.

"You missed your calling Lydia," John complimented her teasingly.

"You should have been a snorkeling tour guide."

Lydia laughed with him as she related her adventure with a real live tour guide, Jose, at Ixtapa Island.

John looked upon her admiringly and then suggested a drink might be in order.

"I could use a beer. How about you?" he asked as they walked back to their belongings.

"Make mine a margarita," she called gaily over her shoulder as she moved in the opposite direction to return their equipment back to the rental shack.

Later as they lay back in their chairs watching the sun sink lower in the sky, Lydia, voice contrite and low, offered an apology.

"I'm sorry I've been so touchy lately John. Believe me it's not you, it's me."

"No apology needed Lydia," he allowed generously, "although I can't help wondering what's up with you. Is there something I should know? Something you want to talk about?"

Lydia froze. *He knows!*

Masking her turmoil she answered lightly, "No John, it's nothing at all. If you want to blame it on anything, blame it on stress. PMS. Whatever. But I am sorry and I will try to control myself better."

She sealed her promise with a long kiss on his mouth.

John shrugged, and pulled her closer. He held her for a minute before letting her go, relieved that he could blame her wild mood swings on 'female problems.'

"Why don't we go to Heiko's tonight," he suggested. "I saw it the other day on the way to the pier. Is it any good?"

"It's wonderful," Lydia affirmed, wondering if she was going to be able to slip away before dinner without arousing his suspicions.

As it happened, there was no need to make any excuses at all. On arriving at the hotel John told her he was beat and wanted to take a nap before they met on the balcony in a couple of hours.

"Say around six? I know you probably could do with some time on your own too, so if you don't mind I'll just go to my own room."

Elated that she could carry out her plan and grateful for his consideration she readily agreed. She kissed John impulsively before she hurried to her room. As the door closed behind her she checked her watch. Time enough to shower, change and still catch Rodolfo at the restaurant before he became inundated with customers. More excited than she had felt in days, she tore around the room, trying on clothes and then discarding them in a heap as she went.

As she raced down the stairs she bumped into Ana, sending her parcels flying over the railing.

Apologizing profusely, she helped Ana retrieve them. Lydia gave her the good news.

"I've decided to stay on a few extra days after John leaves," she told her happily. "I went there today and the airline said there would be no problem with changing the flight. Isn't that wonderful?"

Ana straightened the parcels, once more firmly in her grasp as she contemplated the woman before her.

"I suppose that's good news Lydia," she told her slowly, "but I guess I have to ask why do you want to stay? I mean, after all I thought you made your decision to be with John. Have you had a change of heart?"

She peered closer, "It's Rodolfo, isn't it?"

Lydia nodded silently, not sure how to answer the questions. Ana felt no such restraint in speaking her mind, which she did without further preamble.

"You may not like what I have to say Lydia but I'm going to say it anyway," Ana began brutally. "

"Just what the hell kind of game are you playing here?"

"What do you mean," Lydia stammered, hurt by Ana's attitude.

Ana was relentless as she attacked her friend.

"You know exactly what I mean. For one thing, how are you going to explain your extended stay to John? The man's not stupid you know. Anyone with half an eye can see that. Do you think you can just play around with him while he's here and then run and jump into bed with Rodolfo the minute his back is turned? And what's this," she grabbed hold of Lydia's hand.

"An engagement ring?"

Taken aback, Lydia opened her mouth to protest but snapped it shut as Ana held up an imperious hand.

"Let me finish Lydia. Someone has to talk some sense into you. I told you this before. You've managed to beguile the most beautiful man in Zihuatanejo. You've broken his heart and now you want another fling with him before you go back to your rich boyfriend? Rodolfo is a proud man, a Latin man. Do you really think you can wiggle your little finger and he'll come running back to you, arms wide open so you can hurt him again? My God Lydia, Rodolfo is the son of a powerful Shaman, a Tarhamaraha Indian. You have no right to treat him like your newest toy. And," Ana relented seeing the utter misery on Lydia's face, "I don't know John very well at all Lydia, but I don't think he deserves this, do you?"

Her legs threatening to give from under her, Lydia abruptly sat down on the cement steps, Ana joining her to place a comforting arm around her friend's shoulders.

"I am only saying these things because I care about you Lydia and I don't want to see you get hurt either."

"You're right Ana," Lydia began quietly, her voice void of emotion. "Neither John nor Rodolfo deserve this. All I do know for sure is that I can't go back yet without seeing Rodolfo again. That's all I know. What I don't know is what I'm going to say to him when I do see him. What if he won't talk to me? Maybe this is all academic and he really doesn't care about me at all? Maybe I imagined the whole thing and by staying I am making a huge fool of myself? I just don't know Ana, but I have to find out."

For a long while Ana said nothing as she sat beside her friend, unsure of where to go from here.

"All right then Lydia," she allowed, standing up and moving away. "Do it your way. Go see Rodolfo and see how you feel, then talk to John. As long as you're honest with everyone things will turn out the way they should. But," she warned, "You have to be honest. And one more thing Lydia," she threw over her shoulder as her small feet already cleared the next flight of stairs.

"What Ana?"

"To thy own self be true," she intoned as she floated down the hallway and disappeared from sight.

# Chapter Twenty

From the far side of the room the early staff watched Rodolfo as he set up the tables in his section of the restaurant. Normally a job for his busboy, he had curtly brushed him aside, anxious to wear off some of his frustrations with physical labor. His day spent with Ralph and his family playing music had been a pleasant one but had only served to remind him how much was lacking in his own life. As he organized his workstation, he tried to ignore the comments of his co-workers.

"Look at him," Arturo spoke loudly enough for Rodolfo to hear, "this guy's in bad shape. And all over a woman, too."

He pretended to spit disdainfully.

"*Si*," Carlos nodded enthusiastically, "but what a woman," and his large hands traced a curvy body in the air as the others laughed lewdly in agreement.

Rodolfo's could feel the tips of his ears redden. His lips begin to twitch as he tried not to laugh at the antics of his friends. He didn't want to encourage them so he continued to work steadily until satisfied everything was perfect for tonight. What he couldn't shake from him was the feeling that Lydia had tried to make a fool of him. A slow anger began to burn in the pit of his stomach. Moving to the bar-cabinet behind the sinks, he pulled wine glasses down and began to place them carefully on a tray.

A shadow moved behind him, reflected in the overhead mirror. Thinking it was Arturo coming back to tease him, Rodolfo turned quickly; harsh words ready to leap off his tongue. Hands clenched reflexively when he saw who it was. He was holding two glasses so tightly that he caused them to snap at the stems and shatter into a million pieces on the terra cotta tile floor. Without a word to the figure before him he bent and began to pick up the larger pieces with his bare hands, cutting him in the process.

Straightening he wrapped a napkin around the cut to staunch the flow and regarded the woman with a pained, haunted look in his eyes.

Instinctively Lydia took a step back, her smile fading rapidly in the face of his scowling demeanor.

Ana was right. This wasn't going to be easy.

Rodolfo once more bent to clean up the glass. Defeated, Lydia moved to the bar a few feet away to wait. Pauley smiled a warm, sympathetic greeting and made her a drink before turning away to polish glasses at the far end of the massive counter.

A few agonizing minutes passed with Lydia feeling more uncomfortable and foolish as time went on. Finishing her drink, she laid a few pesos down and gathered up her purse to leave. Before she had time to place one sandaled foot on the ground, Rodolfo stood in front of her and barred her way. Her heart leaped as she scanned his features eager for some hint of what he was feeling. There was only a cool calculating look that confused her and kept her silent. Heart plummeting, she managed to get off her stool and excusing herself she tried to brush past him.

"What are you doing here Lydia?" Rodolfo asked harshly as one hand clamped around her arm, halting her in her tracks.

"I had some news to tell you, but I don't think that's a good idea anymore," she said so softly he could barely hear her.

"Tell me anyway," he demanded, folding his arms across his chest as he waited for her reply.

This is a Rodolfo I have never seen before, she thought, uncertain what to do next.

Taking a deep breath, she bravely plunged forward.

"I came to tell you some good news. I have decided to stay a little longer than I originally had planned. I was supposed to leave Thursday with John but now I've delayed my trip. I won't be leaving for another five days."

"Really?" he asked coolly. "I suppose that's good news – for you."

With that he let her go and spun on his heel to walk back to the glass cabinet.

Feeling more foolish and confused than ever, Lydia turned to leave. She was halted by the thunderous sound of many glasses breaking at once. Startled, she jumped and looked back. Rodolfo looking both angry and sheepish was holding the remnants of two more glasses. Embarrassed he shrugged his shoulders high around his ears.

A giggle escaped Lydia and she placed a small hand to her mouth in an attempt to stifle it. Dropping the broken glass from his hands into the bucket, he strode toward her purposefully. Hidden in the shadows the staff watched as the drama enfolded before them. Reaching her side, Rodolfo roughly pulled her closer to him and looked down, a set look on his face, mouth inches from hers. She wanted to reach up and pull it down toward her.

"What do you want from me?" he demanded ferociously.

Lydia stared up at him for what seemed like forever, thrilled to be this close to him again no matter how angry he looked..

"I need to talk to you Rodolfo. Will you meet me later? After work?"

He nodded once, letting her go so abruptly she momentarily lost her balance.

"Be here at 11:30," he commanded before striding away without another word or backward glance.

Shaken but triumphant Lydia hurried out the door and across the street before he could change his mind.

As Lydia had claimed earlier, dinner at Heiko's was exceptional; deliciously prepared and well served. They had both ordered starters. For her, a creative pumpkin soup steeped in sherry, while he settled for a Caesar salad made at their table by Antonio, their affable waiter. Main course was slow roasted duck in a honey glaze with a side of tenderly steamed fresh vegetables. Later as they spooned Cherries Jubilee in their mouths, John remarked how pleasantly surprised he was by number of good quality restaurants Zihuatanejo now boasted.

"When I first started coming here over eight years ago, dinner usually consisted of some rice, beans and a beef taco. Now look at this!"

Preoccupied, Lydia nodded her head. As delicious as everything was she had done little more than push the food around her plate from one side to the other, finally giving up and covering the leftovers with a napkin.

Sipping Spanish coffees they settled back comfortably in their chairs, listening to the strolling mariachi bands as they serenaded the restaurant's clientele. John unwrapped and lit one of his treasured Cuban cigars and was now puffing contentedly, the aroma pleasant as it drifted on the night air.

"Something wrong Lydia?" he asked her with a touch of concern in his voice. "You've hardly touched your dinner or said a word all night."

Surprised he had noticed she replied, "I guess I just wasn't all that hungry," she told him with a small smile, hurrying to add, "But it was delicious, thank you."

He waved his cigar, the smoke following in a thin blue line as he persisted, and his eyes sharp as he scanned her face closely.

"What's up, kid?"

At the nickname John sometimes called her, although she ceased to be considered one for many years now, Lydia lifted her head. Normally his pet name for her would bring a smile to her face, but tonight she only felt inadequate. She looked at him fully for the first time all night.

Why can't I love this man? She asked herself outright for the first time. She was perplexed by the feelings she did have for him. *Because you love someone else,* the voice whispered close to her heart.

Lydia let out her breath in a ragged sigh, smiling gently at the man facing her before speaking, "There is something John. Something we need to talk about. Do you mind if we go back to the hotel? We can sit on the balcony and talk there if that's alright with you?"

"Certainly," John readily agreed, waving Antonio over.

He requested the bill, which he paid as soon as it was brought to him. Walking back to the Citlali John took her hand, the gesture more companionable than romantic, and Lydia once more thought what a truly good man he really was. Excusing herself for a minute, she hurried to her room to freshen up, while John went out on the balcony to wait for her return. She switched on the light, and her eyes rested immediately on her jade pendant, placed lovingly on the pillow of her freshly made bed. Joyfully she reached for it and clasped it around her neck. Then she left to join John on the terrace.

Once on the balcony, firmly entrenched in comfortable seats, John opened the discussion in his usual forthright manner.

"A few days ago Lydia right here on this very balcony I asked you a question. I would like an answer to that question now. Will you marry me?" he asked her again, earnestly.

Not wanting to prolong the inevitable any longer than was necessary and afraid that she would lose courage if she did, Lydia sadly shook her head her answer clear in that one simple gesture.

Disappointed, John leaned back in his chair, his breath leaving him in a rush. Taking a minute to compose his emotions he glanced over to see tears glistening on Lydia's face. He softened, and putting aside his feelings in his concern for her, leaned forward to take both of her small hands in one of his. With the thumb of the other he brushed away the tears from her cheeks gently.

"Care to tell me why Lydia?" he asked, for some reason feeling the need for an explanation.

Lydia debated on ways to answer, finally deciding that the direct way was the best. As he listened intently she told him about her feelings for Mexico and how much she had been drawn to it from the very beginning—as if, in some strange way, it was her destiny to be here at this time and in this place.

"The thought of leaving here is almost unbearable to me and as much as I try to imagine myself going back with you to Canada and going on as before, I simply cannot do it."

"I see," said John slowly. She continued.

"I admire you more than any man I have ever known," she told him, honest finally with herself about her true feelings for him.

"You are a powerful man, an honest one and anyone would be proud to be your wife."

"Except you," he noted sadly.

"Except me," she agreed. "I'm not the woman for you John. You need someone who is more ambitious than I am. The way I used to be before I came here. It's not that I am coming here to drop out," she hastily assured him at his raised eyebrow, "it's just that I need to take myself out of the race for awhile."

"I think you're making a big mistake," John told her. "You may think that you need to chill out for a while. That's fine Lydia, do that. In fact, why not stay here for another week or so, get it all out of your system? Then you can come back home where you belong," he leaned forward his voice persuasive as he pulled her toward him.

"You're just tired Lydia, I can see that. I could see it before you left. You need a longer vacation that's all."

Lydia pulled back angrily.

"There you go again, John telling me what I need. I know what I need and I need to be here with…" she stopped abruptly.

"With whom?" His eyebrows knit together suspiciously. "Is there someone else Lydia? Is that what this is all about?"

Lydia remained silent for a moment, unsure how to answer. Certainly her feelings for Rodolfo made her realize she couldn't possibly marry John, but to say that he was "the someone else" as John had put it, would be stretching it. At this point he had barely agreed to talk to her. Finally, seeing John's look of utter confusion she replied noncommittally.

"I need to be here with myself John. To find the person I used to be and who I can be in the future."

He relaxed visibly, shaken more than he was willing to let on at Lydia's refusal to marry him. At the same time, he was hopeful he might still have a chance with her. Her next words crushed that idea.

"The airline said it wouldn't be a problem to change my ticket. There is a very good chance I may extend it even longer to up to six months."

"I see," John said inanely. He felt like he was looking at a stranger in front of him.

"'This all has to do with my forgetting your birthday party and Christmas present, doesn't it?" he demanded.

Lydia laughed shortly.

"I won't pretend those things didn't upset me John, nor will I tell you that your refusal to let me know when you were coming here didn't make me angry either. Really John," she patted his hand fondly, "those things are minor compared to how I feel inside about my life. I think my life is here, at least for now. I only know that I have to find out for myself."

Considering her determined look, he knew when he was beaten. He'd seen that same look in the business world many times. Graciously, to her vast relief, he conceded.

"Alright Lydia, if this is what you want, I accept that. I only want you to be happy. If you find that things don't work out the way you want them to, then you know…" he let the last words dangle unspoken in the air, a safety net for her to latch on to if she ever needed one.

Gratefully, Lydia stood and looked down at him. Sliding the ring off her finger she held it in the palm of her hand. For a while he just looked at it, then with a crooked smile and shrug he took it and slipped it into his pocket. Without a word, Lydia leaned over and kissed his cheek. Briefly his arms reached up and tightened around her and then quickly let her go. Uncurling her body from his, tears threatening once again to spill, she hurried swiftly away.

"Good luck," he whispered into the dark after her, unsure if she heard him or not, knowing it wouldn't change anything if she did.

Rodolfo was finding it difficult to concentrate on the conversations going on a round him. Slumped deep in his chair, legs stretched out in front, he checked his watch for the hundredth time that night.

"She'll be here," Carlos assured him knowingly, noticing the motion again. "Will you relax?"

"She's late," he shot back pointing at his watch for emphasis.

"I'm not waiting for her any more." He started to get up angrily but Carlos roughly pulled him back.

"She's not that late," he reminded him. "And yes, you will wait a little longer," he commanded him. "We have a bet remember and I want to collect."

Earlier Rodolfo had told Carlos that Lydia wanted to talk to him, but that he doubted she would show up. Carlos bet him a case of beer that she would.

"Fine," Rodolfo grumbled, then stopped as Carlos nudged him painfully in the ribs.

"She's here," he whispered triumphantly, already anticipating drinking his winnings on his day off tomorrow, "Go get her *Camello*," he teased him, calling him by the nickname which meant Camel. They had named him that because of the way he used to carry his boat motor on his back years ago when he'd been a fisherman.

Obediently, Rodolfo stood and drained his beer in one long swallow. He put the empty glass down on the table before him and turned to see Lydia standing uncertainly in the shadows. The others snickered as they watched him cross the room to where she waited for him, a shy smile of greeting on her face.

Without a word, he grabbed her by the elbow and pulled her gently but firmly out of the restaurant to the catcalls and whistles of the men behind them. He noticed the necklace around her neck, but made no comment. It pleased him just the same.

Outside she pulled her arm away from his grasp and let her hand fall into his. Trying to look indifferent, he nevertheless made no attempt to remove her hand and even squeezed it briefly in response.

For a while they walked along in complete silence, each lost in their own thoughts. By unspoken consent they found themselves near the pier, quiet at this time of the night except for two young lovers wrapped in a passionate embrace. Embarrassed, Lydia glanced away to find Rodolfo's amused eyes on her.

Moving to the end of the pier as far away from the couple as they could, Rodolfo led her to a wooden bench and indicated a place for her to sit down. He took the space beside her. Still silent, they watched the waves slap against the sides of the boats in the harbor, inky black as they swept their way to shore. The sound of the water calmed and lulled her and for a time at least she could pretend that all was perfect in her world.

It was Rodolfo who broke the stillness, a small, self-conscious laugh escaping him as he began.

"You have something to say to me, Lydia?" he asked. "And I have something to say to you, too, hmmm? But ladies first."

Relieved that the wall of silence had been scaled, she answered him as her stomach flipped in a crazy dance of nervousness and anticipation.

"Yes, I do want to talk to you Rodolfo. I have a great deal to say to you but it is not easy for me. I hope you will let me explain."

He nodded. Encouraged by the open expression on his face, she took a deep breath to calm, fingering her pendant for courage.

"Coming to Mexico has been the most life-changing thing that has ever happened to me," she held up a hand to prevent him from saying anything. Her eyes on her lap, she missed the sudden smile that twitched on Rodolfo's lips.

"I know you must be very angry at me because of coming to Coconuts that night after I promised you I wouldn't and I don't blame you."

"Lydia..."Rodolfo began to tell her he knew but Lydia stopped him again.

"Please Rodolfo this is hard enough. Let me just say what I have to say and then I will leave you alone."

Trying to keep a straight face he waved his hand giving her permission to continue, curious now as to what she would say next.

"I want to apologize to you. I never meant to lead you on or embarrass you or hurt you in anyway. And I am sorry. Today I told you that I was going to stay for a while longer and not go back when John does. That is true, I am not. I have decided to stay here for a while, maybe even a few months. I realize now that I could never be happy with John and I don't think he could ever be happy with me, knowing what I do now."

"And what is it that has changed, Lydia?" he asked, holding his breath as he awaited her answer.

She turned to look him full in the face before replying.

"I know that I belong here in Mexico. That I have always belonged here. This is my home," she paused before plunging bravely ahead.

"And most of all Rodolfo I know that I love you, and that I don't want to be anywhere that you are not."

She let her head fall forward, afraid to look at him now. She was sure that she would see ridicule in his eyes at her confession. Feeling more foolish as the minutes ticked agonizingly by in complete painful silence she decided there was nothing more to say. She began to rise from the bench to leave. Before she could take one step Rodolfo pulled her abruptly down on his lap. Cradling her gently in his arms, as he would a child, he held her for a long time. Stroking her hair gently he began to speak, Lydia relaxed in relief against him at the sound of his voice.

"I love you too, *querida. Te quiero mucho*," he whispered against her hair and held her tighter against him.

"I don't have very much to give you Lydia. I am not a rich man and you are a rich woman. But all that I have is yours."

Lydia moved away to look at him, worry written on her face.

"I am not rich Rodolfo, at least not anymore. John gave me the news a few days ago. My business is gone. I'm broke."

Rodolfo started to laugh as Lydia stared at him, surprised by his reaction.

"Don't worry Lydia, about the money. I am not rich but I have enough to take care of you, don't you worry. We will work it out."

Lydia sagged against him once more, a smile on her lips as she thought about her future with this man and what it would be like. His next words surprised her.

"Your friends Richard and Ingrid came into Coconuts for dinner the other night. After they heard about my experience at the Bay Club," he told her proudly. "They offered me a job to manage their restaurant this summer. If you want, we can go to Canada together for a few months make some money and then come back here. How does that sound?"

Lydia twisted her head to stare at him in amazement, a huge smile breaking across her features at his enthusiasm. The plan has definite merit, she thought, already thinking of things she could do to help when he placed his fingers under her chin and kissed her. All rational thoughts fled as she threw her body and soul into the caress. Their pendants hung around their respective necks rubbing together, united again.

When they finally parted many moments later, Lydia grinned impishly up at him.

"You said you had something to say to me," she said, not knowing how close she had been to bearing the full brunt of his anger.

"Yes," he told her. "Carlos was right. He bet me you would leave your boyfriend and come back to me."

You bet against me?" she asked in mock anger. "Well I am sorry to tell you that you lost."

"No Lydia," he answered as he pulled her up to meet his lips again, their matching pendants pressed close together, "I would say that I definitely won."

*The End.*